FORGET ME NOT

Aloha Cove

Theresa Kelly

CPH.
SAINT LOUIS

Glory be to the Father, and to the Son,
and to the Holy Spirit!

For Terrence, Doreen, Jackie, and Tim—
family is a wonderful thing!

Cover Illustration by Sandy Rabinowitz.

Scripture quotation are taken from the HOLY BIBLE, NEW INTERNATIONAL VERSION®.
NIV®. Copyright © 1973, 1978, 1984 by International Bible Society. Used by permission
of Zondervan Publishing House. All rights reserved.

Copyright © 1999 Concordia Publishing House
3558 S. Jefferson Avenue, St. Louis, MO 63118-3968
Manufactured in the United States of America

Library of Congress Cataloging-in-Publication Data

Kelly, Theresa, 1952-
    Forget me not / Theresa Kelly ; cover illlustration by Sandy Rabinowitz.
        p. cm. -- (Aloha cove)
    Summary: Cass has trouble dealing with her mother's pregnancy, her "perfect"
stepsister, and the absence of her boyfriend, who has left Kwajalein Island to attend
college at West Point.
    ISBN 0-570-07033-3
    [Stepfamilies--Fiction. 2. Kwajalein Island (Marshall Islands)--Fiction. 3. Christian
life--Fiction.] I. Title.
PZ7.K2985 Fo 2000
[Fic]--dc21

99-053127

1 2 3 4 5 6 7 8 9 10   08 07 06 05 04 03 02 01 00

CHAPTER 1

"Logan leaves for West Point in exactly 78 hours," Cass Devane announced, coming into her stepsister's bedroom late Tuesday night. "I can't believe how fast the time is going."

"I know." Tabitha Spencer looked up from the book she'd been reading and patted the bed beside her. "I have to hand it to you. You're handling it pretty well. I keep waiting for you to fall apart."

Cass sank down next to her and frowned. "I plan to throw a major fit the moment Logan's plane takes off. You're going to be treated to weeping and wailing the likes of which you've never seen before."

"That's okay," Tabitha assured her. "You're entitled to a few hysterics. After all, who knows when you'll see Logan again? New York is a long way away."

Cass glared at her. "You're not helping. Don't you know anything about how to comfort somebody in the midst of a crisis?" she complained. "You're supposed to pat my arm and say things like, 'There, there. Everything's going to be fine.' " She elbowed Tabitha in the ribs. "Go on," she urged. "Give it a try."

Tabitha swept a stray blonde curl behind her ear then

obediently placed a soothing hand on Cass' arm. "There, there," she crooned. "Even though Logan will be 9,000 miles away, I'm almost positive things will be sort of okay." She grinned. "How was that?"

Even though she tried to scowl, Cass wound up laughing. "You're hopeless. Don't ever plan on going into counseling. You're a complete failure when it comes to cheering people up."

"I beg your pardon," Tabitha said hotly, although her blue eyes danced. "As a matter of fact, I'm a whole lot better than you realize. My goal was to make you smile, and you did." She stuck out her tongue. "What do you think of that, Miss Smarty-Pants?"

"I think I'd rather talk to Mom." Cass stood up and started for the door. "She wasn't in the living room when I came in. Is she on the porch?"

Setting aside her book, Tabitha shook her head. "No, she went to bed about an hour ago."

"At 9:00?" Instead of leaving, Cass perched on the edge of Tabitha's desk. It was immaculate as always—much different than her own. Her hazel eyes narrowed with concern. "Is she sick?"

"No sicker than a three-months pregnant woman usually is, I guess." Tabitha shrugged. "She said she was so tired she couldn't keep her eyes open. Dad checked on her a few minutes ago and said she was sleeping like a baby."

"She sure sleeps a lot." Cass glanced at the wall to her right as if she could see through it into Mom and Dad's room. "Do you think that's normal?"

"How should I know? I've never been pregnant." Tabitha dismissed Cass' worry with an airy wave. "Dad wasn't concerned so I don't see any reason why we should be."

"Still—" Cass impatiently twitched her shoulders, "when Mom first announced she was pregnant, I didn't know it was going to be like this. If I had, I wouldn't have been so happy."

Drawing up her knees and clasping her arms around them, Tabitha frowned. "What are you saying? You're not glad about the baby?"

Cass frowned and glanced out the window to avoid looking at her stepsister. "It's not the baby so much as the pregnancy. I'm used to Mom being up and going and involved in everything. About all she does anymore is sleep. When she's not throwing up, that is," she added sourly.

Tabitha arched an eyebrow. "Aren't you exaggerating just a tad?"

"If I am," Cass defended herself, "it's a whole lot less than a tad. It's more like a smidgen. A teensy-weensy smidgen." Pushing off from the desk, she crossed the room and plopped down on the foot of the bed. "Don't tell me you're okay with the way things have been lately. You actually like cooking and cleaning and doing the laundry?"

This time Tabitha avoided Cass' gaze, studying her nails instead. "I'll admit it gets old sometimes." She shrugged. "But, if it helps Mom out, I'm happy to do it."

Cass snorted. "Oh, puh-leeze. It's just the two of us. You don't have to put on your usual show." She smirked. "You know, the one where you try to impress the folks with what a good sport you are."

"I don't know what you're talking about." Tabitha's expression was as frosty as her tone. "If I didn't like pitching in, I'd say so."

"Whatever." Cass stood up and smoothed her shorts. "Since this discussion is going nowhere, I'm heading to bed."

"You'd better check in with Dad first so he knows you're home."

"Hey, thanks." Cass flashed her a grateful smile. "No sense letting him think I broke curfew and getting on his bad side, especially since he's the one in charge lately."

"If you want to be technical about it," Tabitha pointed out with a sniff, seeming to regret her helpful advice, "you did get in almost five minutes late."

"You know that, and I know that." Cass danced to the door then paused to look back at Tabitha and wink. "But Dad doesn't have to know it."

"And what if I decide to tell him?" Tabitha asked.

Cass could plainly hear the challenge in her voice. "I wouldn't do that if I were you. Don't forget I know of at least two calls you made to Micah after 11:00 at night. In case you've forgotten, 10:00 is the cut-off time for phone calls."

They glared at each other for several seconds before Tabitha broke off eye contact. Picking up her book, she made a show of flipping pages to find her place.

"Shut the door on the way out, will you?" She faked a yawn. "I'm not up to anymore company tonight."

"Will do."

Realizing she'd won, Cass sent Tabitha a triumphant look, but it was wasted. Tabitha's nose was already buried in her book. Letting herself out, Cass went in search of Dad.

CHAPTER 2

The next morning Cass awoke to the smell of breakfast cooking. The delicious aromas of bacon and French toast tickled her nose and set her stomach to rumbling. Pushing back the covers, she shrugged into her robe and hurried down the hall to the kitchen. She stopped short at the sight of Mom at the stove.

"Hey, what are you doing up?"

Mom looked up from the French toast and smiled. "Good morning to you too."

Cass ran a hand through her sleep-tousled hair. "Morning. Now, back to my question. Why are you up?"

"I don't know. It seemed like the thing to do." Mom flipped over two pieces of toast. "It wasn't dark outside anymore. Your Dad was getting ready for work, and I thought to myself, 'Maybe lying in bed all day isn't a good idea.' So here I am."

Cass made a face. "You know what I mean," she said. "It's been a couple of weeks since you got up and made breakfast. Why this morning?"

Mom transferred several slices of bacon from the frying pan to a plate lined with paper towels. "First of all, it hasn't been weeks since the last time I cooked breakfast. What about Sunday?"

Cass wrinkled her nose. "That doesn't count. You served us store-bought muffins."

Propping her fists on her hips, Mom pretended to scowl. "I heated them up first, didn't I?"

"It's not the same thing, and you know it."

Mom smiled. "You're right. The reason I'm cooking a real breakfast is that, for the first time in a long time, the thought of food doesn't make me ill. In fact, I actually woke up hungry instead of feeling queasy the way I usually do."

Cass' eyebrows arched in surprise. "You did? Does that mean you've turned the corner and things will start getting back to normal around here?"

"I hope so." Mom glanced up when Dad entered the kitchen and lifted her face for his kiss. "Hey there, handsome. What would you say if I told you there's bacon and French toast for breakfast?"

Chuckling, Dad tapped her nose. "I'd say, who are you and what have you done with my wife?"

"See?" Cass said. "Even Dad knows it's been ages since we had anything but cereal around here."

"To be fair," he reminded her, "we did have muffins on Sunday."

"I wouldn't mention the muffins if I were you," Mom advised as Cass threw up her hands in disgust. "For some strange reason, they seem to upset her."

After helping himself to three pieces of French toast and two slices of bacon, Dad carried his plate to the table. Cass remained in the kitchen with Mom.

"So, Cassandra," Dad began once he'd said a silent blessing over his food, "what are your plans for the day?"

"Logan and I are going snorkeling this morning, then we'll probably head over to his house to get some lunch." When Mom wasn't looking, Cass snitched a piece of bacon and popped it into her mouth.

"His mother will be there, won't she?" Dad shot her a quick look.

Cass hastily chewed and swallowed the bacon. "What do you think?" she drawled. "You and Mom have drilled it into our heads that we're not to be alone in a house with a boy. Tabitha and I consider it the number one rule in the Steve and Donna Spencer dating handbook."

"Okay, just checking." Dad turned his attention back to his meal. "It never hurts to remind you girls of the rules."

"As if we ever get a chance to forget them," Cass good-naturedly retorted. "Don't worry. Logan and I will be properly chaperoned. His little sisters will probably hang all over us the way they usually do. Logan thinks his mother pays them to follow us from room to room."

"Actually, Mrs. Russell and I split the cost," Mom joked. "It's expensive, but we've decided the peace of mind is worth it."

"Very funny," grumbled Cass. She accepted the plate of food Mom held out to her. "If I didn't know better, I'd think you were serious."

Mom grinned. "Keeping you guessing is one of my favorite pastimes."

Cass walked to the table and sat down across from Dad. "Part of me hopes the baby isn't a girl. Maybe if it's a boy, you'll cut him a little more slack than Tabitha and me."

"Don't count on it." Dad passed her the syrup. "Since a boy would be a new experience for us, we'd probably be even tougher on him."

"Poor kid." Shaking her head, Cass flipped the top on the syrup bottle and began smothering her French toast. "Either way, he or she is in for it."

"Looks like you and Logan have a picture-perfect day to go to the lagoon," Dad said, glancing out at the clear blue sky, swaying palm trees, and unending ocean in their backyard.

Cass nodded. "I guess God wants to make sure Logan's last memories of Kwaj are good ones. I'm glad he didn't leave in the middle of the rainy season."

"Way to look on the bright side of things," Dad congratulated her, carrying his plate to the sink. "I know how hard Logan's leaving is for you."

A shadow passed across Cass' face. "I don't want to talk about it. I just want to make the most of the three days we have left."

"I understand." Dad patted her shoulder as he passed her on the way to the kitchen. "Farewells are never easy."

"Dad." Cass shot him an irritated look. "Didn't you hear me? I said I don't want to talk about it."

"Oops. Sorry." Out of the corner of his mouth, he mumbled, "You won't hear another word out of me."

Cass snorted. "Yeah, right. That'll be the day. You mean well, but you just can't help yourself. That's one of the reasons why you and Mom are so well matched. You both love to talk things to death."

Shaking his head, Dad said to Mom, "Honey, I do believe our daughter just managed to insult both of us in one fell swoop."

"Yes, she did." Mom played along with his mock complaining. "I'd be upset, except she's right. We do tend to go on and on at times."

"At times?" teased Cass. "Try day in and day out, seven days a week, 52 weeks a year."

Mom wagged a warning finger. "I wouldn't push my luck if I were you. We gave you a pass the first time. Things might not go so well for you if you start getting sassy."

"Me? Sassy?" Assuming her most innocent expression, Cass pressed a hand to her chest. "Why, I'm the poster girl for respecting one's parents. You must have me confused with Tabitha."

Her comment brought a roar of laughter from her parents, and Cass smiled with satisfaction. Few things pleased her more than making people laugh. The day was definitely off to a good start.

It took a nosedive a short while later when Dad left for work. The moment the porch door closed behind him, Mom moved to the table and took the chair next to Cass. "Sweetie, I'd like to chat with you if you have a few minutes."

Although an alarm went off in Cass' head, she shrugged. "Sure. What's up?"

"I'm concerned about you and Logan," Mom said without hesitation.

Cass felt a blush creep up her neck to stain her cheeks, and she hunched her shoulders to hide the telltale glow. "What do you mean?"

Mom's gaze pinned Cass until she felt like a bug under a microscope. "I know this is an uncomfortable subject for you, but we have to talk about it. The next couple of days are going to be very difficult for you and Logan. Because you care for each other so much, you're going to be tempted to take your relationship further than you should."

This isn't happening, Cass groaned silently. *Mom didn't really say what I thought she said.* Cringing, she wished the floor would open up and swallow her, chair and all.

"In fact," Mom continued when Cass didn't respond, "you may have already found yourself being pulled in that direction. Your emotions are running high, and things that were definite no-no's up until now may suddenly seem more inviting."

Thoroughly embarrassed, Cass would have preferred to run from the room. However, she forced herself to remain seated and reply in a strangled voice, "You're worrying about nothing, Mom. Logan and I know right from wrong. Believe me, nothing's happened, and nothing's going to happen. When he leaves Saturday, I'll still be as pure as the driven snow."

Please let that be enough for her so she drops this, Cass implored God.

"I trust you're telling me the truth." Mom said, smiling. "If you're not careful, though, things can get out of hand, and you could find yourself taking more liberties than you would under normal circumstances."

Cass gave an impatient flounce. "You make it sound like Logan and I are thinking about..." She couldn't bring herself to say it. "Well ... you know. And we're not. Honest. We've never done anything more than kiss good night. It's not like we're about to go from that to ... to ..."

"Good morning," Tabitha broke in, treating Mom and Cass to a sleepy smile. "Did I interrupt something? You look like you were in the middle of a serious discussion."

Sensing a potential ally in her stepsister, Cass eagerly turned to her. "Mom thinks Logan and I are going to do something stupid before he leaves."

"Now, Cass, I didn't say that," Mom chided while Tabitha cocked an eyebrow and inquired, "Oh, yeah? Like what?"

"She didn't come right out and say it," replied Cass. "But she's scared I'm going to ..." She made a disgusted face. "You know."

"You're kidding," Tabitha said, as understanding flooded her face. Her gaze shifted to Mom. "You really think that?"

"I was merely cautioning Cass to be careful," Mom explained. "I'll have the same talk with you before Micah leaves for college next month."

Cass stifled a smile when she saw Tabitha bristle. *Here we go*, she privately crowed. *At least the spotlight's off me.*

"Excuse me?" Tabitha tossed her head and glared down her nose at Mom. "Are you suggesting that Micah and I might actually ..." Like Cass, she didn't say the words out loud. "Need I remind you about my commitment ring?"

She raised her left hand and pointed to the simple gold band on the fourth finger. "This is proof of my vow to remain a virgin until I marry. Cass has one too. Do you honestly think we'd wear these rings if we weren't planning to keep our promise?"

You go, girl! Cass silently cheered, shooting Mom a smug look.

Mom's expression was unruffled. "Dad and I are proud of you girls for choosing abstinence. But we still have the responsibility of pointing out potential dangers in your relationships. And, like it or not, we'll continue to do that until the day Dad walks you down the aisle."

"Oh, great." Tabitha rolled her eyes at Cass. "We have years of these lectures to look forward to."

"That's the first good reason I've heard for marrying young," Cass quipped, earning herself a playful swat from Mom.

"Don't even think about marriage until you've graduated from college." Mom included Tabitha in her stern glance. "Either of you."

"If Dad had his way, we wouldn't be allowed to date until we're 30," Cass said darkly.

"I'm beginning to think he might have the right idea." Mom laughed. "But don't worry. I wouldn't dream of depriving you of your precious social life."

"Only because you'd wind up being stuck with us at home night after night, and you and Dad like having time to yourselves," Cass shot back.

"I'll have you know Dad and I are still newlyweds," Mom said over Tabitha's laughter. "We're supposed to enjoy each other's company."

"You're newlyweds for three more weeks," Cass pointed out in a longsuffering tone. "Your anniversary is July 5th. Don't you think you've milked this thing for all it's worth?"

"Not quite." Mom placed her hands on the table and

pushed herself to her feet. "But that doesn't mean I won't offer to cook you breakfast."

"Wow, you're all heart," Tabitha drawled.

Mom fixed her with a teasing frown. "I wouldn't push my luck if I were you. I could suddenly develop an irresistible urge to go back to bed, and you'd be stuck eating cereal."

Tabitha gasped in pretended horror. "Please! Anything but that. If I sit here and keep my mouth shut, would you be so kind as to make me French toast?"

"I do believe that would do it." As Tabitha sank into the chair at the end of the table, Mom kissed the top of her head then moved into the kitchen. "I'm afraid I'm a big softie when it comes to you girls."

Stacking her plate and glass, Cass observed, "And getting bigger by the minute. Are you sure you should look this pregnant when you're only three months along?"

Tabitha gaped at Cass as she got up. "Don't say things like that," she hissed.

"It's okay," Mom assured her. "She's right. I am showing a little earlier than usual." She paused for dramatic effect. "That's why the doctor wants to do a sonogram to see if I'm carrying twins."

Cass and Tabitha glanced at each other, then at Mom. They wore matching expressions of disbelief.

"Twins?" Tabitha whooped with delight. "You're kidding! That would be so neat!"

"You are not having twins," Cass declared forcefully. "The four of us barely fit in this house as it is. Where would we put two more people?"

Tabitha brushed aside her concern. "Don't be silly. They'd hardly take up any room at all. Babies are little people."

"They're little, smelly, noisy people," grumbled Cass. "And, if you ask me, one of them would be plenty. Two would be a nightmare."

"That's a terrible thing to say." Tabitha's eyebrows slammed together in a thunderous scowl. "I, for one, think twins would be wonderful."

"Of course you do." A sneer curled Cass' lip. "You're the original Miss Goody-Two-Shoes, always trying to score points with the folks. If you think twins would be so wonderful, try letting them sleep in your room for a week. Then we'll see how you feel about them."

"Fine," snapped Tabitha. "They can sleep with me until I leave for college. I promise you I'd never get tired of having them around."

"Yeah, right. That's easy for you to—" Cass began.

"Girls, that's enough," Mom broke in.

They had the grace to look chastened, each mumbling, "Sorry."

Cass sidled into the kitchen and deposited her dishes in the sink. "Do you want me to wash these?" she asked, avoiding Mom's eyes.

"No, thank you. I'll do them." Mom smiled at her. "I know you're anxious to get to the lagoon."

"Logan's coming by to pick me up in about 15 minutes." Cass suddenly laughed. "Listen to me. I talk like we still live on the mainland. Actually, he's coming by so we can ride our bikes to Eamon together."

Glancing up from her food, Tabitha rolled her eyes. "I'm sure Mom knew what you meant."

"Why don't you mind—" With Mom's scolding fresh in her head, Cass bit off the rest of her retort and mumbled, "Forget it. I'm going to get ready."

Chapter 3

She had just finished packing her beach bag when the doorbell rang. A smile curved her lips when she heard Logan's response to Mom's greeting. Hoisting the bag onto her shoulder, she hurried down the hall to the living room.

Logan's face lit up when he saw her. "Hey."

"Hey, yourself." Cass waved then turned her attention to Mom. "What time do I need to be home?"

Mom glanced at Logan. "Cass said something about eating lunch at your house."

He nodded. "If that's all right with you."

"Of course it's all right. It means I'll have one less mouth to feed," Mom joked. Looking back at Cass, she added, "Why don't we make it 3:00? That'll give you more than enough time for both snorkeling and eating."

"Apparently you've forgotten how much your daughter can eat," Logan said, earning him a loud sniff from Cass.

"What is this? Gang up on Cass day?" she asked darkly.

"Ooh, if it is, can I get in on it?" Tabitha said from the dining room table, where she lingered with a glass of juice.

"I should be so lucky to have you limit your insults to one day." Without giving Tabitha a chance to reply, Cass gestured to Logan. "Let's go. Time's a-wasting."

"Micah and I might join you in a little while." Tabitha wandered into the room and smiled a hello at Logan. "In fact, we all talked about heading to Eamon this morning—Kira, Rianne, and Randy."

Cass didn't mind the others, but she was still mad at Tabitha and wasn't happy at the thought of her showing up. "It's a free beach." She waved a hand dismissively. "I can't keep you out if you decide to come."

Mom frowned and Logan looked puzzled, but Tabitha's eyes narrowed to angry slits. "That's right, and don't you forget it." Tossing her head, she pasted on a more cheerful expression. "While I'm thinking about it, I'm going to call Micah and the Thayers and tell them to meet me at the lagoon at 11:00."

With that, she spun on her heels and headed for the phone in the kitchen. Mom transferred her gaze to Cass.

"I don't know what's up with you two, but I'd advise you both to knock it off. You're going out of your way to needle each other, and I don't like it."

Embarrassed at being scolded in front of Logan, Cass thrust her chin out in a show of defiance. "How come you're just telling me? Shouldn't Tabitha hear this too?"

Mom fixed her with a stern look. "Don't worry. She will."

Yeah, but she won't have an audience like I did, Cass thought resentfully.

Aloud, she said, "If you need me, we'll be at Eamon until one or so. Otherwise, I'll be back at 3:00."

"Have a good time." Mom patted Cass' cheek, then surprised Logan by patting his. "I'm sure going to miss you after you're gone."

Logan walked Cass to the back door and out onto the lanai where the family parked their bikes. A warm breeze caught and lifted Cass' hair as she stepped outside. When she reached up to smooth it, Logan caught her hand.

"Leave it," he requested. "One of the ways I'm going to remember you is with your hair dancing in the wind."

Cass bit her lip and sighed. "Don't say things like that. It's only going to make it worse when you leave."

Logan squeezed her hand before releasing it. "Nothing can make it worse. It's already the pits. I ask myself a hundred times a day why I had to pick West Point. I should have gone with a closer school."

"But West Point's your dream," protested Cass. "You wouldn't have been happy at another college."

"You're my dream." Logan got her bike from the corner where she'd left it and began wheeling it toward the front lawn where his bike was parked. "West Point means nothing compared to the way I feel about you."

"Oh, Logan." Cass briefly rested her hand on his back. "What difference does it make if you're 2,000 miles away or 9,000? The bottom line is, come Saturday, I won't be able to see and talk to you every day anymore." She blinked back the tears that sprang to her eyes. "Like Mom said, I'm sure going to miss you."

Logan was grim-faced when he handed Cass' bike to her. "Let's not ruin the time we have left by talking about it. I've made up my mind that our last couple of days together are going to be fun." He forced a smile. "Even if it kills me."

"That's the spirit. You really know how to make a girl feel special."

Her teasing lightened the mood for the ride to the beach. When they arrived, they found it deserted except for a mother with three young children in tow. After claiming a spot on the sand, they peeled off their T-shirts, strapped on swim fins, and, carrying masks and snorkels, waded into the surf.

"I'll never get over how warm the water is," Cass said, bending down to splash her arms.

"Yeah, I'm not looking forward to being in New York

and having to swim in freezing lake water." Logan spit on his mask to keep it from fogging up.

Cass frowned. "When are you going to have time to go swimming?"

Chuckling, Logan tapped her nose. "Don't you remember me telling you about the first six weeks at West Point?"

"Oh, yeah." Cass snapped her fingers. "There's a name for it. Beast Barracks, right?"

Logan nodded. "It's army basic training, and, from everything I've read, it's not going to be easy. Part of it will involve being in water."

"Which will be freezing." Cass sighed sympathetically. "I'll think of you while I'm swimming in this wonderful 80-degree ocean."

"You're all heart." Logan waded out to where the water was waist-high. "You remember when you swore you'd never go in any deeper than your ankles because you were afraid of sharks?"

Cass, who'd followed him, laughed. "I was such a wimp when I first got here. Fortunately, I got over my fears pretty fast."

"Are you going to get over me just as fast after I leave?" If Logan was trying for a lighthearted tone, he failed miserably.

Taking his hand, Cass threaded her fingers through his. "You have my word. I will never, ever get over you."

"How can you be sure?" Logan asked softly.

"I don't know." Cass shrugged then grinned up at him. "I just am." She abruptly sobered. "Why? Aren't you?"

Logan hesitated before admitting, "Not really. I mean, who knows what the future holds?"

"God does," Cass replied promptly, despite the sudden lump in her throat. "It's like Mom says. We may not know what the future holds, but we know Who holds the future."

"But that's no guarantee it'll work out the way we want

it to." Logan stared at the horizon for a few seconds then shook himself. "All right. We already said enough of that kind of talk. Are you set?"

Cass settled the mask over her eyes and nose. "Yup. Let's dive."

Once their breathing tubes were in place, the couple dove into the crystal clear water and swam toward the rock jetty. If they were lucky, they might discover a school of brightly-colored tropical fish feeding on the algae clinging to the rocks.

By the time Cass and Logan emerged from the lagoon, Tabitha, Micah, Kira, Rianne, and Randy were gathered in the picnic pavilion adjoining the beach. Retrieving their towels, the pair crossed the sand to the shelter, drying off as they went.

"Did you see anything interesting?" Rianne greeted them.

Logan's green eyes slid sideways to teasingly ogle Cass. "Other than my companion you mean?"

"Ooh, you're good," Kira said in approval. Her smile flashed blindingly white against her dark skin. "No wonder you have Cass eating out of your hand."

"Excuse me?" Cass pretended to huff, propping her fists on her hips. "I'll have you know I don't eat out of anyone's hand. I'm my own woman."

"That's not what we hear." Micah nudged Kira and winked. "Isn't that right, Sis?"

"You said it, Bro." She sashayed to within a few inches of Cass. "I hate to be the one to break it to you, but it's all over the island that Logan has you exactly where he wants you."

"Smack-dab in the center of my heart," Logan explained hastily when Cass turned to him with a questioning look. "They're teasing you. I never said I have you eating out of my hand. If anything, it's the other way around."

"Yeah." Dropping the pose, Kira walked to a picnic table and sat down. "We're just giving you a hard time."

Cass' gaze darted to Tabitha. She suspected her sister of putting the Alexanders up to the teasing, but decided not to pursue it. Changing the subject, she asked Rianne, "Are y'all having a picnic?"

"Yup. You want to eat with us? We have more than enough."

Before Cass could answer, Logan replied, "No, thanks. My mother's expecting us for lunch."

Randy, who'd been sitting quietly in his wheelchair, spoke up. "How about we squeeze in one more round of golf before you leave?"

Logan's face lit up. "Great. When?"

"Tomorrow morning works for me." Randy glanced at Micah. "Is that good for you?"

He shrugged. "Any time is fine. My calendar isn't exactly full." A discontented expression flitted across his face. "I mean, what's there to do here? I can't wait to get to Hawaii and start living it up."

Taken aback by his remark, Cass shot Tabitha a sidelong look. The hurt in her sister's eyes was enough to make her forget their recent fight.

What a rotten thing to say, she fumed. *Doesn't Micah care Tabitha's standing right here? Honestly, talk about insensitive.*

Smoothing over the awkward moment, Rianne declared, "I don't know about the rest of you, but I'm starved. Randy," she addressed her brother, "you're closest to the basket. Break out the sandwiches, will you?"

While Randy obediently lifted the lid on the basket, Cass noticed Tabitha carefully studying her feet. Kira glared daggers at her brother, who seemed blissfully unaware of the tension.

Logan tapped Cass' shoulder. "Speaking of food, I'm ready to eat. How about you?"

Grateful for the chance to escape, she nodded. "You know me. I'm always ready to eat." She waggled her fingers at the group. "See y'all later."

"See you," everyone but Tabitha responded.

As much as she wanted to leave, Cass couldn't go with her sister so obviously upset. "Uh ... Tabitha? I need to ask you something. Can we go outside and talk a second?"

"Sure." Tabitha was the picture of dejection as she followed Cass out onto the sand. "What's up?"

"Nothing." Cass kept her voice down so the others couldn't hear. "Are you okay? After what Micah said, I mean."

Instead of taking offense, Tabitha shrugged in defeat. "No, I'm not okay. I hate it when he pulls stuff like that. He goes along for awhile, acting like he can't stand the thought of leaving. Then, out of the blue, he says something about looking forward to it. It drives me crazy."

"Have you told him how you feel?" Cass glanced over her shoulder to make sure no one was eavesdropping. To her relief, the others were too busy pawing through the picnic basket to pay any attention to them.

"I'm not you," Tabitha defended herself. "I don't like confrontation."

"But you can't let it go on, especially since it bothers you so much," Cass argued. "Do you want me to talk to Micah?"

Tabitha's laugh was incredulous. "Yeah, right. Like that's a better idea than me doing nothing."

Stung, Cass glowered at her. "Excuse me for trying to help. That's the last time I offer to do anything for you. Honestly," she added, shaking her head, "you're such a snot sometimes." Waving at Logan to get his attention, she informed him, "I'm done. We can go now."

He detached himself from the group and joined her. "You may have to carry me. I'm about to collapse from hunger."

Cass arched an eyebrow. "Not that you're exaggerating."

"Me?" Logan pressed a hand to his chest. "Never."

As the pair turned to leave, Tabitha caught Cass by the arm. "About what I said," she began.

Cass shrugged off her hand. "You don't have to say anything else. You made yourself perfectly clear the first time, so I have a deal for you. I'll stay out of your business if you'll stay out of mine."

Without giving Tabitha a chance to respond, Cass whirled around and stalked across the sand to where she and Logan had left their things. Snatching up her T-shirt, she jerked it over her head.

"You two really aren't getting along, are you?" Logan observed mildly as he too donned his shirt.

"I'll give you three guesses as to whose fault it is." Cass scraped her hair into a ponytail and anchored it with a scrunchy. "And the first two don't count."

Logan handed Cass her bag before picking up his own. "That narrows it down."

"It's not funny," Cass said. "I have one nerve left, and she's been all over it lately."

"Have you prayed about the situation?"

Logan's quiet question stopped Cass in her tracks. Her lower lip protruded in a pout. "No. I don't feel like praying."

"Ah." Logan nodded sagely. "So you're enjoying being mad."

"That's not ... I mean ..." A reluctant smile curved Cass' lips. "Okay, maybe I am." She leaned her head against his shoulder for a moment. "What am I going to do without you around to keep me in line?"

"The same thing I'm going to do without you around," murmured Logan. "Rely on God's grace and count the days until we see each other again."

The afternoon passed quickly. Cass couldn't believe it

when 3:00 rolled around, and it was time to head home. *Another day closer to Logan leaving*, she thought sadly as they wheeled her bike to the road in front of Logan's house.

"I'm sorry we can't get together tonight." Logan played with Cass' fingers, bending them back and forth. "My Mom wants to do the family thing."

"I understand." She did, but that didn't mean she liked it.

"I'll call you as soon as we're through golfing in the morning. Is there something special you'd like to do?"

"Being with you is all I want."

Logan sighed. "Same here." After a quick look around, he leaned forward and kissed Cass goodbye. "I'll call you later."

"You'd better." She wagged a warning finger. "I don't want to sit by the phone the rest of the day for nothing."

With that, Cass climbed on the bike and took off. She was just in time. The tears that continually threatened of late started to fall the moment she pulled away from Logan's house. Instead of turning to wave goodbye, she raised her hand in a farewell salute and kept pedaling. She didn't want Logan's last memories of her to be a tear-stained, splotchy face.

CHAPTER 4

By the time Friday rolled around, Cass' emotions were running at a fever pitch. She and Logan decided their last evening together would include dinner at the Yokwe Yuk, followed by a walk on the beach.

They spent most of the time at the restaurant reminiscing about the past year. Beginning with the day they met, they recalled their first date, the Christmas party on the neighboring island of Ebeye, and prom, which had just been a month ago. Cass was grateful for the trip down memory lane. It kept her tears at bay for the duration of the meal. The moment they hit the beach, however, they welled up.

"I can't believe this is it," she whispered bleakly, clutching Logan's hand as if it were a life preserver. "You'll be boarding the plane in less than nine hours."

"It's going to take every last ounce of courage I have to actually go through with it." Logan's profile appeared to be carved in stone as he gazed out at the moonlit ocean. "I want you to be at the airport in the morning. But part of me is scared I won't be able to make myself get on the plane if you are."

"You know how much I want to be there. But—" Cass

swallowed hard, "if it'll make it easier on you, I'll stay home."

Pulling her to his side, Logan draped his arm across her shoulders. "I want your face to be the last one I see before I walk onto the plane. I want you there."

"Then it's settled." Cass slid her arm around his waist. "I'll meet you at the airport at 5:30." She pretended to shudder. "Only for you would I get up at such a crummy hour."

"I'm honored." Spying a crop of boulders, Logan led her to them, and they sat down. "Uh ... Cass, I ... uh ... I've been wanting to say something to you, but I can't decide if I should. The problem is I'm running out of time. If I don't say it now, I may never get the chance."

Cass' heart slammed against her chest. She wasn't sure if she was more frightened or eager to hear what he had to say. "Is it something bad?" she asked cautiously.

"I ... don't think so." Logan smiled crookedly. "Maybe I should just tell you and let you decide." Taking a deep breath, he rubbed damp palms down his shorts. "Okay, here goes. We've never talked about ... love. When Pastor Thompson led the True Love Waits program for the guys, he said we shouldn't throw the word around the way most people do because it loses its meaning. He told us we should wait for the woman we're to marry before using it. But the way I feel about you—"

"Shh." Cass placed her finger against his lips. "Don't say it, okay?" When Logan nodded his agreement, she removed her finger. A smile briefly touched her mouth. "It's funny. A couple of days ago, Mom warned me to be careful about getting in over my head physically. She didn't say anything about emotionally."

Logan looked puzzled. "What do you mean? Why would it be wrong for us to say we love each other?"

"Because—" Cass took his hands and tightly gripped

them, "it changes everything. At least it does for me. When I finally tell someone I love him, it's going to mean I plan to spend the rest of my life with him. And I expect it to mean the same thing for the guy. We're not ready to make that kind of commitment."

Logan frowned slightly. "What would you say if I told you I am?"

The breath whooshed out of Cass, and, for a moment, she couldn't speak. Visions of engagement rings and wedding dresses danced in her head until she pushed them away.

"I'd say I'm flattered, but that I don't believe you know what you're talking about." When Logan opened his mouth to protest, she raised a hand to cut him off. "Let me finish. Are you saying you don't ever plan to date—not even once—while you're at West Point?"

"Well ..." Logan hedged.

"As long as either one of us entertains the possibility of going out with other people, we're not ready for the commitment that saying 'I love you' brings."

Logan's expression grew stormy. "You're planning on dating?"

"I don't have anyone in mind," Cass replied, adding honestly, "but, if somebody does come along, I don't see myself sitting home every weekend while everyone else goes out and has a good time." She regarded Logan with a steady gaze. "Do you?"

He squirmed and avoided her eyes. "Well ... no."

Even though she felt as if a fist were squeezing her heart, Cass forced herself to declare, "There you go. I rest my case."

"But—" Logan raised troubled eyes to her, "the thought of you dating someone else makes me sick to my stomach."

"I'm not too crazy about the idea myself." Cass sighed deeply. "And I don't know what I'll do the first time you write and tell me you've taken some girl out."

His face awash with misery, Logan squeezed Cass' hands. "I wish it didn't have to be like this."

"That makes two of us."

"Promise you won't wind up liking another guy more than you like me."

As much as she wanted to, Cass couldn't. Instead, she countered, "Can you make me that kind of promise?"

Logan's jaw rhythmically clenched and unclenched for several seconds before he shook his head. "Man, this stinks. I don't want it to be over between us."

"Nobody's saying it is." Cass sandwiched his hand between hers and peered earnestly at him. "We don't know what God has planned for us."

"Then you think it's possible a few years down the road that you and I might ..." Logan's voice trailed off.

"Who knows?" Cass shook back her hair with a saucy toss of her head. "God has done some pretty strange things in my life."

"Are you calling me strange?" Logan teased.

"Hey, if the weirdness fits," Cass shot back.

Glancing at his watch, Logan reluctantly stood up and pulled Cass to her feet. "We'd better get going. It's close to 11:00. I don't want your folks mad at me my last night here."

"Aw, I think they might cut you a little slack if we're a couple of minutes late."

Since they hadn't ridden their bikes, they turned left and started toward the Spencer house. Cass swallowed so many tears that they formed a golf ball-sized lump in her throat. As if sensing her predicament, Logan kept up a steady stream of conversation until they reached the back door. There, he swung Cass around to face him and leaned his forehead against hers.

"I know we agreed not to use the L word, but I want you

to know I care about you more than I've ever cared about anybody."

Not trusting herself to speak, Cass merely nodded.

"And unless you tell me not to," he continued, "I'm going to pray every night that God clears the way for us to be together someday."

"That sounds good to me," Cass managed to croak.

"Starting right now."

For the next several seconds, Logan softly asked God to watch over their relationship, to keep it strong, and to help it grow. When he finished, he tenderly kissed Cass, turned her, and gave her a playful push toward the door.

"I'll see you bright and early tomorrow morning."

"I don't know how bright I'll be," Cass grumbled, "but it'll definitely be early. 'Night now, and thanks for a good time."

"The pleasure was all mine. Good night."

From the porch, Cass watched Logan disappear into the darkness and stifled a sob. *Lord, please keep him safe. Not just tonight, but during the flight tomorrow, and until we meet again.* With that, she spun around and went inside.

CHAPTER 5

"Hey, how are you doing?" Trailed by her brother and the Alexanders, Rianne came up to Cass the moment church was over Sunday morning. The friends surrounded Cass, forming a circle of support and encouragement. She produced a wan smile. "As well as can be expected, I guess. When I got here, I automatically looked around for Logan. Then it hit me like a ton of bricks that he's really and truly gone. I just about lost it."

"She did," confirmed Tabitha. "It was touch and go for a couple of minutes. I thought we might have to leave."

With a stab of envy, Cass noticed Micah move to Tabitha's side and take her hand. She forced herself to look at Rianne.

"Fortunately, I got myself under control so I could stay. I'm glad I did. Worshipping with you guys in that setting and taking communion was important, I think, and Pastor Thompson's sermon about God being sufficient for our every need was exactly what I needed to hear."

"I'm glad." Rianne reached over and squeezed Cass' arm. "What are your plans for the rest of the day? Can Randy and I treat you to lunch at the Yokwe Yuk?"

Gently bumping her with his wheelchair, Randy pretended to gripe, "What's with this we? You never checked with me about spending my hard-earned money on Cass."

Rianne snorted. "What do you mean hard-earned?" she scoffed. "You don't work. You get an allowance."

"I have to live with you 24/7, don't I?" Randy shot back. "I'd call that earning my keep."

After the laughter died down, he turned to Cass. "All kidding aside, it would be my pleasure to escort you to lunch."

"I'm touched. Thank you." She silently consulted Tabitha, whose shrug indicated it was her decision. "I think I'll head home. Mom didn't feel up to coming to church, and Dad stayed with her. I should probably check on how she's doing."

"Since Cass is taking care of things at home," Micah immediately said to Tabitha, "how about you and I go to lunch?"

Cass noted with irritation that Tabitha didn't even hesitate.

"I'd love to have lunch with you," Tabitha said. She glanced at Cass. "Would you tell the folks where I am and that I'll be home around two?"

The best Cass could manage was a curt nod.

Slipping her arm through Micah's, Tabitha smiled up at him. "Let's go. The Yuk fills up quickly after church, and we don't want to have to wait."

Hand in hand, they walked away to retrieve their bikes. Cass didn't realize she was glaring at them until Kira tapped her on the shoulder.

"If looks could kill, my brother and your sister would be a couple of corpses lying on the grass right now," she observed softly.

Cass started and dragged her gaze away from the pair. "Sorry. I didn't mean to stare."

"Girl, you weren't staring." Kira snickered. "Your eyes

were two laser beams burning holes in their backs."

"Can you blame me?" muttered Cass. "My heart's broken, and Tabitha doesn't even have the decency to see if I need her to stick around. Talk about insensitive."

"Talk about selfish." Kira's tone was as challenging as her expression. "Just because Logan's gone doesn't mean Tabitha should give up what little time she has left with Micah to baby-sit you."

Cass' eyes narrowed to pinpoints. "I should have known you'd be on Tabitha's side, seeing as how you're best friends and all."

"You're her sister." Crossing her arms and tilting back her head, Kira glowered right back at Cass. "If anybody should be on her side, it's you."

"Aw, come on, you two." Rianne, the group's peacemaker, stepped between them. "Why don't you stop before you wind up saying something you regret?"

Although she itched to continue the argument, Cass realized Rianne was right. With tempers running as hot as they were at the moment, it wouldn't be long before somebody's feelings got hurt. Taking a deep breath, she turned to the Thayers.

"Like I said, I'm going home. Rianne, Randy, thanks again for the invite. Maybe we could have lunch some other time."

"Absolutely," declared Randy while his sister nodded vigorously.

Cass barely glanced at Kira. "See y'all later."

"See you," the Thayers replied.

Cass returned home in time to find Mom had just gotten out of bed. Looking pale and strained, she had settled down on the couch, and Dad was hovering over her with a cup of tea. She waved a limp hand at Cass.

"Hi, Sweetie. How was church?"

"Good. I liked the sermon." Cass walked to the recliner across from the sofa and sat down. "How are you feeling?"

"I've been better." Mom managed a small smile. "But I'm holding my own. The doctor is confident the morning sickness will pass in another month or so."

Cass' spirits plummeted. She couldn't imagine one more week, let alone another month, of this.

"At least we're not having twins," Dad commented, trying to inject a cheerful note. He handed Mom the tea and sat down on the other end of the couch. "I have to admit, I was relieved when the sonogram Friday showed only one baby."

"That makes two of us," Cass agreed fervently. "Tabitha thought twins would be cute. As far as I was concerned—" she gave a delicate shudder, "it was a fate worse than death. One baby is bad enough."

The silence in the room alerted her to the fact she'd said something wrong. Realizing what had popped out, she clamped a hand over her mouth and muttered around it, "Oops."

Tears welled in Mom's eyes. "You're not happy about the baby?" She placed a protective hand over her stomach.

"Of course I'm happy. I am," Cass insisted when Mom continued to look unconvinced. "I don't know why I said that. The only possible reason is I'm not thinking straight because I'm still wrung out from yesterday. I've told you a hundred times how thrilled I am about having a brother or sister."

"Speaking of sisters," Dad put in before Mom could respond. "Where's Tabitha? Didn't she come home with you?"

Relieved at the change of subject, Cass shook her head. "She and Micah went to the Yuk for lunch. She said to tell you she'll be home around 2:00."

Mom frowned. "Weren't you invited?"

The hurt Cass had felt at Tabitha's abandonment returned full-force. Her mouth tightened with anger, and she shook her head. "Not by Tabitha. Rianne and Randy asked me to eat with them."

Blowing on her tea, Mom hesitantly took a sip. "Why didn't you go?"

"I was worried about you," explained Cass. "I told them I wanted to come home and see how you were."

There, she thought with satisfaction. *That should earn me a few brownie points.*

"Thank you." Although Mom inclined her head in appreciation, she didn't smile. "But, really, it wasn't necessary. You should have gone with your friends. Dad was here." This time she did smile, but it was directed at him. "He does a wonderful job of taking care of me."

"Well, excuse me for being concerned," Cass muttered. Getting up, she stomped across the floor toward her room. "I can't do anything right anymore. First Kira, now you. I don't know why I even bother."

Without a backward glance, she stormed off to her room.

Fifteen minutes later, Dad knocked on the door.

"Yes?" Cass called from her bed. She had changed into shorts and a T-shirt, and had sprawled out to take a nap.

"Room service," Dad replied.

Rolling over, Cass stood up and padded to the door. "Wow, what's all this?" She eyed the plate in his hand, piled high with grilled cheese sandwiches, chips, and pickles, and her stomach rumbled. "I wasn't expecting you to make me lunch."

"I know." Dad set the plate and chocolate milk shake he had in his other hand on the nightstand. "It's compliments of the house. Mom and I thought you could use a little extra TLC."

"Thanks." Cass picked up the sandwich and milk shake,

and laughed. "What an interesting combination. Is it possible to overdose on calcium?"

"I'm sure you'll be fine as long as you eat slowly." Dad turned to leave, but Cass' voice stopped him.

"Would you like to share?" she offered, then admitted in a rush, "I ... I really don't feel like being alone right now."

"I'd love to stay and eat." Taking the sandwich half Cass held out to him, Dad walked to the desk and sat down. "Your Mom always says I make enough to feed an army."

Cass licked the cheese oozing out of the sandwich. "I know. I love that you use two slices of cheese when you grill sandwiches. It makes them all gooey, the way they're supposed to be. Not to complain or anything, but Mom just uses one."

"Her way is healthier and more economical." Dad winked. "But my way is more fun. And, every now and then, we could all use a little more fun in our lives."

At his leading, Cass bowed her head while he said a blessing over the lunch. When she looked up, she found him smiling at her.

"What?" She took a drink of the milk shake.

"I was just thinking how proud I am of you for the way you're handling Logan's leaving." Dad bit into the sandwich.

Cass shook her head. "I'm not handling it well at all. I almost broke down and bawled in church this morning."

"But you didn't," Dad pointed out. "Doesn't that tell you you're made of stronger stuff than you're giving yourself credit for?"

"I guess." Cass nibbled at a potato chip. "I feel so empty inside though. It's awful. And the worst part is I don't know when I'm going to see Logan again. He's pretty much stuck on the mainland since he doesn't have the money to fly back here for Christmas."

"I know it's hard," Dad sympathized. "Now's when you really have to draw on Christ to see you through."

"It's the not knowing how things are going to turn out that gets to me." Cass tore off a corner of the sandwich. "Don't you ever wish God would let you see into the future?"

"Sure." Dad shrugged. "But then we wouldn't need faith, would we?"

Cass gave him a half smile. "I hate it when you're logical." She chewed thoughtfully on the piece of sandwich. "If I knew everything was going to work out for Logan and me in the end, I don't think being separated would be so difficult."

"What do you mean by work out?" Dad asked carefully.

Color blossomed on Cass' cheeks. She suddenly busied herself with fussing with her napkin and rearranging the chips.

"Well?" he prompted when she didn't say anything.

"You'll think I'm silly," Cass said in a muffled voice. "That I'm too young to even be thinking about ... you know ... marriage."

"Sweetie, when two people care as much for each other and have as much in common as you and Logan do, then it's natural to think ahead to what might happen." Dad paused for effect before adding, "Years and years down the road."

Cass laughed. "You always have to get that in, don't you?"

"What can I say? I hate the thought of losing you. The longer I can stave it off, the happier I'll be. But," Dad continued, "to get back to the subject. Don't forget the future is in God's hands. If He wants you and Logan to wind up together then nothing can keep it from happening."

Instead of comforting Cass, his statement caused her shoulders to droop. "That means the opposite is also true. If it's not God's will that we get married someday, we won't."

"That's true," acknowledged Dad. "The bottom line is you have to trust God's will for your life, no matter what."

"Sometimes I really hate the no matter what part," Cass said darkly. "I still struggle with wanting things my way."

"Welcome to the club. I don't know if that ever changes." Dad popped the last of the sandwich into his mouth and wiped his hands on his shorts. "When you get to feeling that way, I have a bit of advice for you. Go back over the things you dreaded in your life, and you'll see how God has brought good out of them."

"You're talking about your marriage to Mom and our move here, aren't you? I really didn't want that to happen, but look how well it turned out."

"Exactly," Dad said. "We can only see a tiny part of the picture, but God sees the whole thing. For instance, think of His death on the cross. If you stopped the video—so to speak—right there, things look really awful. But if you fast forward, you see His resurrection, and the ultimate purpose—His death meant salvation for all. I know it's hard, Cass, but God always knows what's best for us, even when we don't."

"So I'm supposed to be happy about Logan leaving?" Cass knew she looked as skeptical as she sounded.

Dad shook his head. "Of course not. You have every right to be sad and to miss him. But you need to trust that God is working everything out according to His plan for your life."

"Even when that's the hardest thing I've ever had to do?"

He smiled tenderly. "Especially then."

"Well, all I can promise is that I'll try." Cass picked up what was left of her sandwich and waved it. "Is there any way I could talk you into making another one? I have a feeling a half just isn't going to cut it today. I'm going to need food—and lots of it—to see me through this crisis."

Dad immediately stood. "One grilled cheese sandwich coming right up."

"Be sure to make yourself one," Cass called after him as he headed out the door. "I'm not sharing this time."

Chapter 6

Cass was on the porch struggling with yarn and a crochet hook when Tabitha returned from her lunch with Micah.

"What are you doing?" Tabitha asked, plopping down in the wicker chair across from the swing where Cass sat. Cass huffed her impatience with the question. "Building a rocket ship. Honestly, what does it look like I'm doing?"

"I have no idea." Instead of taking offense, Tabitha laughed. "That's why I asked."

Holding each item up in turn, Cass drawled, "Hook. Yarn. Hmm, do you think maybe I could be crocheting? Duh."

Tabitha shrugged, then asked mildly, "What are you so crabby about?"

"Come on, you're a smart girl. You can put two and two together. Logan left yesterday. Then today my own sister couldn't be bothered to stick around and give me moral support." Cass glared across the space separating her from Tabitha. "Wouldn't you agree that adds up to me having the right to be crabby?"

"Look—" her eyes flashing, Tabitha sat up straight in

the chair, "I'm not going to let you make me feel guilty because my boyfriend's still here and yours isn't."

"Ooh, low blow, Sis." In her anger, Cass dropped a stitch and had to go back and pick it up. "If you're going to take that attitude, don't expect any sympathy from me when Micah packs up and heads out next month." She trilled a laugh designed to get on Tabitha's nerves. "How's this for a deal? I'll treat you the way you're treating me. That's fair, don't you think?"

"What have I done?" Tabitha flung out her arms in a gesture of innocence. "I've been there for you, and you know it. I've sat with you while you cried. I've listened to you talk about how scared you are about the separation. I've done my level best to cheer you up. What more can I do? So I had lunch with Micah? Big deal. I was gone a grand total of two hours. I'm not allowed one little break?"

Chastened, Cass had to admit she had a point. "Okay, maybe I overreacted. So—" she forced herself to smile, "did you and Micah have a nice time?"

"It was all right." Suddenly, Tabitha got up and began to pace. "All he ever wants to talk about anymore is school. He keeps going over the same territory. What he's taking with him. What he'll need to buy once he gets to Honolulu. The activities he's going to participate in at school. It's like—" she hesitated, and her voice dropped to a near whisper, "he can't wait to get there."

"I'm sure that's not true," Cass said.

"He never says he's going to miss me." Stopping by the window, Tabitha perched on the ledge, crossed her arms, and stared at Cass.

"Oh. Well." Disturbed by the remark, Cass wracked her brain for something to say. "Maybe that's not his way. A lot of boys aren't comfortable talking about their feelings."

Tabitha sniffed her disgust. "He doesn't have any problem talking about how excited he is about school and how much he's looking forward to it."

"That's different."

"How?" Tabitha challeneged.

Cass was stumped, but she didn't want to admit it. "It just is," she replied crossly. "This conversation is going nowhere. Go away and let me crochet in peace."

A mischievous grin tugged at the corners of Tabitha's mouth. "First you jump all over me for leaving you alone. Now you want me to go away." She threw her hands up in mock exasperation. "I can't win."

Cass frowned. "Don't try to make me laugh. I'm in a bad mood, and I want to stay that way."

"Suit yourself." Tabitha pushed off from the window ledge and sauntered over to the swing. Sitting down, she set it in motion. "So, what are you making?"

"A baby blanket." Cass consulted the pattern in her lap, sighed gustily, and began unraveling several stitches. "At this rate, I'll probably have it done in time for the kid to bring it to college."

"Wait a minute." Tabitha looked confused. "I thought you weren't that thrilled about the baby. Why are you making it a blanket?"

"Like I've said, it's not so much the kid I'm put out about. It's Mom." Cass lowered her voice. "Did you see her asleep in there? How are we supposed to have a youth group meeting tonight if she's still sick and tired the way she's been all day? I was looking forward to the meeting to help take my mind off Logan."

"Aren't you being kind of selfish?" Tabitha asked, her tone and facial expression dissaproving.

Cass gave an irritated flounce. "I'm getting a little tired of people accusing me of being selfish."

"Who else said you were?"

"Kira." The moment the response was out of her mouth, Cass wished she could take it back.

"Kira?" Tabitha's eyebrows arched. "When? Why?"

Mentally kicking herself, Cass explained, "This morning after church. I made some comment about you going off with Micah, and she said I was selfish."

"You know," Tabitha coolly informed her, "if you have something to say, I'd rather you said it to my face."

"How could I?" Cass shot back. "You were gone."

Silence reigned for several seconds. Cass finally produced a sheepish smile.

"This reminds me of a year ago when I first moved down here. Back then every conversation ended in a fight."

"Yeah." Tabitha slid her arm along the back of the swing and gazed out the window at the ocean. "We're both on edge and, as usual, we're taking it out on each other."

"At least Mom's so out of it most of the time that she doesn't notice." Cass stifled a giggle. "Remember how we used to drive her crazy with our arguing?"

Tabitha nodded. "I miss the way she was always on top of things. I hope this phase of the pregnancy doesn't last too much longer."

"Aha!" Cass crowed triumphantly. "So you're not as deliriously happy about the baby as you pretend to be. I knew it."

"How many times do we have to have this discussion?" Tabitha sighed to express her annoyance. "I'm more than happy about the baby. I'm positively delighted. But that doesn't mean I like what the pregnancy's doing to Mom. It would be nice to talk to her about Micah. But either she's asleep or she's too sick to think straight."

"Tell me about it." Cass' mouth tightened into a discontented line. "I spend half my time worrying about her and the other half resenting the fact that she's pregnant. I'll tell you one thing. If this is what being pregnant is like, I'm never having kids."

"Maybe it's easier when you're younger," Tabitha suggested hopefully. "After all, Mom is 38. That's practically ancient as far as having a baby is concerned." Tabitha picked up the ball of yarn lying on the seat between her and Cass and began tossing it from one hand to the other. "Anyway, to get back to the meeting—do you think they're going to cancel it?"

Cass shrugged. "Who knows? So far, Mom's always rallied enough to have them. Let's hope her nap gives her the energy she needs for this one."

As it turned out, Mom didn't make it to the meeting. Dad carried on alone while she retreated to the bedroom to lie down. Although he did a good job leading the Bible study and discussions, Cass and Tabitha agreed later that it wasn't the same without Mom. For Cass, it also wasn't the same without Logan.

Standing at her bedroom window later that night, she leaned her head against the glass as the tears that had threatened all day finally spilled down her cheeks. She didn't bother wiping them away, but let them drip onto the front of her nightshirt.

Lord, I miss Logan so much. Wherever he is, and whatever he's doing, please watch over him. I know Your will for us is perfect. But, if it's all right with You, please don't let our friendship die. It happened with Jan back in Tennessee, and I don't think I could stand it if it happened with Logan. Also, help Mom get over not feeling well and being exhausted all the time. Tabitha and I need her. In Jesus' name, thank You and amen.

Cass felt slightly better as she turned away from the window and walked to her bed. Pulling back the quilt, she slipped between the sheets then snuggled the covers around her ears. Her last thought as she drifted off to sleep was of Logan, and she sent up a quick prayer that he would call her soon. She was sure that hearing his voice would boost her spirits like nothing else could.

CHAPTER 7

"Sweetie." Cass woke to someone gently shaking her shoulder. "You have a phone call."

Blinking, Cass rolled over and pushed the hair out of her eyes. "Huh?" She glanced at the clock. 9:30.

"You have a phone call," repeated Mom.

Cass startled her by bolting upright and grabbing for her robe. "A call? For me? Who is it?"

"Rianne."

Mom's answer affected Cass like a punch in the stomach. She collapsed on the bed, flung her arm over her eyes, and burst into tears.

Dropping down beside her, Mom took her hand and anxiously rubbed it. "Honey, what is it? Why are you crying?"

"F-for a few seconds there ... I-I thought it might be Logan," Cass wailed.

"Oh, my." Getting up, Mom moved to the door. "You wait here. I'll be right back."

By the time she returned, Cass' sobs had subsided to hiccups. Bleary-eyed, she looked up when her mother bustled into the room, carrying a glass of milk and a doughnut.

"Why do you and Dad think food solves everything?"

She struggled to a sitting position and reached for the napkin-wrapped doughnut. Mom set the milk on the nightstand.

"Because we're parents. Food is something we can do. Besides—" Mom smoothed Cass' hair, "it usually works, doesn't it?"

Nodding, Cass licked the powdered sugar off her lips. "I'm not complaining. What did you tell Rianne?"

"That you couldn't come to the phone and you'd call her back."

"Thanks." Cass leaned back against the pillow. "I really lost it for a couple of minutes there."

Mom pulled the chair from the desk and set it next to the bed. "I feel awful. I thought you were doing well. I didn't realize how distraught you still are about Logan's leaving."

"That's okay."

Cass ducked her head so Mom wouldn't see what she was thinking. *How could you know? We've barely talked since he left.*

Mom seemed to know her thoughts anyway. "I know I haven't been much help to you. I promise I'll do better once I get past this part of the pregnancy."

"You're doing fine. Don't worry about it." Cass hoped God wouldn't consider that lying. "As far as my hissy fit, I went to sleep thinking about Logan. So, naturally, he was the first one I thought of when you said I had a phone call."

"When do you expect to hear from him?"

"That's the thing." Cass' brow furrowed. "I'm not sure. He reports in at West Point on July 1st, so sometime between now and then, whenever he gets a chance to call."

"I guess you won't be leaving the house until he does, huh?" Mom quipped.

"Only if it's an emergency." Setting the doughnut in her lap, Cass picked up the glass of milk. "When I talk to

Rianne, I'll see if she can come over here."

Mom's expression grew concerned. "Sweetie, you need to get out. It's not good to stay cooped up."

Cass rolled her eyes. "I was kidding. I plan on doing my usual stuff. If Logan calls while I'm out, he can either call back or you can get a number where I can reach him. See?" she teased. "I really do have a few functioning brain cells."

Mom had the grace to look chastened. "Sorry. It seems I'm losing my sense of humor along with my waistline."

"You're feeling better this morning?" Finishing off the doughnut, Cass crumpled the napkin and tossed it at the wastebasket beside the desk. It bounced off the rim and onto the floor.

"So far, so good." Mom got up, retrieved the napkin, and dropped it into the basket. "I know you must be tired of me being sick all the time."

"It has gotten pretty old," Cass conceded. "But, once the baby gets here, I guess it'll all be worth it."

"You guess?"

Cass held up a hand. "Don't start analyzing everything I say. I get enough of that from Tabitha. I'm glad you and Dad are having a child to keep you company in your old age." Her face briefly lit up with an impish grin. "I just didn't count on the first few months being like this. If you think that's a terrible thing to say, I'm sorry. But," she added firmly, "I don't take it back."

"Fair enough." Mom smiled slightly. "I'll let you in on a little secret. I don't like it, either. I sailed through my pregnancy with you, and that's the way I expected this one to go. But there's a world of difference between having a baby at 21 and having one at 38. Sometimes I think you're right, and I am too old to be doing this."

"I never said you were too old," Cass protested. As Mom stood, Cass reached up and patted her rounded stomach. "I said you were *almost* too old. Besides, it's very trendy nowadays for women in their late 30s and early 40s to be having babies. But I do think 40 should be the cutoff. What teenager in their right mind wants a mother in her 60s?" She shuddered. "Talk about embarrassing."

Erupting with laughter, Mom drawled, "Thanks for the pep talk. I always feel so much better after one of our little chats."

"That's what I'm here for," Cass called after her as she exited. "To spread sunshine and good cheer wherever I go."

"Nobody spreads it like you do," Mom shot back before disappearing down the hall.

Before getting out of bed, Cass spent a few minutes studying the picture on the nightstand. It was of her and Logan, taken at the prom last month. Their brilliant smiles and clasped hands proclaimed to the world their joy at being together. Although the picture made her feel like crying, Cass found herself smiling instead as she traced Logan's face with her fingertip.

"Logan Michael Russell, I miss you like crazy. But I'm also so proud of you for achieving your dream of going to West Point. I pray God protects and blesses you today and every day." She started to get up, hesitated a moment, then added, "But, if you don't call me soon, I take it all back. No more prayers for you, pal." After making sure no one was around, she leaned over and quickly kissed the picture. "Just kidding."

Cass was enjoying a breakfast of bacon and eggs when Tabitha wandered into the dining room. Halting behind Cass' chair, she yawned and stretched.

" 'Morning. What's going on?"

Cass shot her a wry glance over her shoulder. "Uh ... breakfast."

"Anything else?" Tabitha helped herself to a sip of juice from Cass' glass.

"I'm expecting the acrobats and dancing elephants to show up any minute now. Hey!" Cass swatted Tabitha's hand when she went for the juice again. "That's mine. Go get your own."

"Okay." Tabitha shrugged agreeably and moved to the refrigerator. "Good morning, Mom."

Mom looked up from the bowl of eggs she was beating. " 'Morning, sweetie. How do scrambled eggs sound?"

"I have no idea. I've never heard them say anything."

While Mom chuckled, Cass covered her face with her hands and groaned.

Tabitha plucked a grape out of a bowl in the refrigerator and threw it at her. "Oh, hush. That's the best I can do this early in the day."

Cass snagged the grape before it rolled off the table. "Why do you insist on trying to be funny? That's my job. You're the pretty one, and I'm the funny one. When are you going to get it straight?"

"Maybe when you finally start being funny." Preening, Tabitha fluffed her curls. "As for me, I have being pretty down cold."

"You're both beautiful, and you're both funny," Mom said quickly, before Cass could respond. "I don't want to hear any more talk about who's better at what."

"But, Mom," Cass began.

"But nothing," Mom broke in. "No more discussion, and that's that."

Although she never would have had the nerve to say it out loud, Cass thought resentfully, *Why don't you go back to bed? That way you wouldn't be out here taking Tabitha's side against me.*

Glancing her way, Mom remarked, "And just so we're clear, I'm not taking anyone's side. I'm doing my job and heading off an explosion."

Cass gaped at her. *How does she do that? Sometimes I*

believe she can actually read my mind. In case it were true, she cleared her head of negative thoughts and concentrated on finishing her breakfast.

"Are you doing anything today?" Tabitha carried her plate to the table and sat down across from Cass.

"I talked to Rianne, and we're going to meet at the pool." Cass shoveled the last forkful of eggs into her mouth. "We'll probably spend the morning there. After that, I don't know."

"How about the two of us do something?" Tabitha offered.

"Like what?"

"You want to check out Macy's and see if they've gotten in any new clothes?"

Cass made a face. "You know I don't like to shop, especially for clothes."

"Well, then you suggest something," Tabitha said quickly, a note of annoyance in her voice. She lifted her glass so abruptly that juice sloshed over the side.

"Why me?" countered Cass. "It was your idea that we do something."

"Honestly!" Tabitha plunked the glass down on the place mat, causing another spillover. "Forget it. I didn't mean for it to turn into a big hassle."

Cass assumed her most innocent expression. "What are you talking about? I just asked a simple question."

Clutching her midsection, Mom turned from the sink. "I'm afraid you girls are going to have to clean up. I'm not feeling well."

Cass jumped out of her chair. "Do you need me to help you to the bathroom?"

Mom waved her off. "No, thanks. This has become such a daily routine I could get there with my eyes closed."

"Okay." Cass reluctantly stepped aside. "Holler if you need me though."

"I will." Mom disappeared down the hall.

"Wow, she actually looked green," Tabitha said, biting into a piece of bacon.

"Yeah, I'm surprised she's gaining any weight with how often she gets sick." With a last, worried glance down the hall, Cass shifted her attention back to the task Mom had assigned them. "So, do you want to put the stuff in the dishwasher or scrub the pans and wipe the stove?"

"Neither."

Cass sighed in exasperation. "Fine. I'll load the dishwasher."

"Cass?"

Her sister's plaintive tone stopped her, and she turned around. "What?"

"Are you really not interested in doing something together?"

"I never said I wasn't interested. I hate it when you put words in my mouth."

Tabitha stiffened. "Never mind. Maybe some other time."

"Whatever."

Making as much noise as possible, Cass did her share of the cleaning up. She hoped the clatter of dishes and the slamming of doors made it impossible for Tabitha to enjoy her meal, but she also hoped Mom couldn't hear the racket. She wanted to annoy her sister, not get in trouble.

The moment she was done, she hurried down the hall to her room to change into her bathing suit and grab a T-shirt and towel. Before leaving, she knocked softly on Mom's door.

"Come in," came the muffled reply.

Opening the door, Cass found Mom curled up in a miserable ball. "I'm leaving for the pool. Is there anything you need?"

"You wouldn't happen to have a cast-iron stomach lying

around anywhere, would you?" Mom joked weakly.

"I wish I did." Cass walked to the bed and gently stroked Mom's hair. It was strange to be the one doing the comforting. "Would you rather I stay here?"

"As the old saying goes, 'This too shall pass.' You go on. I'll be fine." Mom carefully eased onto her back. "Besides, Tabitha's here if I need anything."

A familiar spurt of jealousy shot through Cass. *I can take care of you 10 times better than she can,* she wanted to say.

Instead, she nodded and replied, "In that case, I'm out of here. I should be back around lunch."

"Of course you will." Mom's smile was mischievous. "I don't believe I've ever known you to miss a meal."

"Fine." Pretending to be insulted, Cass flounced toward the door. "See if I ever volunteer to baby-sit you again."

"Aw, don't go away mad." When Cass glanced back, Mom grinned. "Just go away."

Cass left the room on a wave of laughter. It quickly died when she saw Tabitha coming toward her down the hall.

"How's she doing?" Tabitha asked in the hushed tone usually heard around hospital rooms.

Holding out a hand, Cass waved it from side to side. "So-so. She seems a little better, but she still looks rotten. I offered to stay home."

Tabitha's eyebrows shot up in surprise. "Why? I'll be here."

"That was Mom's response too." Cass hid her disgruntlement over not being needed behind a casual shrug.

"Then I'd say it's unanimous." Tabitha's challenging stare dared her to argue.

Cass didn't. Slinging the towel over her shoulder, she gave a jaunty wave. "If Mom gets to feeling better, why don't you come over to the pool? I'm sure Rianne would like to spend some time with you."

"What's that supposed to mean?"

Pleased to have the upper hand, Cass took her time answering. "Oh, just that everyone's noticed how you're spending all your time with Micah. People are starting to feel left out."

"You mean like you did with Logan before he left?" Tabitha returned sweetly.

"I—" Cass drew herself up to her full height, taller than Tabitha, "wasn't half as bad as you. I made time for my friends."

"Funny, but that's not how I remember it," Tabitha shot back.

"Then maybe you should have your memory checked." Folding her arms, Cass summoned up her fiercest scowl. "I went out of my way to keep doing stuff with y'all."

"Look, I don't want to argue. If you choose to believe you divided your time equally between Logan and the rest of us, fine. But I'm not going to let you make me feel bad for wanting to spend as much time with Micah as I can before he leaves."

"All I'm saying is, don't forget who'll be staying behind. Once Micah's gone, you're going to need your friends. Don't do anything that might keep us from rallying around you," Cass advised, her tone ominous.

Instead of responding, Tabitha brushed past Cass and went into her room without a word. She closed the door with a distinct thud, and Cass was left to fume in the hall alone.

Sometimes she can be the most annoying person on the face of the earth, Cass grumbled to herself as she stalked down the hall to the front door. *I'm only trying to be helpful. But is she grateful? No, of course not. She's the original Miss Know-It-All. Well, she can just be that way. I wash my hands of her.*

51

CHAPTER 8

Settling into a poolside lounge chair, Cass felt her tension melt away in the heat of the tropical sun. Rianne hadn't arrived yet so she amused herself by watching a group of mothers playing with their toddlers in the kiddie pool. She tried to imagine Mom with a 6-month-old baby a year from now, but couldn't picture it. She would look ancient compared to the young women gathered here this morning.

I wonder why her age bothers me so much, she mused. *Maybe Rianne has an answer to that.*

She almost forgot to ask because the combination of the heat and the sound of the surf had nearly lulled her to sleep by the time her friend arrived. Rianne had to call her name twice before Cass finally pried open her eyelids.

"Oh, hi." Stifling a yawn, Cass struggled to sit up. "I didn't hear you come up."

"Of course you didn't." Rianne dragged over a lounge chair and sat down. "You were lost in dreamland. I think I even heard you snore a couple of times."

Cass frowned. "No, you didn't! I don't snore."

Rianne wagged a chiding finger. "I've slept over at your house too many times for you to get away with pulling that one. Sometimes you get to snoring so loud you sound like a chain saw."

Sliding down, Cass glanced left then right to see if anyone was within earshot. "You're lying."

"About the snoring just now, yup," Rianne confessed without a shred of remorse. "But not about the chain saw thing. Honestly, there have been times I've woken up, expecting to see a tree falling on me."

"That's not funny." Cass folded her arms and glared. "I don't know why I put up with you."

"Because—" stripping off her T-shirt, Rianne stretched out on the chair, "right now, I'm about the only friend you have. Logan's gone. Kira's put out at you for what happened yesterday. And you're put out at Tabitha because she still has Micah. Face it, I'm the only show in town."

Although she hated to admit it, Cass recognized the truth of what Rianne said. "If I'm so awful, why do you still like me?" she asked stiffly.

Rianne slid her sunglasses down her nose in order to look Cass in the eyes. "I'm your friend. Don't you remember the birthday card I gave you? It said a friend is someone who knows everything about you and loves you anyway. That's the kind of friend you are to me so that's the kind of friend I try to be to you."

"But everything I know about you is nice," Cass pointed out. "It's not hard to like you."

Rianne's laugh was genuine. "Then you don't know me as well as you think you do." Assuming a mysterious expression, she intoned, "I have secrets so deep and so dark they'd make your blood run cold if I ever revealed them to you."

"Yeah, right." Cass flashed her an affectionate smile. "You're the least secretive person I know. Your life is an open book."

"I know." Rianne wriggled around in her chair to find a more comfortable position. "But a girl can dream, can't she?"

"You're nuts." Laughing, Cass shook her head.

Rianne reached over to pat her arm. "I love you too."

"You think you know me so well, don't you?"

"Nope. I know I do." Folding her arms beneath her head, Rianne looked at Cass. "For example, I know you have something on your mind. So give. What's up?"

Cass looked at her, filled with both admiration and bewilderment. "How do you do that? Never mind," she went on when Rianne opened her mouth to respond. "I'll just accept it as one of your gifts and go on. Anyway, before you showed up, I was lying here wondering why it bothers me that my Mom's having a baby at 38."

"Hmm." Rianne took a few moments before she continued her response. "I can think of a couple of reasons right off the top of my head. First of all, it's not her age so much as the fact that she's having a baby. You were an only child for 16 years. Soon you'll be one of three kids. That takes a lot of getting used to."

"Okay. I'll buy that." Cass nodded her agreement. "What else?"

"Secondly, her age does have something to do with it." Rianne wrinkled her nose. "I've thought about how I'd feel if my parents decided to have another kid. I'd hate to be a senior in high school and have my mother walking around pregnant. The timing is all wrong. Your parents should be done having kids by the time you're ready for college."

Cass threw her hands up in relief. "That's exactly how I feel. I'm glad you understand. Is that it as far as theories go?"

Rianne nodded. "That's all I've got."

"It's good enough. Thank you." Cass turned a wry face to her. "Now if only you could help me solve my problems with Tabitha. We're getting on each other's nerves something fierce, and I don't know how to stop fighting with her."

"Sorry. You're going to have to call in the U.N. to work on that one," Rianne joked. "Your relationship with Tabitha is way out of my league."

"I was afraid of that." For a few seconds, Cass' shoulders slumped. Then she shook herself and stood up. "I'm not going to let it ruin the day. I'm burning up, and the water looks very inviting. What do you say we swim awhile?"

"I say—" flinging off her sunglasses, Rianne jumped up, "out of my way, girl. Last one in is a rotten egg."

For the rest of the morning, Cass was able to keep thoughts of Mom, the new baby, Logan, and Tabitha at bay. She made sure to thank God for the break as she headed back to the house shortly before one. Whatever the rest of the day held for her, at least she'd had a fun couple of hours.

Chapter 9

"I have mail, and guess who it's for." Afraid to hope, Cass raised dull eyes to Dad as he came into the living room. It was the second week of July and, except for a postcard and a brief phone call, Cass hadn't heard from Logan. She'd gotten to the point that she hated to hear mail had come in because she was sure there'd be nothing for her.

Dad stopped in front of the recliner where Cass was diligently working on the blanket for the baby. His hands were behind him, and he rocked back and forth on his heels, brimming with excitement.

"Come on," he wheedled. "Aren't you going to guess?"

Setting aside the blanket, Cass scowled up at him. "With the way you're acting, you'd better have mail from Logan or I won't talk to you for a month."

"You consider that a threat?" Tabitha teased from the couch where she sat with Mom.

"Stop. You're killing me." Cass slapped her knee with pretend glee before holding out her hand to Dad and snapping her fingers. "Okay, no more games. If there's something from Logan, fork it over."

He produced several envelopes and made a show of flipping through them. "Let's see. Here's one from a Cadet

Russell. Oh, look, here's another one. And another one. I do believe we've hit the jackpot."

Suddenly, Cass was on her feet, eagerly grabbing for them. In all, Dad presented her with five letters which she promptly carried off to her room to read in private.

Curled up in a corner of the sofa, Tabitha saw Mom and Dad exchange relieved smiles the moment Cass' door closed behind her.

"You remember how we used to pray for letters from home for her last year?" Mom said to Dad. When he nodded, she shook her head. "This is 10—no, make that 100—times worse than that."

"I know." Dad cleared a space on the coffee table and sat down. "I nearly jumped for joy when I saw the letters, and Logan's not even my boyfriend."

Mom leaned over and patted his knee. "You're a good dad. The girls' feelings are very important to you."

"Does that include me and my feelings?" Tabitha asked suddenly.

"You're one of my girls, aren't you?" He shifted on the table so he faced her. "Is there some particular feeling you'd like to talk about?"

Tabitha pulled a needlepoint pillow onto her lap and began tracing the design stitched into it. "Micah's leaving in 10 days."

"So soon?" Dad's eyebrows shot up, and he glanced at Mom. "Did I know about this?"

"I've told you at least a dozen times," Tabitha said darkly before Mom could respond. "I guess you didn't remember because it's not as big a deal as Logan being at West Point."

Dad wearily rubbed a hand over his face. "Please don't

start the sibling rivalry stuff. I'm not in the mood. I'm sorry I forgot. If you tell me again, I promise I'll remember. Why is Micah leaving so early when school doesn't start until the middle of August?"

"He has relatives in Hawaii he's spending time with. They'll shop for school and help him brush up on his driving." Having finished a flower, Tabitha moved on to outlining a butterfly. "If he weren't going so early, we'd have almost another month together."

"But he is leaving," Mom pointed out. "So that's the reality you have to deal with."

Tabitha sighed impatiently. "I know that. Can't I make a simple comment without you jumping all over me?"

"That's enough." Although he didn't raise his voice, Dad's disapproval came through loud and clear. "Don't take your unhappiness out on Mom."

Instead of backing down, Tabitha asked, "Why not? Cass does it all the time."

"Not when I'm around," he assured her.

"True. She does tend to be sneaky when it comes to stuff like that." Deciding she'd pushed her luck far enough, Tabitha stretched and stood up. "I'd better get ready. Micah and I are going to the movies."

"I assume you've checked with Mom about this?" Dad cocked a brow at her.

"Yes, Dad," Tabitha drawled, propping a hand on her hip. "Believe it or not, I do follow the rules."

"Not all of them," he retorted. "You're not doing too well at respecting your elders."

Although she hated letting him have the last word, she couldn't think of a snappy comeback. With as much dignity as she could muster, she exited the room and stalked down the hall.

Cass emerged from her room a short while later. She figured the goofy smile she couldn't wipe from her face would let her parents know that Logan's letters had succeeded in lifting her spirits. She returned to the recliner and picked up the yarn and crochet hook.

"How's Logan?" Dad prompted when she didn't volunteer any information.

"Doing well, all things considered." Cass looped the yarn around her finger and began stitching.

"What do you mean, all things considered?" Dad asked patiently.

"They get up before dawn and run every morning. Can you imagine?" Cass shuddered. "Then they spend the rest of the day learning army stuff, like how to shoot and hand-to-hand combat. He said it's hard, but he likes it."

Dad laughed. "Good for him. He'll do well as long as he keeps a positive attitude."

"He said the worst part is being tired all the time. He can't remember the last time he slept more than a few hours at a stretch." Frowning, Cass continued, "He also said he's meeting people from a lot of different places. Not just the United States, but foreign countries too."

"How interesting," Mom said. After a pause, she added, "Does that bother you?"

Cass made a face. "I can't help wondering how many of them are girls."

"Since it's not an all-male school, he's bound to meet girls," Mom replied with a smile.

Folding her arms, Cass frowned. "Well, I don't want him to." She suddenly laughed at herself. "Not that I can do anything about it with him 9,000 miles away."

"Spoken like a true realist," Dad said.

Cass shrugged off the compliment. "It's easy to be realistic when you don't have a choice. Now if Logan were still here," she added menacingly, "I'd break every bone in his body if I caught him talking to another girl."

"Which may explain why he found it necessary to move so far away," Dad said, laughing.

"Men." Cass rolled her eyes at Mom. "They always stick together, don't they?"

"This from someone who can't even go to the ladies' room by herself?" Dad retorted. "For the life of me, I'll never figure out why women travel in packs to the restroom."

Winking at Cass, Mom said, "I'm afraid it'll have to remain a mystery, dear. There are some things women are sworn to secrecy about, and that's one of them."

"I hope the baby's a boy." Dad pretended to sulk. "I'm tired of being outnumbered around here."

"Micah's coming over in a few minutes," Tabitha chirped, having come from her room. "I'm sure he'll be happy to take your side in whatever's going on." She perched on the edge of the rocking chair and expectantly looked around, as if waiting for someone to fill her in on the conversation so far.

"Nothing specific," explained Dad. "I'm just generally tired of having three females gang up on me."

"Poor Dad," Tabitha cooed. "No one knows what a nightmare your life is."

Her false sympathy grated on Cass' nerves. She hated it when her sister got cutesy. About to make a snide comment, she was interrupted by the doorbell.

"There's Micah now." Tabitha jumped up, the skirt of her sundress swinging around her tanned legs. She hurried to the door and opened it with a flourish. "I knew it was you," she greeted Micah. "In all the time I've known you, I don't ever remember you being late."

"Yeah, I'm a regular clock." Micah strolled into the living room and lifted his hand to the Spencers and Cass. "How's it going?"

"Not bad," Dad replied, and Mom nodded in agreement. "How about you? Are you all set for school?"

"Just about." Micah's dark eyes gleamed with anticipation. "I'm counting the hours until I leave. I can't believe I'm actually starting college next month."

Cass' gaze flew to Tabitha's face in time to see her crestfallen expression before she hid it behind a bright smile. *He did it again*, Cass fumed, annoyed at Micah's thoughtlessness. *It's one thing for me to bug Tabitha. But I don't want any outsiders upsetting her.*

"Honestly, Micah," she complained, "you make it sound like you can't wait to get off the island. Isn't there anything or any*one* you're going to miss?"

Suddenly aware of what he'd said, Micah reached for Tabitha's hand and pulled her to his side. "How can you ask a question like that when everyone on Kwaj knows how crazy I am about this beautiful lady?"

Instead of being satisfied with his response, Cass tilted back her head and regarded him with a cool gaze. "Maybe it's because you never miss an opportunity to talk about how much you're looking forward to leaving."

Micah's jaw tightened, and he returned Cass' gaze without flinching. "I think I'm entitled to be excited about going off to college. It's a big step, you know."

"There's a big difference between being excited and being insensitive," Cass countered.

Micah glared at Cass and seemed about to respond, but Tabitha laid a soothing hand on his arm and summoned up her most charming smile. "We can stand here all night and argue the meaning of various words or we can go to the movie like we planned. I vote for going to the movie."

Although Micah looked like he preferred to continue the discussion, he grudgingly gave in. "I guess you're right." He couldn't resist having the last word, though. "For the record, Cass, I hate the thought of being away from

Tabitha. She's very special to me."

"Then why don't you try mentioning that at least as often as you talk about how wonderful college is going to be?" she suggested sweetly.

"Why don't you—"

"We're out of here," Tabitha broke in before Micah could finish his sentence. "After the movie, we're going to get something to eat at the bowling alley. I'll be home by 11:00." Fluttering her fingers, she tugged Micah toward the front door. "See you later."

"Have fun." Mom had to raise her voice to be heard over Micah's growled protests. The moment the door closed behind the couple, she turned to Cass. "You sure have a way with words. Have you ever thought about becoming a diplomat?"

"Okay, I might have put it nicer," Cass conceded. "But I'm tired of Micah hurting Tabitha's feelings." She grinned. "That's my job. Anyway," she went on, growing serious again, "did you see her face when he said that about counting the hours? What's he thinking when he says stuff like that?"

"He's not thinking." Shifting position, Mom drew her legs up beneath her and rested her elbow on the arm of the couch. "I don't believe he intends to hurt Tabitha. He just doesn't think before he speaks."

"Maybe now he will." Cass treated Mom and Dad to a defiant look. "I'm not sorry for what I said. Somebody had to. It just happened to be me."

"Are you sure there's not a tiny part of you that enjoyed telling Micah off?" Dad teased.

Cass tried not to grin and failed. "If you have to know, I liked doing it. A lot."

Mom and Dad just shook their heads and laughed.

CHAPTER 10

"You put Cass up to that, didn't you?" Micah started in, several yards down the road. "What have you been telling her?"

"Nothing," Tabitha said defensively. "I was as surprised as you were at what she said."

Micah snorted his disbelief. "Then where did she get the idea that I'm being insensitive?"

Maybe because you are? Tabitha wanted to snap, but couldn't bring herself to do it.

Aloud, she said, "You know Cass. She likes to pick fights. She's been in a bad mood ever since Logan left, and you were a handy target to take it out on."

After the way Cass had stuck up for her, she felt a twinge of disloyalty talking about her like this. However, she didn't want Micah mad at her for something that wasn't her fault.

Her answer seemed to satisfy him. They walked in silence for several seconds then he turned to her with a curious look.

"Do you think I talk about going off to school too much?"

Here's my chance to tell him how I feel, Tabitha thought. *Jesus, please give me the right words.*

"You're excited about college, and you have every right to be," she responded carefully. "But I don't like thinking about you being gone. When you talk about school, it reminds me you're leaving in just a few days, and it makes me sad."

When Micah spoke, his voice was cool. "What are you saying? I shouldn't talk about it because it upsets you?"

Tabitha stifled a sigh. This was why she disliked these conversations. They always ended up with Micah's feelings getting hurt.

"No. Like I said, you're entitled to be excited about school. Aren't I just as entitled to be unhappy about the prospect of you leaving?"

Micah frowned. "You should be happy for me. You know how worried I've been about making it in the real world. I could be walking around all scared right now, but I'm not. Isn't that a good thing?"

"Of course it is." Tabitha bit back her impatience. "But can't I be happy and sad at the same time?" She slid him a sidelong glance. "Aren't you?"

Her heart sank when he didn't answer right away. *I guess that says it all*, she lamented. *He really isn't all that upset to be leaving.*

In response, Micah took her hand and laced his fingers through hers. "You know how much I'm going to miss you. In fact, I'm counting on you coming to the University of Hawaii too, next year."

Although Tabitha allowed her hand to rest in his, it remained limp. She couldn't bring herself to hold onto someone who was so eager to be gone.

"We'll see about UH," she hedged. "Cass and I are still talking about going to college together."

At the mention of Cass' name, Micah's face hardened. "You don't owe her any loyalty. At least not as much as you owe me. You've known me longer than Cass."

"But ... she's my sister," sputtered Tabitha, amazed at his attitude.

"Stepsister," Micah corrected. "And I'm your boyfriend. Who would you rather be with in college? Someone who's practically a stranger or someone who loves you?"

Tabitha's breath caught in her throat. In all the time they'd been together, they'd never talked about love. Instead of thrilling her, Micah's use of the word made her uneasy.

Affecting a tinkly laugh, she brushed aside the question. "This is silly. It's too early for me to be talking about college. I still have one more year of high school."

Micah didn't flinch. "Didn't you hear what I just said?"

"Yes." Rubbing her sweaty palm on her dress, Tabitha stared down at her feet. "It's just that I'm really not comfortable talking about ... you know ... love."

"But doesn't the fact that I said it prove Cass is wrong about me not caring about you?" persisted Micah.

If I were Cass I'd come right out and ask him if he used the word love because he's trying to show her up. But I'm not Cass, which means I'm going to have to find a way to weasel out of this.

"She never said you don't care."

"Maybe not in so many words, but that's what she meant."

There was a stubborn set to Micah's jaw that told Tabitha there was no way she was going to win this argument. She wracked her brain for a way to change the subject.

Tugging on Micah's hand, she pouted at him when he turned to look at her. "Why are we talking about Cass? I want to talk about us and all the things we're going to do before you leave next week." She summoned up her most persuasive smile. "Okay?"

Micah hesitated, clearly wanting to continue the discussion. Finally, pulling her close, he draped an arm across her shoulders.

"Okay, you win. Any more talk about Cass is off-limits. From now on, the only people we discuss are you and me."

Tabitha heaved a silent sigh of relief. For the moment, the issue was settled and she could relax and enjoy herself for the rest of the evening.

Over the course of the next week, Tabitha found herself caught in a dilemma. On the one hand, she wanted to spend as much time as she could with Micah. On the other, it was increasingly difficult to be together. All Micah wanted to talk about was the future, which was the last thing Tabitha wanted to discuss. She wished she could talk over the situation with Cass, but she didn't know how to confess that a secret part of her actually looked forward to Micah leaving. It was the only way to end the tension that had sprung up between them.

Four weeks after Logan's departure it was Tabitha's turn to head to the airport early Saturday morning to see Micah off. As the sun rose in a blaze of glory, she huddled with Micah in a corner of the terminal, unable to believe the time had actually come for him to leave.

"Promise you'll write to me every day," Micah whispered, his mouth close to Tabitha's ear.

She nodded. "Every day and twice on Sunday." She lifted tear-filled eyes to his. "You'll write too, won't you?"

"Probably not every day since I'll be busy getting used to college," replied Micah. "But as often as possible. Plus, Christmas isn't that far off. I'll be home for the holidays."

Tabitha did her best to be a good sport. "The months will fly by," she agreed.

The announcement was made that the plane was ready for boarding. Micah squeezed Tabitha's hand one last time before releasing it.

"I'd better go and say good bye again to my family." He lifted his chin in the direction of his parents and sister standing a few feet away. Leaning close to Tabitha, he murmured, "I love you."

"I ..." She swallowed hard. Mom's warnings about not saying "I love you" until the time was right echoed in her ears. *But this is Micah, and I do love him,* she reasoned. Straightening her shoulders, she looked directly into his eyes. "I love you too."

He broke out with a megawatt grin. "Wow! Talk about a great going-away present." He gave her a quick kiss. "Thank you."

Instead of feeling exhilerated that she'd finally said the words out loud, Tabitha discovered the declaration left her uneasy. She hoped no one else had heard her.

If I made a mistake, Lord, I'm sorry. I'll never say it again.

The next few minutes were a blur as Micah bid his family farewell, hugged Tabitha, and headed out the door and across the tarmac to the plane. The last glimpse Tabitha had of him before he disappeared into the craft was of a gleaming smile and a raised arm. She couldn't help thinking he didn't look the least bit upset.

"That's it." Standing beside her, Kira slipped her arm through Tabitha's. "He's on his way."

"Yup."

Kira shot her a concerned glance. "How are you holding up?"

"Pretty well." Although she'd shed some tears, Tabitha wasn't anywhere near as devastated as she'd expected.

"I thought you'd be a basket case." There was a hint of disapproval in Kira's voice.

Hearing it, Tabitha explained hastily, "I think I'm numb. It'll probably hit me in a little while. Then you'll see the waterworks."

As the plane taxied into position for take-off, Kira choked back a sob and wiped her cheeks on a sleeve. "It's going to be so weird having him gone. He's been around my entire life. It'll almost be like I'm an only child."

"I remember what that was like." Tabitha chuckled. "It's not bad."

"You know," huffed Kira, "you could at least try acting like you're sad he's leaving."

"I am sad," Tabitha defended herself. "Just because I'm

not all weepy right now doesn't mean I'm not falling apart inside. Not everybody," she added pointedly, "displays their emotions for the whole world to see."

Kira's eyebrows arched then came together in a scowl. "Don't jump on me for being emotional. That's the way I am. If you don't like it, that's tough."

Instantly apologetic, Tabitha butted shoulders with her. "Sorry. I guess I'm more upset than I realized, and I'm taking it out on you."

"That's okay." Kira's irritation passed, and she produced a wan smile. "You want to come back to the house and have breakfast with us?" Glancing to her right at her weeping mother, she added, "Not that Mom's going to be in any shape to fix anything. We have tons of cereal, though. And I do know how to scramble eggs."

Tabitha shook her head. "No, thanks. I'm going to head home. I want to curl up someplace by myself and cry until I get it all out of my system. Then maybe I'll be ready for company."

Seemingly pleased that she was showing signs of grief, Kira sympathetically patted her arm. "You go on then. I'll call you later and see how you're doing."

Feeling like a fake, Tabitha waited until the plane was airborne before saying goodbye to the Alexanders and starting for the door. She had no intention of curling up anywhere and crying. She'd said that to get out of having to act depressed in front of Kira and her parents. The truth of the matter was she felt like a huge weight had been lifted off her shoulders. The moment she exited the terminal, she jumped on her bike and pedaled home as fast as she could.

CHAPTER 11

To her surprise, Cass was waiting for her as she crept quietly into the house. Wrapped in a blanket, she was snuggled in a chair on the porch.

"What are you doing up?" Tabitha plopped down into a wicker chair.

"I thought you might need to talk to someone when you got back." Cass emitted a jaw-cracking yawn. "I've been up since 6:00."

Tabitha was touched. "Gee, thanks. You're not nearly as rotten a sister as everyone says you are."

Cass fixed her with a baleful stare. "You're the only one who says that."

"Oh, yeah." Tabitha snapped her fingers. "I forgot."

Studying her, a small frown puckered Cass' forehead. "Either you've made a remarkable recovery or you haven't been crying."

"I cried." Tabitha self-consciously lowered her head so her curls bounced forward to cover her face.

"I'm not talking about a few tears," countered Cass. "I mean the all-out carrying on that leaves you with a red nose and squinched up eyes. You didn't do that kind of crying."

"Nope." Tabitha didn't see any sense in pretending she

had when it was obvious she hadn't. "Micah left. I sniffled a few times, and that was it. I assume I'll cry later when it really sinks in."

"Maybe." Cass looked doubtful. "I was a mess when Logan left, but there's something different about this. I can't quite put my finger on it."

Here's my opening to tell her how I feel. Fully intending to, Tabitha took a deep breath. At the last second, she chickened out. *What if she doesn't understand and thinks it means I don't like Micah as much as I used to? I don't want anyone to think that, especially when it's not true.* In an effort to distract Cass, Tabitha smiled smugly. "Maybe I'm not as upset as you think I should be because Micah told me he loved me right before he left."

Cass' jaw dropped open. "You're kidding! You mean he actually came right out and said, 'I love you'?"

Tabitha nodded.

"Wow, how did that make you feel?"

Weird, Tabitha wanted to respond. Instead, she replied, "Wonderful. Better than wonderful. Fantastic."

"Did you say it back to him?"

Tabitha hesitated before admitting, "Uh-huh."

"Holy smokes." Cass pulled the blanket more tightly around her. "Did you mean it?"

About to say she did, Tabitha abruptly decided it was time to be honest. "I don't know. He said it to me so I felt like I should say it back. But—" she hesitated, chewing on her lower lip, "it didn't feel right."

"I know what you mean." Cass sighed deeply. "Logan wanted us to say it before he left, but I couldn't. I like him a lot, and I dream about us getting married someday way in the future." The look she gave Tabitha was confused. "But I don't know if that adds up to love."

"I don't, either." Resting her elbow on the chair arm, Tabitha propped her chin on her hand. "This isn't an excuse, but Micah kept pressuring me to say it the last week or so. I finally caved in." She smiled sadly. "I guess I'm lucky he didn't try to pressure me into anything else."

"Things haven't been quite right between you and Micah, have they?" Cass asked quietly.

Tabitha shook her head. "It was like I couldn't be myself with him. I had to act happy all the time or he'd get mad."

"That was probably his way of dealing with leaving," suggested Cass.

"Did Logan do the same thing?" Tabitha mentally crossed her fingers that he had.

"Well ... no," Cass was forced to admit. "But everybody handles stress differently."

"Yeah." Unconvinced, Tabitha's mouth drooped. If she was ever going to come clean with Cass, now was the time. "Can I tell you something? You have to promise not to breathe a word to another soul, though."

Cass frowned. "Is it something Mom and Dad should know about?"

"No, nothing like that," Tabitha assured her. "I meant I don't want Kira or Rianne knowing. You can't even tell Logan. I can't risk this getting back to Micah."

"In that case, wild horses couldn't drag it out of me. Cross my heart. What's up?"

"I—" Tabitha suddenly busied herself with smoothing imaginary wrinkles out of her shorts, "don't feel all that awful about Micah leaving," she finished in a rush. She shot Cass a tentative glance. "Are you surprised?"

"I'm not sure." Cass suddenly shrugged off the blanket. "I don't think so. Like I said, I thought things were kind of off with y'all."

"Do you think I'm a terrible person for feeling this way?" ventured Tabitha.

"Don't be silly." Cass' tone was brisk. "I figure you have a good reason for not being upset."

"Thank you." Tabitha expelled her breath in a whoosh

of relief. "I was scared you'd be mad." She wriggled around in the chair, making herself comfortable. "When I was riding home from the airport, I was thinking how glad I am to have a break from Micah."

"Aren't you going to miss him at all?" wondered Cass.

Tabitha carefully chose her words. "I'm going to miss the way things were. Not the way they've been the past month or so."

Cass nodded her understanding. "It was obvious you weren't having fun, what with Micah talking about leaving all the time."

"He told me I should be glad he wasn't as scared of living in the real world as he used to be." Tabitha made a face. "He spent a lot of time telling me what I should and shouldn't be feeling."

"How thoughtful of him," Cass drawled, which made Tabitha laugh.

"I've missed talking to you," Tabitha said wistfully. "How did we get so off track with each other?"

"It's been a weird summer. There've been so many changes." Cass leaned her head back against the cushion. "We still have Randy's leaving to get through, then maybe life will return to normal."

"How's Rianne doing with the thought of him going?"

"She's fine. Ever since they cleared the air about how she'd felt since his accident, they've been getting along great." Cass shrugged. "She'll miss him, of course. But they're really close. A few thousand miles aren't going to make a difference in their relationship."

"I wish I could say the same about Micah and me." As soon as the words were out of her mouth, Tabitha shook her head. "No, I don't. I'm hoping, once he gets to Hawaii, he realizes how self-centered he's been. It got so bad that, towards the end, every conversation revolved around him. It was almost like I didn't exist."

"He told you he loved you," Cass reminded her.

"I know, but—" Tabitha struggled to find the words to express her feelings. "I kept thinking it had become a game to him. He was going to make me say I loved him if it was the last thing he did." She growled low in her throat. "I could shoot myself for saying it."

"Oh, well. Live and learn." Cass tossed aside the blanket and swung her feet to the floor. "If I'm going to stay up, I've got to eat. Are you hungry?"

"Starved." Tabitha trailed her to the kitchen. "Are you cooking something?"

Cass turned from the cabinet where the cereals were kept. "Now that you mention it, I think I will. What are you in the mood for? Eggs? Pancakes? Your wish is my command."

Tabitha hoisted herself onto the counter. "Do you know how to make waffles?"

"Sure. How hard can they be?" Cass located a box of pancake mix in the pantry. "I've never made them before, but I can follow directions." She turned the box around so Tabitha could see the instructions printed on the back. "Get out the waffle iron and grease it while I mix the batter."

The girls were in the middle of their preparations when the phone rang. The sound was so strident in the early morning stillness that they both jumped then turned anxious eyes to each other.

"Uh-oh. Maybe something's wrong," Cass said.

Tabitha hurried to the phone and snatched it up before it could ring again. "Hello?"

There was a pause, then a male voice crackled over the wire. "Tabitha?"

"Yes," she replied cautiously.

"What are you doing up so early?"

Her eyes narrowed. "Who is this?"

"I've only been gone a few weeks, and you've forgotten me already," teased the caller. "I'm crushed."

"Logan!" Tabitha turned a jubilant face to Cass. "It's Logan!"

CHAPTER 12

Cass lunged at Tabitha and practically ripped the receiver out of her hand. "Logan! Is it really you?"

"That's what it says on my name tag," he said, laughing. "How are you doing?"

"I'm missing you like crazy, but I'm fine." Cass was so excited she could barely breathe. "The real question is how are you?"

"So far, so good. I haven't blown myself up yet or shot off any toes. We're on a short break, then we're heading out to the confidence course. My roommate's sleeping, but I decided to take a chance on getting through to you. By the way, what are you and Tabitha doing up?"

"Micah left for college this morning," explained Cass. "We were just about to make waffles when you called."

"I didn't disturb your folks, did I?"

"They haven't come down the hall so I guess not," Cass assured him.

"How's your mom?"

"She's doing a little better. She actually stays up most of the day, and she's usually just sick in the mornings."

"Tell her I said hello. Your dad too." Logan's voice softened so that Cass had to strain to hear him. "Thanks for all your letters. They keep me going. I don't know what I'd do without them."

"You'll never have to find out." Cass moved onto the porch for privacy. "Hearing from you makes my day too."

"I wish I could write more often, but most days I'm swamped." Logan sighed. "It's tougher than I thought it would be."

A tingle of alarm shot up Cass' spine. "You're not thinking of quitting, are you?"

Logan's bark of laughter was reassuring. "Hey, you know me better than that. I'm the original 'never say die' guy. When it gets really bad, I crawl into my bunk with your letters and pretend I'm back home, snorkeling at Eamon with you. I have your picture on my desk. Mark—that's my roommate—says you're a looker."

Cass blushed. "Tell him he needs his eyes examined."

"No way," Logan laughingly protested. "The man has excellent taste."

Unsure how to respond, Cass changed the subject. "Before I forget, I've been meaning to ask you if your father had any luck tracking down your brother when you were in Pennsylvania."

"He got a lead from one of Sean's friends who thought he was in Pittsburgh. I don't know if Pop's been able to get an address on him."

"I'll keep praying." Cass walked to the window and leaned her forehead against the glass as she gazed out at the ocean.

"Thanks. As soon as I hear something, I'll let you know." In a tone Cass thought sounded unnaturally casual, Logan asked, "So, have you found anyone to replace me yet?"

"How could anyone replace you? You're one of a kind. Besides, I'm not looking." Cass traced a heart on the glass and wrote her and Logan's names in it. "Have you met anybody?"

"No one special. There's this girl in my company—her name's Shiloh—I talk to every now and then. She's from Kentucky, and her accent reminds me of you."

"Oh." Just the thought of Logan talking to another girl made Cass stiffen. "I'm glad you're making friends."

"You make it sound like I'm in kindergarten," Logan observed wryly. "Maybe I should wear a sign that reads, 'plays well with others.' "

Cass wasn't amused. "I hope I never hear that you've been playing with Shiloh."

There was a long silence then Logan said quietly, "I told you I talk to her because of her accent. Does that sound like I'm interested in her as a person?"

"No," Cass admitted. "I'm sorry. I guess the green-eyed monster took over for a few seconds there."

"I don't mind. I'd be worried if you weren't jealous. One of the ways I psyched myself up for bayonet training was to imagine the dummy was some guy who'd been hitting on you," confided Logan.

Cass immediately felt better. "You're nuts. Then again, there must be something wrong with me because I think that's sweet."

Logan laughed, then quickly sobered. "I hate to cut this short, but I've got to go. Break's almost up. I'm glad you were there so we could talk."

"Me too." A lump formed in Cass' throat, and she had trouble talking around it. "Thanks for calling. Take care of yourself out on the confidence course."

"I will." Logan hesitated then asked in a rush, "Is it okay if I end with a prayer?"

Cass didn't know whether to smile or cry. "I was hoping you would."

"Father, thank You for giving us this chance to talk. Go with us through the rest of this day, keep us safe, and draw us closer to You. In Jesus' name, amen."

"Amen," echoed Cass. "I'll talk to you soon."

"Bye. I'd blow you a kiss, but I'd feel dumb."

"Goodbye." Giggling, Cass hung up.

Leave it to Logan to end with a joke, she thought. *No*, she corrected herself, *leave it to him to end with a prayer. Am I blessed or what to have him as my boyfriend?*

Carrying the receiver back to the kitchen, Cass replaced it in its holder. As she walked to the counter, Tabitha never took her eyes off her. Her face was alight with curiosity.

"Don't leave me hanging," she ordered when Cass didn't say anything. "Did you and Logan have a good talk?"

"Very good." Cass opened the refrigerator to retrieve eggs and milk.

"Does that mean he's still being true-blue to you?" Tabitha reached into the cupboard for the oil to grease the waffle iron.

"He says he is." Cass measured the mix and milk into a bowl then cracked the eggs and added them.

Frowning, Tabitha looked up from her task. "You believe him, don't you?"

"Absolutely." Cass erupted in a huge grin. "He prayed before we hung up."

"Wow," Tabitha said, her voice envious. "That's something I always wanted Micah and me to do. I figured it was up to him to suggest it, but he never did."

"It means a lot," acknowledged Cass. "For a couple of moments, I felt close enough to Logan to touch him. If he ever quits praying with me, that's when I'll know it's over."

"He won't."

At this confident prediction, Cass glanced over her shoulder at Tabitha. "How do you know?"

"It's just a feeling I have. You and Logan—" her hands fluttered as she tried to explain, "have something special. The kind of thing that lasts. I can't see either of you with anybody else."

"From your lips to God's ears," Cass replied fervently.

"Mark my words." Tabitha plugged in the waffle iron. "I'm going on record that you and Logan will wind up together."

Cass laughed with delight. "This is one time when I won't mind you being right."

Following breakfast, Cass disappeared into her room for a nap. When Mom woke her up at 10:00, she stretched and protested before dragging herself out of bed. Meeting up with Tabitha in the hall, they exchanged bleary glances.

"I sure could have used another couple of hours," grumbled Cass.

"Couple of hours?" Tabitha yawned. "I wouldn't have minded sleeping the whole day away."

"Has it hit you Micah's gone?" Cass wanted to know.

"Yes, but that doesn't mean I want to crawl into a hole and die. As a matter of fact—" Tabitha shook off her weariness and straightened her shoulders, "I'm ready to throw myself into doing girl stuff. What do you say we plan a slumber party? We haven't had one in ages."

Cass perked up. "Hey, good idea. When do you want to have it?"

"The sooner, the better." Crossing her arms, Tabitha leaned against the wall. "How about tomorrow night?"

"After the youth meeting? Sounds good to me." Cass moved past her and ducked into the bathroom. "You call Kira and Rianne while I take my shower."

"Why do I have to call?" Tabitha griped.

"Because it was your idea. Plus—" Cass stuck out her tongue before shutting the door—"I beat you to the bathroom."

The next night, Cass, Tabitha, and the others gathered in the Spencer living room after Mom and Dad headed off to bed. After spreading their sleeping bags, they trooped into the kitchen to pop popcorn for the movie Rianne had brought to watch.

"Did Micah call you last night after he got to my aunt's house?" Kira asked Tabitha as she rifled through a cupboard for something to munch on while she waited for the popcorn. Locating a bag of potato chips, she ripped it open, took a handful, then passed it around.

"He called this morning while we were at church. The service went longer because of John MacAdams' baptism." Tabitha dropped ice cubes in each of their glasses. "He left a message that he'd call back at one, which he did."

Kira grinned. "You must have been thrilled to talk to him."

Tabitha hesitated, and Cass knew she was having trouble figuring out an answer for Kira. Tabitha had told her about the conversation. Micah had gone on and on about the fun he and his cousin had hitting several night spots around Honolulu. He didn't ask about her and hung up shortly after informing her that he was heading to a party with his cousin.

Finally, Tabitha drawled, "Thrilled to death."

Kira's head jerked up, and she shot her a speculative look. "Gee, try to show a little enthusiasm."

Tabitha bristled at her sarcasm. "Maybe I didn't like hearing about how he went club-hopping last night and the wild beach party he was planning to go to tonight."

"Don't tell me you expect him to sit home every night," retorted Kira. "Besides, who are you to talk? He's only been gone a day, and you're already throwing a party."

Tabitha emitted a most unladylike snort. "There's a big difference between this and what Micah's doing tonight."

"Are you saying you don't trust him?" Eyes flashing, Kira glowered at her.

"All I'm saying is—"

"Come on, you two," Rianne broke in. "We're supposed to be having fun. Quit going at each other like a couple of alley cats."

Cass laughed at her description. "Rianne's right. What's the point in having a party if we're going to spend all our time arguing?" The microwave beeped and she reached over to take out the bag of popcorn. "Why don't you agree to drop it, and let's put in the movie." She glanced first at Kira then at Tabitha. "What do you say?"

"I'm willing if she is," Tabitha grudgingly agreed.

Kira responded with a shrug.

"And no more talk about Micah for the rest of the night," Rianne added. "If you two want to fight about him, do it on your own time."

Although the matter was settled for the time being, Cass suspected it wouldn't be long before it once again became an issue. Kira was understandably protective of her brother, and she'd made it clear she'd even do battle with her best friend in order to defend him.

As she carried the drinks to the living room, Cass sighed to herself. *This doesn't bode well for the future. I guess we'll just have to wait and see. And,* she added, *pray Christ gives them the strength to apologize to each other and forgive each other in Him, so that when this is all over—they're still friends. So that we're all still friends.*

CHAPTER 13

"Hey, Red. Is this seat taken?"

Cass immediately bristled and looked up from the magazine she was reading. No one ever called her "Red." She couldn't believe the nerve of the stranger grinning down at her.

"Excuse me?" She injected as much ice into her tone as she could muster.

"I asked if this chair—" the boy gestured behind him, "was taken."

Impatiently brushing aside his question, Cass explained, "What I meant was, what did you call me?"

The boy didn't seem the least bit fazed by her obvious irritation. "Red. I'll admit it's not original, but it sure fits."

"My name is not Red." Cass spoke slowly and distinctly so he'd get the message. Having informed him of this, she lowered her gaze to the magazine so he'd know the conversation was over.

Unfortunately, he didn't get the hint. After spreading a towel on the lounge chair next to Cass', he plopped down and asked, "Then what is your name?"

"None of your business," Cass retorted without looking up.

"Weird." The boy stretched out on the chair and folded his arms behind his head. "What do your friends call you? None?"

A reluctant smile tugged at Cass' mouth, but she bit it back. She'd rather eat a lizard than let the boy know she found him amusing.

"Ah—" he nodded sagely, "the strong, silent type. Cool." Raising up on his elbows, he leisurely scanned his surroundings. "Nice pool. You come here often?" Before Cass could respond, he laughed. "Listen to me. Is that the oldest pick-up line in the book or what?"

Cass found it harder and harder to ignore him. There was something irresistible about his cheerful attitude. To her surprise, she heard herself say, "I'm Cass Devane."

The boy lifted a hand in greeting. "Nice to meet you, Cass Devane. My name's Sam Steele." He laughed when Cass arched her brows. "I know. It sounds like something out of a detective novel. Sam Steele, Private Investigator. I've asked my parents what they were thinking when they came up with it, but all they ever say is it's a good name."

Unable to resist his good humor, Cass closed the magazine. "I take it you're new on Kwaj."

"My family and I arrived yesterday." Rolling onto his side, Sam propped his head on his hand and gazed at her. "How long have you been here?"

"A little over a year. I moved here last July when my mother married my stepfather. My stepsister, Tabitha, has lived here practically her whole life." Cass reached for her sunglasses so she could study Sam without being too obvious about it. "How old are you?" she asked bluntly.

"Seventeen. I'll be 18 in January." Sam made no secret of the fact that he was checking Cass out. His gaze slid from the top of her head to the tips of her toes.

Although his open scrutiny unnerved her, Cass was determined not to show it. "So you'll be a senior?"

"Yup. One more year of high school then this bird's flying the coop."

"How did you feel having to switch schools right before your senior year?"

Sam shrugged. "I'm used to it. My father's in the army so we move every couple of years. My parents gave me the option of staying with a friend's family in Virginia—we were living at Fort Belvoir right outside of Washington D.C.—and finishing school. But I thought, why not? I like seeing new places, and I've never lived on an island before. So—" he flashed a broad grin, "here I am. That's my life story in a nutshell."

Cass admired his adventurous spirit. "Do you have any brothers or sisters?"

"I have three younger sisters who make my life a nightmare." Sam's affectionate tone let Cass know he was kidding.

"My mother's expecting a baby in December," she confided. "I can't decide if I'm looking forward to it or not."

"Since there's nothing you can do about it, you might as well sit back and enjoy the ride," Sam suggested. "My baby sister's almost 3, and she's a hoot to have around. I'd never tell the other two, but she's my favorite."

Laughing, Cass decided she appreciated Sam's outspokenness. "You're not shy about expressing your views, are you?"

"Life's too short to waste time beating around the bush." He watched a little girl catapult off the diving board before turning his attention back to Cass. "I figure the world would be a much better place if people would just say what's on their minds and get on with it."

"Amen to that," agreed Cass. She squinted up at the sun. "In case you didn't think to put on sunscreen before you got here, you might want to borrow mine. Otherwise, you could wind up with a nasty burn."

"Thanks for the advice, but I've already taken care of it.

I'll tell you what, though—" Sam swung his legs off the chair and stood up. "You feel like going for a swim?"

Cass shook her head. "Not right now. The water's so cold I have to be roasting before I get in it."

"Yeah, well, I'm beginning to get that boiled lobster feeling so I'm going to risk it." Sam started toward the steps at the shallow end of the pool then turned back. "Are you planning on leaving anytime soon?"

"I'll be here for at least another hour," she said.

"Great. Save my place, okay?"

Cass nodded. Folding her arms, she watched Sam stick a tentative toe into the frigid water, then slowly descend the steps. Although he wasn't the kind of boy who turned heads, she liked him. Everything about him was medium. He was of medium height and weight, and his hair and eyes were medium brown, neither very dark nor very light. His one outstanding characteristic was his personality. On that, Cass gave him an enthusiastic two thumbs-up.

Wait until I tell the others there's a new boy in town, she thought. *Who might be interested? Tabitha's definitely out because of Micah. Rianne and Greg still seem to be getting along okay. I guess that leaves Kira, especially since Garth isn't due back from the mainland for another two weeks.*

What about you? a separate little voice piped up. *Don't you find Sam attractive?*

Me? Cass silently squealed. *Of course not. My heart belongs to Logan.*

But he's 9,000 miles away, reasoned the voice. *Sam, on the other hand, is nine feet away. Let's see if you can figure out who might be the better choice when it comes to dating.*

I'm not in the market for a dating partner, Cass sternly informed the voice. *It's Logan or nobody. I mean it,* she added when the voice tried to protest.

To distract herself from the argument raging inside her head, she opened the magazine again and flipped through it until she found the article she'd been reading. The idea of dating Sam was ridiculous, and she refused to entertain the possibility one second longer.

Still, Cass kept one eye on Sam even as she pretended to be engrossed in the article. Not even the scolding she gave herself stopped her from tracking his every move. Disgusted with herself, she finally stuffed the magazine into her beach bag, shoved her feet into her flipflops, and got up.

Sam immediately swam to the edge of the pool and hung on. "Hey, where are you going? I thought you said you were staying awhile."

"I changed my mind. I ... uh ... remembered something I needed to do at home."

Like write to my boyfriend, she added silently.

"Hold on." Streaming water, Sam hoisted himself out of the pool. "I'll ride home with you, if that's okay. I'd like to find out where you live."

Cass stepped back so he wouldn't drip on her and gestured beyond the fence. "I just live next door. We're the first house after the empty lot."

"Oh. Okay." Sam appeared momentarily disappointed before brightening again. "That shouldn't be too hard to find. Maybe I'll stop by when I leave."

"I'd like that," Cass replied truthfully. She started toward the gate. "Bye. It was nice meeting you."

"Same here." Sam paused, then added with a devilish smile, "See you later, Red."

Shaking her head and laughing, Cass left. She had no doubt she'd be seeing Sam again, and soon.

As soon as she arrived home, she went in search of Tabitha. She found her sister in the backyard with a notebook in her lap and a pen clenched between her teeth. Cass sank down onto the grass beside Tabitha's chair.

"What are you doing?"

"Trying to write a letter to Micah." Tabitha sighed. "Unfortunately, I haven't gotten very far. All I've written is, 'Dear Micah, How's it going?' Do you find it hard to write to Logan?"

"No. But, unlike you and Micah, we weren't having problems before he left." Drawing up her knees, Cass clasped her arms around them. "Why don't you try again later? Maybe you'll have something to say then."

"Yeah, there's no sense sitting here, wracking my brain to think of things." Tabitha closed the notebook and clipped the pen to the cover. "So, did you come looking for me for a reason or did you just miss me?"

Cass snorted. "That'll be the day." She ducked when Tabitha pretended to swat at her. "I wanted to tell you I met a new guy at the pool. His name's Sam Steele, and he's from Virginia. He's 17, which means he'll be a senior this year."

"Did you get his social security number and favorite color too?" Tabitha drawled. "I don't know how you get people to tell you their life stories the way you do."

"It's called showing an interest," Cass good-naturedly shot back. "You should try it sometime."

"Very funny." Tabitha leaned her chin on her hand and peered down at her. "So, is he cute?"

"Ooh, you'd better not let Kira hear you ask a question like that," Cass warned. "She's already worried you're not going to remain faithful to Micah."

"I think the real issue is whether or not Micah remains faithful to me." Tabitha gave an irritated flounce. "I have a feeling he's going to go a little wild once school starts. I've heard it happens to some people their freshman year."

"You sound so calm about it," Cass said in amazement. "Doesn't the possibility upset you?"

"Of course it does." Leaning back in the chair, Tabitha studied the waves breaking over the rocks. "But worrying about it won't change anything. There's nothing I can do about it if Micah decides to go crazy. I just have to trust he'll get over it."

"Wow." Cass stared at her. "This is a switch. I'm usually the practical one. You're supposed to carry on about how things should be, instead of accepting the way they are."

Tabitha's smile was sad. "Maybe I'm growing up. The last few weeks with Micah taught me a lot."

"You had it way harder than I realized," Cass observed in a subdued voice.

"You were busy. You didn't have much time for me," Tabitha said calmly.

"Still, I should have made it my business to be more aware of what was going on. Sorry."

"Apology accepted. Anyway—" Tabitha shifted in her chair, "tell me more about Sam. What does he look like?"

"He's ordinary, but in a nice way." Cass smiled, thinking about him. "He's about five-nine. Not skinny, not fat, not muscular. Just ... average. He's really funny. I liked his personality a lot."

"Uh-oh. It sounds like Logan might have something to worry about," Tabitha teased.

Cass gave a guilty start before hastening to defend herself. "Nuh-uh! Honestly, can't I say someone has a good personality without you thinking I'm on the verge of cheating on my boyfriend?"

"Whoa! Down, girl." Tabitha held up her hands, as if warding off an attack. "I was joking. Don't be so touchy."

Shrugging an apology, Cass stood and started into the house to shower and change. "I told Sam where we live, and he said he might stop by on his way home from the pool."

"Good. I'd like to meet him. Since he has such a great personality and all," Tabitha added earning a sour look from Cass before she disappeared inside.

CHAPTER 14

As it turned out, Cass wasn't home when Sam dropped by. Rianne had called and invited her to eat dinner with the family. It was Randy's second to last night at home before he left for college in California, and he wanted to share it with Cass. She'd left about 15 minutes before the doorbell rang.

"I'll get it," Tabitha called from the bedroom. She knew Mom was relaxing on the porch, and she didn't want her getting up.

"Hi. You must be Tabitha."

It took her a moment to place the boy grinning at her from the front step. "Oh, yeah." She snapped her fingers. "And you're Sam, right?"

"Guilty as charged." He leaned against the doorjamb. "Is Cass here?"

"She just left a little while ago to go to a friend's house." Tabitha stepped aside. "Would you like to come in for a few minutes?"

Motioning toward his wet trunks, Sam shook his head. "I'd better not. My mother taught me it's rude to drip all over people's floors, especially people I've just met."

"Your mother's a wise woman." The seriousness of

Tabitha's tone was offset by the twinkle in her eyes. "Hardly anyone teaches their kids that anymore."

"And the world's worse off because of it." Sam shook his head in mock sorrow.

Tabitha found herself grinning from ear to ear. *Amazing,* she thought. *I've only known him all of—what?—30 seconds, and I feel totally comfortable with him. This is weird.*

Sam started to edge away. "I guess I should be going. Not that my mother will be worried I've gotten lost. But she'd probably appreciate me taking my sisters off her hands for a little while so she can unpack and stuff."

Wishing she could think of a reason for him to stay, Tabitha reluctantly watched him go. "I'll tell Cass you stopped by."

"Thanks. Would you also tell her I'll be at the pool again tomorrow?" Sam pushed up the kickstand on his bike.

"Same time?" Tabitha asked.

Sam nodded. "Yeah. I'm what you might call a creature of habit." Lifting a hand in farewell, he climbed on his bike. "Nice meeting you, Tabs."

Tabitha stiffened. No one—no one—was allowed to shorten her name. It reminded her of her mother, and that was a memory she'd rather do without. Her positive feelings toward Sam evaporated, and she shut the door with a bang.

Good personality or not, she fumed, *he had no right to call me by a nickname without asking first if it was okay.* She couldn't wait for Cass to return so she could tell her exactly what she thought of her new friend, Sam Steele.

Several hours later, she and Cass were on their way to the Ten-Ten Store to get Mom a candy bar she'd craved since supper. After listening to Cass talk about Randy's excitement over leaving for school in two days, Tabitha finally found the opening she'd been waiting for.

"I met Sam."

"Yeah?" Cass shot her a pleased smile. "Isn't he great?"

"He's rude," Tabitha declared flatly.

"What?" Cass shook the windblown hair out of her face. "He was a perfect gentleman when we talked."

"Are you implying I brought out the worst in him?" Tabitha asked stiffly.

"It has been known to happen," Cass retorted. "There's something about you that rubs people the wrong way."

"Wait a minute." Tabitha fought the impulse to pull ahead of Cass then jam on the brakes. Causing a collision wouldn't do much to convince her sister she was a nice person. "How did the conversation go from being about Sam to being about me?"

"I don't know, and I don't care." Cass glared across the space separating them. "All I want to know is why you think he's rude."

Tabitha suddenly realized she didn't want to reveal the reason. She was sure Cass would ridicule her for it. Mumbling, "Never mind. It's not important," she put on a burst of speed.

Cass quickly caught up with her. "Come on, give. What did he do that ticked you off?"

"Forget it. I don't feel like talking about it."

Tabitha wheeled into the Ten-Ten parking area and skidded to a stop. Cass was right behind her as she jumped off her bike and headed for the store.

"You know I'm going to keep bothering you until you tell me," observed Cass. "So you might as well 'fess up and get it over with."

"Fine." Gritting her teeth, Tabitha spun around so fast that Cass barely avoided running into her. "He called me Tabs."

Cass waited for her to go on. When several seconds passed, it seemed to dawn on her that was all Tabitha was going to say.

"That's it?"

"I knew you wouldn't think it was any big deal." Tabitha threw her hands up in disgust. "That's why I didn't want to tell you."

"I was ... uh ... just making sure you were done before I said anything," Cass said lamely. "So ... he called you Tabs."

"Yes. Without asking." Tabitha scowled at a passing boy who hastily averted his gaze and hurried into the store.

"I see." Cass tried to think of something else to say, but drew a blank.

Tabitha sniffed her disdain. "No, you don't. I guess you've forgotten how much I hate nicknames." When Cass continued to look confused, she prompted, "Because of my mother."

"That's right." Cass hit her forehead with the palm of her hand. "I get it now. Nicknames remind you of Beth." She lowered her hand and peered earnestly at Tabitha. "There's no way Sam could have known."

"He should've asked instead of assuming I wouldn't mind," insisted Tabitha.

"Other than the thing with your mother, I don't see why you're making such a big deal about this. Apparently it's something he does. I mean, he called me Red when he came up to me at the pool."

Tabitha's eyes widened in surprise. "Didn't that bug you?"

"A little," conceded Cass. "But I got over it."

"Meaning I should too?" Tabitha was prepared to start the argument all over again.

Cass shrugged. "Meaning nothing. It was just a comment. Come on." She nodded toward the door. "We should get the candy bar back to Mom before she throws a temper tantrum from having to wait so long."

"She only took one nap today." Tabitha followed Cass into the store.

Cass twirled her finger in the air. "Whoop-de-do. I'll know she's making real progress when she stays up all day, plus does all the stuff she used to do before the baby came on board."

Tabitha giggled. "You really hate pitching in with the chores, don't you?"

"Hate is too mild a word." Cass made a beeline for the candy section. "Call me spoiled, but I liked it when Mom did the cooking and the cleaning." She heaved an exaggerated sigh. "My life was so simple back then. All my needs were met, and I had tons of free time. I wish we could go back to the way things were."

Tabitha reached around her for the candy bar Mom wanted. "You think it's going to get better after the baby is born?"

Frowning, Cass accompanied her to the register. "I haven't thought that far ahead. Are you saying you don't?"

"Well, duh." Tabitha made a face at her before handing over the candy and a dollar. "If you think it's bad now, imagine what it's going to be like then." With a nod to the cashier, she pocketed the change and candy bar. "All Mom's time is going to be taken up with feeding and changing diapers and trying to get the baby to sleep. Everything else is going to be left to us to do."

"But ... but ..." Cass sputtered, trailing her out the door. "That's not fair."

"Who ever said life is fair?" Tabitha wheeled her bike out of the rack and straddled it.

"But I thought Mom having a baby would be fun." Dragging her feet, Cass retrieved her bike. "I knew it would be work, but I figured she and Dad would be the ones doing it."

"Boy, are you ever in for a rude awakening," Tabitha drawled. Pushing off, she began pedaling toward home.

"This is the pits," Cass drew alongside to grumble. "So

what you're saying is we're going to have to live with being their personal servants until we leave for college."

"That's about the size of it." Tabitha treated her to a smirk. "I can't believe I figured this out before you did."

Instead of taking offense, Cass sighed. "Me neither. I've been more preoccupied with Logan than I realized."

After delivering the candy bar to Mom, Cass disappeared into her room. Tabitha did the same, sitting down at her desk to write to Micah. When 10 minutes had passed and all she had to show for her efforts were the pictures she'd doodled in the margin, she crumpled the paper in disgust. Jumping up, she strode over to the window.

"Lord," she whispered, "has it really come to this? I thought Micah and I were soul mates, but he's only been gone two weeks, and I don't know what to say to him. I thought he'd lean on me more for support, but, according to Kira, he's doing just fine on his own. I'm glad about that—I really am—but I don't know where it leaves me. If he doesn't need me to boost his spirits and tell him everything's going to be okay, what good am I to him anymore? I'd really appreciate some guidance here. I wanted a little break from our relationship, but I didn't want to lose it altogether. Micah and I go back too far to throw it all away now. Please help us through this tough time. I care about Micah a lot, and I know he feels the same way about me. Thank You."

More at peace than she'd been in the last couple of days, Tabitha pulled out a book to read before falling asleep.

CHAPTER 15

Two days later, Rianne called bright and early to let Cass know Randy's plane had taken off, and he was officially on his way to college. She asked Cass to accompany her to the library in order to check out pattern books. Her mother had surprised her with an offer to sew her several outfits for the new school year.

"Uh, I'd really like to, but I'm busy." Cass rubbed the sleep from her eyes and glanced at the clock. It was only 8:30. If she got off the phone within the next couple of minutes, she might manage another hour of sleep before Mom roused her and Tabitha at 10:00.

"Doing what?" Rianne asked.

For some reason, Cass felt reluctant to tell her. "Uh ... well ..." Since lying wasn't an option, she had to come clean—sort of. "I'm going on a picnic at the lagoon."

"By yourself?"

"Not exactly." Taking a deep breath, Cass blurted, "With that boy I told you about. Sam."

"Oh." Rianne was quiet for a few seconds. "Who invited who?"

"He asked me," Cass admitted grudgingly.

"Hmm. So it's a date?" Rianne didn't sound at all happy.

"No," Cass hastened to assure her. "We were talking, and I was telling him about Eamon, and he said he hadn't been there yet, and I told him about how beautiful the beach is and that there's a pavilion for picnicking, and the next thing I knew he was asking me if I'd like to go swimming and have a picnic," she explained in a rush.

"Sounds like a date to me." There was a long pause on Rianne's end of the line, then she asked quietly, "Cass, what's going on?"

"Nothing! Honest!" She injected as much sincerity into her voice as she could. "Sam just needs somebody to show him around, and I guess I've been elected."

"By who? Is showing him around his idea or yours?"

"I don't know." Cass was starting to get irritated. "It's not like we've discussed it. He asked me to go to the lagoon. I said yes. End of story. I don't know why you're getting so worked up about it."

"What about Logan?"

"What about him?" Cass retorted coolly.

"How do you think he'd feel about you and Sam going on a picnic?"

"I've already told you Logan and I agreed we're free to date other people," Cass pointed out in a snide tone.

"Aha!" Rianne shouted. "So it is a date."

Momentarily stumped, all Cass could do was huff, "Don't put words in my mouth."

"But you're the one who said—" Rianne began.

"Look," Cass broke in, "it's too early to get into a stupid discussion about what I did and didn't say. I'll call you after I get back from the lagoon. Maybe we can go to the library tonight."

"Fine. Have a nice time. I'll talk to you later." Rianne ended the call without saying goodbye.

"Whatever," Cass muttered, hanging up. Pretending she didn't care, she shuffled back to her room and crawled into bed.

She had just finished getting ready when the doorbell rang at 11:00. She ran out to the living room to answer it, but Tabitha had just opened the door.

"Good morning, Tabs," Cass heard Sam say, bright and cheerful. "Nice to see you again."

"My name is Tabitha, not Tabs," Tabitha replied. Cass smiled when she didn't hear nearly as much tension in her voice as she might have expected. "Not Tabby. And definitely not Beth. Tabitha. Got it?"

"Yes, ma'am." Sam executed a snappy salute. "Your message has been received loud and clear—" he grinned, "Tabitha."

"Good. I'll get Cass."

Sam grabbed her sleeve to stop her. "Before you go, do you mind me asking why you don't like being called Tabs?"

Tabitha leaned close to him, and in a stage whisper replied, "I would tell you. But then I'd have to kill you."

Sam laughed. Tabitha turned quickly and nearly bumped into Cass, who was standing right behind her.

Cass grinned at her. "Way to speak your mind," she congratulated Tabitha in a low murmur. "It's nice to see you standing up for yourself."

Tabitha glowed with pleasure. "Thank you. Too bad I didn't learn to do it before Micah left. But better late than never, I guess."

"Hey, what are you two whispering about?" Sam asked in mock complaint.

"I was just about to ask Tabitha if she'd like to come with us," Cass said, smiling at Tabitha's shocked expression. "If that's okay with you."

The expression on Sam's face indicated he wouldn't mind in the least. "That'd be great. I'll be the envy of all the guys, having not one, but two, gorgeous ladies as my escorts."

Cass and Tabitha rolled their eyes at each other. Tabitha carefully lifted her feet.

"You'd better watch out," she advised Cass. "It's getting awfully deep in here."

Looking stricken, Sam pressed a hand to his heart. "I'm hurt. I meant every word of that compliment."

"Sure you did." Tabitha elbowed Cass. "If you're serious about me going with you, my answer is yes. I just need to check with Mom and make sure it's okay."

"Of course I'm serious," Cass assured her.

"Me too," Sam chimed in.

"Then let me talk to Mom and grab my swimming suit." Tabitha hurried out to the porch.

"That was nice of you to invite her," Sam remarked as they waited for Tabitha to return.

"You're sure you don't mind?"

"Hey—" Sam shrugged, "the more the merrier. You have any other stray sisters lying around you'd like to ask?"

"None that I know of." Cass backed up until she bumped into the recliner where she perched on the arm. "I'm glad you're okay with her coming. She's been having a hard time since her boyfriend left for college a couple of weeks ago."

"She has a boyfriend, huh?" Sam's tone was oh-so-casual. "How long have they been going together?"

"Officially, not quite a year. But they've known each other forever." Cass snapped her fingers and stood up. "Silly me. I'm about to forget the picnic basket. Wait here."

"You need help?" Sam called after her as she headed to the kitchen.

"No, thanks. It's not heavy."

Tabitha, who'd reappeared with her beach bag slung over her shoulder, peered anxiously at the basket. "Is there enough for me?"

"That depends. How much are you planning on eating?" Cass teased.

"My usual amount, about half as much as you do." Tabitha stuck out her tongue.

"Isn't she a riot?" Cass drawled to Sam, who laughed.

"Bye, Mom," Tabitha called as they headed out the front door.

"Bye. Have fun," came her faint reply.

That was precisely what they had. Cass was amazed at how comfortable she felt around someone she had basically just met. Sam entertained them with stories about growing up in a military family. He painted vivid pictures of the various places he'd lived and had them roaring with laughter as he described a close encounter with an alligator in Louisiana. Every now and then, Cass would catch a smile from Tabitha that clearly said *Thank you for inviting me!*

"Well, ladies—" after a glance at his watch, Sam hauled himself to his feet and picked up the towel he'd been lying on. "I hate to break this up, but I told my mother I'd be home by 2:00 to take my sisters to the pool."

"It's been great." Following his example, Tabitha stood up and shook the sand off her towel. "We'll have to do this again, and soon."

"Aw, you're not just saying that to make me feel good, are you?" Sam joked.

"Cass can tell you I never say anything to make a person feel good." Tabitha folded the towel and stuffed it in her beach bag.

"Liar," Cass shot back, adding to Sam, "She's always saying what she thinks our parents want to hear."

"Yeah, but they're parents," Tabitha defended herself. "I was talking about being nice to real people."

"I don't think Mom and Dad would like knowing you don't consider them real people." With a sigh, Cass slowly got up then flipped the towel with her foot and caught it.

"Ooh, I'm impressed." Sam clapped. "Can you also catch a Frisbee in your mouth?"

"No, but I can put a smart aleck in his place," Cass shot back.

Joking and laughing, they made their way to the pavilion to retrieve the picnic basket, then walked to their bikes.

"I wasn't kidding about us doing this again." Straddling her bike, Tabitha leaned on the handlebars. "Maybe next time we can invite Kira and Rianne along."

Sam's eyes widened. "Me and four girls? Man, it just keeps getting better and better. I wish my father had been transferred here sooner."

"Don't get your hopes up," Cass advised with a laugh. "They both have boyfriends."

"So do you two," Sam reminded her. "But a guy can dream." He dumped his things in the basket suspended from his handlebars. "Can I call you tomorrow and see about us getting together?"

Cass and Tabitha exchanged glances, not sure who he was talking to. With a nod, Tabitha indicated Cass should respond.

"That'd be great. You haven't seen the fish pond yet or the high school."

Sam groaned. "Ugh. Don't remind me school starts in two weeks."

"You'll like good old Seaside High," Tabitha assured him. "The classes are small, and the girls wear shorts all year 'round."

Sam's gloomy expression brightened. "Hey, maybe life is worth living after all."

On that note, they took off and went their separate ways home. The moment Sam was out of earshot, Cass turned to Tabitha with a triumphant grin.

"See? I told you he was nice."

"Okay," Tabitha grudgingly conceded. "I'll admit, for once you were right."

"I think he has his eye on you," Cass said.

"That's funny. I thought the same thing about you."

"Really?" Cass' eyebrows formed two perfect arches, and she was sure she was blushing. "Nah."

"Yes, really," Tabitha insisted, shooting her a curious look. "Would you like it if he does?"

Cass hesitated before replying, "I ... don't know."

"What will you do if he asks you out on an actual date?" Tabitha persisted.

Cass' stomach lurched at the suggestion. "I'm not sure I want to think about it. I went out a few times back in Tennessee, but I never had a real boyfriend before Logan. He's the only guy I've ever kissed. The thought of dating somebody else—even someone as nice as Sam—is too weird."

"But you like him," Tabitha pointed out.

"Yes, but not in that way." Cass began pedaling faster so she could get home and escape to her room. She was rapidly tiring of Tabitha's questions.

"How can you say that when you haven't gone out with him yet?"

Cass bristled with indignation. "Are you suggesting that I should date Sam?"

"Why not?" Tabitha drew alongside her, not about to be left behind. "I can't think of a better way to find out how you feel about him."

"If you're so curious to know what it would be like, why don't you go out with him?" Cass challenged.

"I probably would if he asked me."

Tabitha's response caused Cass to almost run off the road. "No way! You're kidding!"

"No, I'm not," Tabitha replied calmly. "There's something about Sam that kind of gets to me."

"But ... he's so ... *plain* compared to Micah," sputtered

Cass.

"So?" The face Tabitha turned to her was cool. "Looks aren't everything." Her gaze narrowed. "Are you giving me a hard time because, deep down, you want Sam for yourself?"

"Absolutely not." Cass' answer was immediate and definite. "I just can't believe you'd choose Sam over Micah."

Tabitha emitted a scornful hoot. "Quit being so dramatic. I'm not choosing anybody. All I'm saying is I think Sam's attractive in his own way, and I'd like to get to know him better."

"You'll die a slow, painful death if Kira ever hears you say that," Cass muttered darkly.

"Don't worry. I'm not that stupid. If Sam and I ever do go out, it'll be the deepest, darkest secret this island's ever known." Tabitha laughed. "I want to live to see my 18th birthday."

"If it ever happens, she won't hear it from me," vowed Cass. "After all, blood is thicker than water."

"You nut." The insult was affectionate. "We're not related by blood."

Cass dismissed Tabitha's remark with a wave. "I don't care about the facts. I consider us real sisters, and that's good enough for me."

Smiling, Cass buried any thought of Sam deep inside, and kept the conversation light the rest of the way home.

Chapter 16

"Hello, Sweeties," Mom greeted them as Tabitha and Cass entered the kitchen. She was at the stove, stirring a pot of something that smelled wonderful. "Did you have good time?"

"Terrific." Tabitha sniffed the air. "What are you making?"

"Homemade chicken noodle soup. Dad called from work and requested it for supper." Mom set the spoon aside. "Before I went to Surfway, I stopped by the post office. You both have mail."

"From Micah?" Tabitha breathed at the same time Cass asked, "From Logan?"

Mom laughed. "Yes, and yes." She gestured toward the dining room. "The letters are on the table."

Dropping their things, they both dashed to the table. Tabitha had two envelopes addressed to her, while Cass had three. They snatched up their letters and raced to their rooms to savor them in private.

The phone rang a couple of minutes later, and Mom knocked on Tabitha's door. "Sweetie," she said, poking her head into the room, "Kira's on the phone for you."

Tabitha looked up from the letter lying in her lap and absentmindedly took the phone. "Thanks."

"Don't forget to take it back to the kitchen when you're done," Mom reminded her.

Tabitha made a face as she brought the receiver to her ear. "I'm not the one who leaves it all over the house. Talk to your other daughter if you have a complaint." Changing her tone, she chirped into the mouthpiece, "Kira, hi."

"Hi, yourself. I just called to make sure Micah wrote to you too. We had a letter from him when I checked our box a little while ago."

"I got two letters." Tabitha smoothed the one beside her on the bed before picking up the one in her lap.

"You'd better not tell my mother you got twice as many she did," Kira warned with a laugh. "She believes a son should write his mother at least once a day. Since Micah doesn't share her belief, she's very disappointed at the lack of mail winging its way here from Hawaii."

"She can have my letters if it'll make her feel better." With a sniff, Tabitha dropped the second letter on top of the first.

"Meaning?"

"Meaning Micah might as well be writing to a stranger instead of to someone who's supposed to be his girlfriend," Tabitha said darkly. "He doesn't say anything personal, and heaven forbid he should ask how I'm doing. All he does is talk about how fabulous life is. He loves the campus, his dorm, the people he's met, his classes. Yada, yada, yada."

"That's pretty much what he wrote to us too." Kira sounded troubled. "I figured he'd go into more detail with you, though, and tell you how he's really doing."

"I think that is how he's really doing." Tabitha scooted back to lean against the headboard and crossed her arm over her midsection. "Everything's turned out great for him. All the stuff he used to worry about hasn't happened. Making it in the real world has turned out to be a snap."

"Do you honestly think it's all fallen into place that easily?" Kira asked.

"How should I know?" Tabitha heaved an exasperated sigh. "He's your brother."

"He's your boyfriend," Kira shot back.

Tabitha snorted. "You could have fooled me." Passing a hand over her eyes, she sighed again. "Maybe it would help if I talked to him. I'm going to ask Mom if I can call him over the weekend."

"Good idea," Kira said. "A nice, long chat will clear things up. It's hard to put stuff in a letter, but the phone works every time."

Although Tabitha didn't share her confidence, she chose not to say so. "I'll ask her as soon as I hang up with you."

"In that case, bye," Kira said quickly, then added, "Seriously, I'll let you go. The sooner you get the go-ahead, the better I'll feel. Call me back after you've talked to your mom."

"Will do." Pressing the off button, Tabitha tossed the phone on the bed. She was about to reread parts of Micah's letters when there was a quick knock on the door. "Come in."

The door flew open, and Cass stormed into the room. Her eyes blazed, and her cheeks were flushed a bright red. "Give me the phone. I'm calling Sam and asking him out."

Tabitha raised an eyebrow. "Slow down. Take a couple of deep breaths."

"I don't want to." Cass thrust out her jaw at a defiant angle. "I'm too mad."

"No kidding," drawled Tabitha. She patted the bed. "Sit down and tell me what Logan's done. It doesn't take a rocket scientist to figure out he's the reason for your temper tantrum."

"I am not having a temper tantrum." Cass enunciated each word slowly and distinctly. "This is a full-fledged fit." Nevertheless, she crossed the room and plopped down next to Tabitha. "Logan's first two letters were bad enough. He must have mentioned that girl, Shiloh, a hundred times. But then I got to his third letter. He wrote that they went to the movies together."

Tabitha's mouth dropped open in shock. "Just the two of them?"

"Well, no," Cass admitted. "They were with a group." Her expression darkened. "But you and I both know it's only a matter of time before they go out on an official date."

"I don't know any such thing," argued Tabitha. "And don't you dare use Sam to get back at Logan for something he *might* do. It's not fair to either of them."

Cass frowned. "Don't be mean to me," she whined. "I'm having a bad day."

"You are not." Tabitha bumped shoulders with her. "We had a great time with Sam, and I bet there's tons of good stuff in Logan's letters. You're just choosing to ignore it right now."

"Gee, thanks for being so understanding." Cass flounced impatiently. "You sound exactly like Mom."

"I consider that a compliment. Now come on," Tabitha wheedled, "tell me something nice that Logan wrote."

"Well—" a reluctant smile tugged at the corners of Cass' mouth, "he really misses me. He's also joined a campus ministry group Pastor Thompson told him about. He said it reminds him of our Sunday night group, only it's not as good. Plus, he said he talks about me all the time. His roommate wants to meet me because he can't believe I'm as perfect as Logan says I am."

"I knew his letters weren't as bad as you were making them out to be." Tabitha gave her a smug look. "It doesn't sound to me like he's on the verge of asking someone else out."

"Maybe you're right," conceded Cass. "I'm glad I came in to talk to you."

"That's what sisters are for." Remembering the phone, Tabitha picked it up. "I'd better put this back. You want to come and split whatever is left of the pie from last night?"

"You're on." Cass bounced off the bed. "Sometimes you have the best ideas."

CHAPTER 17

Two weeks later Tabitha and Cass came into the kitchen following their first day of school. A quick look around told them Mom wasn't anywhere to be seen. Cass' eyebrows knit together in a ferocious scowl.

"I don't believe it!" She smacked her hand on the counter. "There's no grilled cheese and tomato soup for our first day of school. Mom's had grilled cheese and tomato soup waiting when I got home ever since my first day in kindergarten."

Tabitha swallowed her disappointment. "Yeah. After last year, I was looking forward to it too."

"This stinks. I'm going to find out what's going on."

Cass marched down the hall to Mom and Dad's room, Tabitha following close behind. Striding to the bed where Mom lay curled on her side asleep, Cass poked her in the shoulder.

"I thought you'd like to know we're home."

Rolling onto her back, Mom blinked the sleep from her eyes. "What time is it?"

"Almost noon," Cass replied curtly.

"Noon?" Mom's eyes flew open, and she struggled to a sitting position. "Oh, girls, I'm so sorry. I meant to have the soup and sandwiches ready when you got home. Just give me a minute—" she swung her feet to the floor, "and I'll get right to it."

"Don't bother." Cass glared down at her. "Tabitha and I will fend for ourselves. Obviously you don't consider the first day of our last year in high school all that important," she added with a sneer.

Mom frowned. "I will not allow you to make me feel guilty for lying down. I should have set the alarm clock, just in case I fell asleep. I didn't, and I apologize. But I expect you to be a little more understanding about the situation."

Cass abruptly sagged against Mom's dresser. "I'm sorry. It's just ... there have been so many changes over the past few months that I was counting on something being the same. I wanted to walk into the house and smell tomato soup and grilled cheese sandwiches."

"I know." Mom slid off the bed and stood between Tabitha and Cass. She draped an arm across each girl's shoulders. "It's comforting to have something familiar to hang onto."

Cass rested her head on Mom's shoulder. "It's like I'm never happy anymore. I'm upset when I don't hear from Logan; then I get even more upset when I do. I'm mostly excited about having a baby brother or sister, but I resent the way your pregnancy has turned our life upside down. I was looking forward to being a senior, but, now that I am, I don't like it because it's not the way it was last year. Everything's a mess."

"Yeah," Tabitha agreed, wishing for the hundredth time that she could be as honest about her feelings as Cass always was.

Mom gave their shoulders reassuring squeezes. "Ladies, I think it's high time we had ourselves an old-fashioned, clearing-the-air discussion. I propose we eat first then talk. What do you say?"

"I say—" Cass sighed, "that sounds terrific."

"I second the motion." Tabitha leaned over and kissed Mom's cheek.

Taking their hands, Mom pushed off from the dresser. "Then let's get this show on the road. Soup and sandwiches coming right up."

"You know what's weird?" Kira remarked as she and Tabitha made their way into school. "We've been back in school almost a week, and I still can't get used to Micah not being here." She nudged her friend. "How about you?"

"It's strange to have them all gone," Tabitha replied carefully. "Micah, Logan, Randy. I keep expecting to see them walking down the hall, but they've moved on to greener pastures. It's kind of sad."

"But not seeing Micah is the worst, right?" Kira persisted.

"Uh ... yeah." Tabitha squirmed inside, sure Kira wouldn't find her answer satisfactory. She was right.

"Gee, do you think you could try to sound more convincing?" Kira drawled.

"What do you mean?" Tabitha worked hard at sounding innocent. "I—"

"Hey, Tabs! Kira! Wait up!" a shout interrupted her.

The girls glanced over their shoulders to see Sam jogging toward them. As usual, he sported a lazy grin.

"Sorry about the Tabs slip-up," he apologized the moment he reached them. Since Kira wouldn't move over to let him walk between her and Tabitha, he fell into step on Tabitha's other side. "That's how I think of you, but I try not to say it out loud. This time it just popped out." He smiled. "I promise it'll never happen again."

"Don't worry about it," Tabitha said, laughing. "The name's starting to grow on me. Saying Tabitha all the time can be a mouthful."

Kira's jaw dropped, and she jerked her head around to gape at her. "After all these years of insisting people use your real name, you suddenly decide a nickname is okay?" Her eyes narrowed into suspicious slits. "What's gotten into you?"

"Nothing." Tabitha hunched a shoulder and avoided her gaze. "What's wrong with shaking things up and making a few changes?"

"Hmm." Kira looked past her at Sam then back again. Lowering her voice so only Tabitha could hear, she murmured, "Maybe I shouldn't be asking what's gotten into you, but who's gotten to you."

"Don't start," Tabitha hissed. She darted a nervous glance at Sam, hoping he hadn't heard Kira's comment. Pasting on a bright smile, she asked in an attempt to change the subject, "So, did you have a reason for catching up with us?"

"Other than wanting to be seen walking into school with the two prettiest girls on the island?" he teased. Kira emitted a loud snort, and he pressed a hand to his chest. "Do you think I'm lying?"

"To put it in words of one syllable," sniffed Kira, "yes, I do."

"Who's prettier than you two?" Sam challenged. "Come on," he prompted when she didn't say anything. "Tell me so I can track her down and latch onto her. My ego is at stake here."

Kira sighed and ordered through clenched teeth, "Knock it off and answer Tabitha's question. Did you want something or not?"

Sam shrugged. "Actually, I did. I was talking to a couple of people after church yesterday—I went to the early service because they were having communion—and they said something about a youth group that meets at your house, Tabs." He smothered a laugh when she shot him a quick grin. "I was wondering if it's by invitation only. Or can any-body go?"

A spurt of pleasure shot through Tabitha. "It's open to anyone. My parents would love to have you give it a try."

"Just your parents?" purred Kira.

Tabitha flashed her a withering look before continuing, "We meet Sunday night at 6:00. Supper's provided. We fel-lowship first, then pray, then we have Bible study and dis-cussion. We're usually done by 8:00."

"Sounds great." Sam smiled warmly. "Tell your folks I'll be there this Sunday."

"I will." Tabitha did her best to hold in check the smile she felt tugging at her lips. "They'll be happy to hear some-one new is coming. Our attendance has been down since a bunch of kids left for college."

"I'll do my best to be a worthy replacement," Sam solemnly vowed. His attention was caught by a couple of people ahead of him in the crowd. "Hey, there's your sister and her friend. Sorry to chat and run, but I want to talk to Cass."

"So you can use the same line on her and Rianne that you used on us?" Tabitha arched a brow at him.

"Don't you know a gentleman never flirts and tells?" With a playful tap on Tabitha's nose, Sam was off and run-ning. "Yo, Red! Do you have a minute?"

Shaking her head, Tabitha turned to Kira. "Do you believe him? What a character."

Instead of sharing her amusement, Kira's face was tight as she gazed after Sam. "All I can say is it sure hasn't taken you long," she observed tartly.

Tabitha frowned. "What do you mean?"

"To find a stand-in for Micah." With an impatient twitch, Kira shifted her backpack to her other shoulder. "While he's pining away for you in Hawaii, you're down here yucking it up with Sam."

"Excuse me?" Tabitha's frown deepened into a scowl. "First of all, I don't know what makes you think Micah's pining away for me. From everything I've heard, he's having the time of his life. And secondly, where is it written I can't talk to other guys? Sam and I had a pleasant little conversation. Period. End of story."

"He was flirting with you," snapped Kira. "And, if I didn't know better, I'd think you were flirting right back."

Tabitha forced herself to take a couple of deep breaths. She didn't want to say something she'd regret later. "For your information, if Sam is interested in anybody, my money's on Cass. They're a lot alike, and she thinks he's great. He's not my type at all which means there was no way I'd flirt with him, either deliberately or subconsciously."

Her firm response seemed to reassure Kira. Some of the stiffness drained from her shoulders. "I'm just looking out for my brother's interests."

"I know, and I'm sure Micah appreciates it." Tabitha briefly squeezed her arm. "So, no more stupid talk about Sam and me?"

"As long as you behave yourself and don't give me any reason to be concerned." Although Kira kept her tone light, there was no mistaking the veiled threat in her reply.

Tabitha immediately tensed. "Since when is it your job to keep tabs on me? What do you do? Send weekly reports to Micah?"

"Should I?" retorted Kira.

Throwing her hands up in exasperation, Tabitha halted just inside the building. She ignored the students streaming past her as she whirled to confront Kira.

"Don't you ever—" she shook a warning finger in her face, "betray our friendship by spying on me. If Micah wants to know what's going on in my life, he can ask me himself."

"That's ridiculous. You can't tell me what I can and can't

talk about with my own brother." Kira propped her fists on her hips and glowered.

"You're right," Tabitha conceded. "But I will tell you this. If I ever find out you've been talking to him about me behind my back, you can kiss our friendship goodbye."

A sneer curled Kira's lip. "If things between you and Sam are as innocent as you say they are, what are you so worried about?"

"Oh, for Pete's sake!" Tabitha exploded. "You're not even trying to see things my way so forget it."

Utterly frustrated, she spun on her heels and stalked down the hall to her locker. For some strange reason, Kira had made up her mind she was planning to cheat on Micah with Sam, and nothing she could say would convince her otherwise.

Fine then. Tabitha yanked open the locker door. *She can think whatever she wants, but I'm not about to stand around and listen to her drivel. She owes me an apology, and, until I get one, I'm going to act like she doesn't exist. Let's see how she likes being made to feel like an outcast.*

When Kira arrived at her locker a short while later, Tabitha made a point of ignoring her. The problem was, it turned out Kira was playing the same game. As much as Tabitha wanted to shun her, she didn't get the chance because Kira shunned her first. Annoyed, Tabitha stomped off to homeroom.

"Wow, who rained on your parade?" Cass wanted to know as Tabitha slammed her things down on the desk next to hers.

"Kira," Tabitha bit out the name.

"What'd she do?"

"She accused me of flirting with Sam." Tabitha sat down with a thud.

Cass raised an eyebrow. "Were you?"

"No, I was not."

Cass sighed in what sounded like relief. "So tell her you weren't."

"I did. Besides, she was right there. She could see for herself I wasn't. If she didn't have such huge blinders on, that is," Tabitha added bitterly. "Kira's on a mission to make sure I don't cheat on her brother while he's away at school."

"Like anybody here believes he hasn't been partying up a storm ever since he hit Hawaii," scoffed Cass.

"As far as Kira's concerned, Micah can do no wrong. I, on the other hand, should be wearing a scarlet A on my chest because I dared to talk to Sam." Tabitha shrugged. "Go figure."

"Y'all have had your little spats before. You'll make up," Cass predicted.

"Not unless she says she's sorry." Folding her arms, Tabitha glared around the room in case Kira had come in without her noticing. "I'm getting really tired of her watching me all the time. I feel like a bug under a microscope."

"You've said before she suspects you're not all that upset about Micah being gone. Maybe you should explain to her why you feel the way you do," Cass suggested. "She might lighten up if she realizes how things were before he left. She might even agree the break will do your relationship good."

Tabitha stared off into space as she considered Cass' advice. Turning back to her sister, she nodded. "You know, I believe you're right. I haven't said anything to Kira about how Micah acted because I didn't want her to think I was badmouthing him. She's so touchy when it comes to family. But now I think that was a mistake. She needs to know so she'll quit jumping to wrong conclusions about me."

"Now's your chance." Cass' gaze slid toward the door. "Kira just walked in."

Mustering her courage, Tabitha got up, gathered her

books, and moved to the desk behind her friend. Kira made a point of pretending not to see her, so Tabitha tapped her on the shoulder.

"Can we talk?"

Kira tossed her dark curls. "That depends on what you want to talk about."

"Micah and me."

That got Kira's attention, and she turned sideways in her seat. "Go ahead. I'm listening."

"Not here." Tabitha glanced around at the other students. "Let's go to the fish pond after school. We can stop at the Ten-Ten first for snacks and make an afternoon of it. I haven't been there in ages."

"Right after school?" Kira asked. "If so, I'll call my mother during lunch to tell her."

Tabitha nodded. "I'll do the same. As long as it's okay with them, I'll meet you at your locker after the last bell."

"Deal." Kira hesitated then blurted, "Just tell me one thing, though. Do you still like Micah as much as you used to?"

Since the answer was more complicated than a simple yes or no, Tabitha put her off with, "We'll talk later. That way I'll be able to go into more detail."

"Later then." Kira said, then frowned. "I'm warning you, though, this had better be good."

Throughout the rest of the day, Tabitha worked hard at not thinking ahead to their discussion. Every time she did, butterflies erupted in her stomach. As much as she loved Kira, she knew her friend had a nasty temper, and she usually bent over backward to avoid being on the receiving end of it. This afternoon, she might not be able to dodge it, and the thought made her queasy.

CHAPTER 18

"Why so glum, chum?" Sam appeared beside her as she headed to her last class of the day.

Just the sight of his friendly face instantly cheered Tabitha. "There's something I have to do this afternoon, and I'm not looking forward to it."

"So ditch it, and come swimming with me." Sam assumed his most charming expression. Tabitha laughed, then hastily looked around to make sure Kira wasn't anywhere in sight. "I wish I could, but I can't. It's something I really have to do."

Sam lowered his voice. "You're not like a spy or anything, are you? With my father in the military and all, it wouldn't be right if I were friends with a spy."

"Has anyone ever told you you're nuts?" Tabitha shook her head at his joking.

"You mean today?" Sam's brow furrowed as he thought. "Nope, nobody's mentioned it today."

"Remind me to tell you before the day is out." Tabitha halted outside a classroom. "This is as far as I'm going. I guess I'll see you later."

"You'll definitely see me later. Cass invited me over for a study session."

"Then what was that business about asking me to go swimming?" Crossing her arms, Tabitha tried to look stern as she awaited his response.

"Oh, yeah. That. It was one of those spur-of-the-moment invitations." Sam dazzled her with an unrepentant grin. "I'd have been in real trouble if you'd taken me up on it."

"One of these days you're going to get yourself into hot water," Tabitha scolded with mock severity. "Then what are you going to do?"

Lowering his head, Sam peered up at her with a hopeful expression. "Use my gift of gab and talk my way out of it?"

Gosh, he's cute, Tabitha realized with a start. *And he's got a personality to match. I wish I didn't have this thing with Kira so I could stay home and be a part of Cass' study group.*

Giving herself a mental shake, she replied aloud, "With the way you can snow people, it would probably work." She fluttered her fingers. "I'd better get into class. If you're still at the house when I get back, I'll see you then."

"I'll make sure I'm there," vowed Sam. "I'm not dumb enough to pass up a chance to see your smiling face if I can help it."

Tabitha stared after him as he took off down the hall. *Was that just a throwaway line?* she wondered. *Or does he really like the way I look?* She mulled the question over another couple of seconds before firmly putting it out of her mind. Calculus was her last class, and it took every ounce of brainpower she could summon to follow along. Already she couldn't wait until the end of the semester when she'd never have to open another calculus text again.

As planned, Tabitha met Kira at her locker after class, and they walked out front together to find their bikes. They waved to Cass and Sam as they left before backing their bikes out of the rack.

Tabitha placed her backpack in the handlebar basket and, feeling that their silence was awkward, asked, "Do you have anything special in mind for a snack?"

Kira shrugged. "Whatever you want is fine."

"Definitely not ice cream." Tabitha mopped her brow. "Today's a scorcher. I'm starting to look forward to the rainy season."

"Not me." Kira made a face. "I hate it when it gets all dark and dreary. We live on a tropical island. It should look like one."

Debating the merits of the dry versus rainy seasons, they rode to the Ten-Ten store. Once there, they quickly decided on pretzels and Cokes. Since it was her idea, Tabitha paid for the purchases.

"Who were you talking to while I was checking out?" Tabitha asked after they exited the store.

Kira's face instantly lit up. "I've told you about him. That's Jason Howell, the new boy in my Spanish class."

"He's a junior, right?" Tabitha raised the kickstand and climbed on her bike.

"Don't start in about him being younger the way you did with Garth," Kira ordered irritably.

Tabitha let the comment pass. "Speaking of Garth, what's up with you two?"

Kira snorted. "You know how I told you he's been acting funny since he got back from the mainland?" When Tabitha nodded, she continued, "He wrote me a note today and told me why. He had a fling with some girl from his hometown, and they've pledged their undying love for each other. Since he doesn't want to cheat on her, he's breaking up with me." She rolled her eyes. "How humiliating is that? I've been dumped by a sophomore."

"Oh, well. There are worse things in life."

"Yeah? Like what?"

"He could be a freshman."

They both laughed, which lifted Tabitha's spirits. As long as she and Kira could still kid around together, everything would be fine.

Sitting down on the bench beside the pond, they busied themselves opening the bag of pretzels and the cans of soda. Once that was done, they were out of excuses not to talk, and Tabitha took a deep breath.

"Okay, here goes. I don't want to beat around the bush so I'm going to ask you right out. Do you think I'm the type of person to run around on Micah?"

"I don't want to think that." Kira avoided looking at Tabitha by staring intently into the pond. "But, yeah, I'm starting to think you are."

Although that was the answer Tabitha had expected, it still distressed her, and she threw up her hands. "Why? What have I done?"

"It's not what you've done. It's—" Kira hesitated for a moment, "more your attitude since Micah's been gone. You're almost ... happy."

Setting aside the soda can, Tabitha twisted her hands together in her lap. "I'm not happy. I'm relieved. Things got very confusing with Micah before he left. One day all he'd talk about was how much he was going to miss me then the next day he'd go on and on about all the fun he planned to have in Hawaii. I couldn't figure out where I stood with him. Even when he told me he loved me, I—"

"He said he loved you?" Squealing, Kira rounded on Tabitha and grabbed her in a bear hug. "That's so exciting! Did you say it back to him?"

"Well ... yes," Tabitha reluctantly admitted.

"No guy has ever told me he loves me." Kira heaved a rapturous sigh. "It must be the most wonderful thing in the world."

Tabitha decided it was time to burst her bubble. "I didn't like it. I didn't feel wonderful. I felt weird."

The excitement drained from Kira's face, and she looked shocked. "How can you say that?"

"Because it's true." Tabitha's tone was as stubborn as her expression. "Micah and I don't love each other, and we had no business saying we did. If Micah loved me, he'd pay more attention to me. He'd want to know how I'm doing and what's going on in my life instead of always talking about himself. And if I loved him, I wouldn't be relieved he's gone. I'd be missing him so much I couldn't stand it. But the truth is I'm not. I'm happy to have a break from him. It gives me a chance to try to figure out my feelings. I hope he's doing the same thing."

"But ... but ..." Kira sputtered. She jumped up and began to pace. "You're just put out because he's doing so well at school. You expected him to fall flat on his face. He didn't, and now you don't know what to do."

"No!" Tabitha denied heatedly. "He was the one who expected to fail. I kept telling him he'd do great. I'm glad things are turning out the way they are. I'm proud of him."

"Yeah, right," jeered Kira. "Since Micah's doing well, it means he doesn't need you as much as you thought he would, and you don't like that."

"I'll admit I wish he'd talk to me about his hopes and fears the way he used to," Tabitha conceded. "It's like he's cut me out of his life. And it hurts," she added softly.

Instead of being sympathetic, Kira marched over to stand in front of her and scoff, "Who cut who out? You used Micah. Now that he's gone, it's not convenient having him as a boyfriend anymore. You're not about to sit home and miss out on all the fun. So it's out with the old and in with the new."

"Is that what you really think?" Tabitha was so angry she could barely breathe.

"Yup, that's what I really think." Kira's fierce glower dared Tabitha to contradict her.

Tabitha didn't. Without a word, she rose and, summoning all her dignity, walked to her bike. Mounting the bike, she rode away without a backward glance.

Tabitha slammed into the house a few minutes later, ignoring the study group who stared at her as she stormed through the kitchen and down the hall. She tried to slam her bedroom door shut, but Cass was too close behind her and caught the bedroom door with her foot before it banged shut.

"Leave me alone!" Tabitha shouted. "Go back to your friends. At least you have some." Bitterness hardened her features.

"I'm not going anywhere." Closing the door, Cass leaned against it and crossed her arms. "What happened with you and Kira?"

"Our friendship is over."

Cass sagged against the door. "She said that?"

"Not in so many words, but that's what she meant." Tabitha angrily brushed away the tears pooling in her eyes. "She accused me of using Micah and then dumping him because it's not convenient having him as a boyfriend anymore. A friend doesn't say something like that."

"You know Kira," Cass reminded her. "She's says lots of stuff she doesn't mean."

"Believe me, she meant it." Flopping onto her bed, Tabitha stared up at the ceiling. "I don't know what's happened to my life. Last year at this time, I had a whole group of friends. Now Micah acts like he couldn't care less about me. Kira thinks I'm a two-timing sleaze. Logan and Randy are gone, and Rianne's your best friend." She sniffled loudly. "I have nobody."

"Why don't you come join the study group?" Cass said

calmly. "Rianne, Greg, and Sam are here. We're working on economics."

"You don't want me. I'd just be in the way." Tabitha flung an arm over her eyes. "Besides, you're all paired up. I don't want to be a fifth wheel."

"Oh, for pity's sake, it's a study group, not a date. Nobody's paired up. Okay, technically," she corrected herself, "Rianne and Greg are, but Sam and I aren't. You wouldn't be in anyone's way."

"You're just being nice." Rolling onto her side, Tabitha curled up into a miserable ball.

"So?" challenged Cass. "What's wrong with being nice?"

"I don't need your pity."

"That's obvious," Cass drawled, "since you're wallowing in a tubful of it."

"Hey!" Tabitha jerked upright to a sitting position to glare at her. "I could use a little sympathy here."

"Honestly!" Cass exploded. "I can't win. Whatever I do, you jump all over me."

The girls glowered at each other for several seconds before Tabitha reluctantly smiled. "You're right." Lowering her head to her knees, she thought a moment. "You said you're studying economics? Is it for the test Friday?"

Cass nodded.

"If the offer's still open, I'd like to join you. I need to get my mind off Kira, plus I could use the help studying." Her expression was hopeful as she gazed up at Cass.

"Get your book and come on then." Reaching behind her, Cass found the knob and opened the door. "Time's a-wasting. We decided we'll study till 5:00 then head over to the bowling alley for pizza."

In the process of sliding off the bed, Tabitha hesitated. "You're sure it's okay for me to tag along?"

Cass responded with an exasperated growl and left. After a quick stop in the bathroom to splash cool water on her face and brush her hair, Tabitha made her way to the dining room. She immediately relaxed when Sam pulled out a chair and invited her to sit next to him.

"Yo, Tabs, take a load off."

"Tabs?" echoed Rianne. Her eyebrows disappeared under her bangs.

Sam blew on his knuckles and polished them on his chest. "Yup. We have a deal. I get to call her Tabs, and she doesn't beat me up."

"So I noticed. If any of us ever dared to call her that, we'd be sporting black eyes." Rianne slanted Tabitha a curious look. "What gives? How come he's privileged?"

Before she could reply, Sam said quickly, "Because I'm so good-looking?"

"Oh, puh-leeze! Be serious," Cass said, laughing.

Listening to them, Tabitha realized how long it had been since she'd been with people who enjoyed teasing one another. She was suddenly grateful to Cass for including her.

"Maybe we should let Tabs answer," suggested Sam. He elbowed her in the side. "Go on. Tell them why I'm allowed to call you by a nickname."

"Well, Sam—" Tabitha batted her eyelashes and tried not to giggle, "it's exactly like you said. Because you're so good-looking."

While the others erupted in laughter, his mouth dropped open. Reaching over, Tabitha used her index finger to shut it for him.

"Watch it. You're drooling on your book."

The look Sam gave her was composed of equal parts amusement and admiration. For reasons she didn't care to examine, it sent shivers up Tabitha's spine.

After a while, they managed to settle down and actually study. But at 4:45, Sam suddenly shut his book with a thud. "I don't know about the rest of you, but my brain's about to explode. If I don't take a break, it could get pretty messy."

Sighing loudly, Greg closed his book. "I hear you. Who invented this stuff, and why do we have to learn it?"

"It was invented by grown-ups who don't want teenagers to have any fun," explained Rianne. "And we have to learn it because those same grown-ups decided we can't graduate unless we do."

"I say we find them and make them sit through economics classes for the rest of their lives," Sam declared.

"Good luck trying to find them," Cass said darkly. "Nobody in their right mind would admit to making this stuff up."

Laughing, they piled up their books and, after Cass let Mom know they were going, left for the bowling alley.

CHAPTER 19

"Hey, there's a message for you," Cass announced to Tabitha when they returned home two hours later.

Tabitha, who had lingered on the porch to enjoy the sight of the moonlight shimmering on the water, turned from the window. "I didn't hear you turn on the answering machine."

"Not on the machine, silly." Snatching up the note, Cass carried it out to the porch. "Mom left it. It says Micah called—"

Tabitha grabbed the piece of paper. "Hey, that's my note. I want to read it."

"Suit yourself." Shrugging, Cass disappeared into the house.

After reading the message twice, Tabitha entered the kitchen. She found Cass with her head in the refrigerator, searching for dessert.

"Don't tell me the pizza didn't fill you up."

"Okay, I won't." Cass pulled out a lemon meringue pie and set it on the counter. "You want some?"

Tabitha pressed a hand to her midsection. "No, thanks. My stomach's tied in knots right now."

Cass gave her a curious look. "You're nervous about calling Micah?"

"Petrified is more like it." Tabitha leaned against the counter and watched while Cass cut herself a hefty slice of the pie. "I figure Kira already talked to him, and he called to chew me out."

"That's not a very positive attitude," Cass said.

"All right, then I'm positive he wants to chew me out." Tabitha's expression was as gloomy as her tone.

"So don't call him." Cass took a bite of pie and heaved a blissful sigh. "If you're not in the mood to be yelled at, wait until he calls you."

"That would probably make him more angry." Confused about what to do, Tabitha nibbled at her thumbnail.

"Don't do that." Cass reached over and pulled Tabitha's finger out of her mouth. "You don't know for sure that's what he wants. He might have called to tell you he's come to his senses and realizes he's been treating you like trash."

"Yeah, right."

"Anything's possible." Cass chewed and swallowed another bite of pie before continuing, "For all we know, he wants to pledge you his undying love and devotion."

"Did the pizza fumes go to your head or something?" Tabitha muttered. "You're talking crazy."

"I'm just coming up with alternatives," Cass defended herself. "You shouldn't automatically assume Micah's call means something bad."

"After my discussion with Kira this afternoon, that's the only logical explanation for his call." Squaring her shoulders, Tabitha pushed off from the counter. "I guess I shouldn't put it off any longer. The sooner I call, the sooner I can quit guessing how mad he is and know for sure."

"You want me to go to my room so you can talk in private?" Cass offered.

"Nah, I'll take the phone out onto the porch." Tabitha attempted a light laugh. "If I start yelling too loud, I'll go outside."

"Ah—" Cass nodded wisely, "disturb the neighbors. Good idea. That'll thrill the folks to no end."

"Put a cork in it," Tabitha retorted good-naturedly.

Feeling slightly better, she picked up the receiver and carried it out to the porch. It took almost a minute to muster the courage to dial Micah's number. Then it took all her courage not to hang up when the phone began to ring on the other end. After four rings, she expelled the pent-up breath she'd been holding.

Good, he's not in. I'll try again tomor—

"Hello, you've reached the Honolulu Zoo. Head zookeeper speaking."

Tabitha frowned at the receiver. "Uh ... hello. I'm ... uh ... trying to reach Micah Alexander. Is he—"

The phone was set down with a clatter. "Yo, Mike. It's for you. Don't be long, man. I'm waiting for Mindy to call."

"Yeah?" Micah's familiar voice came on the line.

To Tabitha's surprise, tears sprang to her eyes. "Hi, Micah. It's me."

There was a slight pause. "Tabitha?"

Stung that he didn't immediately recognize her voice, she stiffened and blinked away the tears. "Yes. My mother left me a note that you'd called."

"So you made it back from the bowling alley." Micah's tone was cool. "Did you have a nice time?"

"Very nice, thank you."

Two can play at this game, Tabitha thought.

"Who'd you go with?"

Tabitha hesitated at the edge in Micah's voice. "Uh ... Cass, Rianne, Greg, and Sam."

There was a long pause. "Sam. Would that be the Sam Steele Kira's told me about?"

"I don't know any other Sam."

"How'd he wind up going?"

"He was part of a study group Cass invited over."

Tabitha affected a tinkly laugh. "Don't tell me you called all the way from Hawaii to check on Cass' and my social life."

"I couldn't care less about what Cass does in her free time. That's Logan's problem. But," Micah continued harshly, "after talking to Kira today, I thought you and I should have a little chat."

"So, chat away." With effort, Tabitha managed to sound breezily unconcerned.

"What's this about you needing a break from me?" Micah didn't bother beating around the bush.

"I ... uh ... that is ..." Tabitha stammered.

"You did say that, didn't you?" interrupted Micah.

"Yes, but I didn't mean it in a bad way." Not sure how to proceed, Tabitha fell silent.

"Go on," Micah urged. "I'm listening. I'd really like to know what's going on."

Heartened by his encouraging tone, Tabitha took a deep breath then blurted in a rush, "First off, I want you to know I miss you. A lot. But, in another way, I'm glad you're not here so I can sort out our relationship. By the time you left, I was pretty tired of you acting like you couldn't wait to get away from Kwaj. And me," she added, her voice temporarily dropping to a near whisper. "You stopped talking to me about the things you were scared of. I used to feel like you needed me. I don't anymore. I'm not sure if I even have a place in your life."

"Are you done?" Micah asked stiffly. When Tabitha assured him she was, he continued, "I don't know how you can question my feelings for you. I told you I loved you, didn't I?"

"Yes, but—"

"But nothing," he broke in. "I don't make a habit of telling girls I love them, you know. You're the only one I've ever said it to. Now I wonder if I made a mistake. You should be glad I'm doing well in school. I'm involved in lots of activities, and I've made a ton of friends. Not to brag on myself, but I'm pretty popular. I can find my way around Hono with my eyes closed. I worried for years about making it in the real world. I've found out I can, and I'm really proud of myself."

"I'm proud of you too." Tabitha wasn't sure how it had happened, but suddenly she felt like she was the one in the wrong.

"You don't act like you are," countered Micah. "I get the feeling you wish I'd fallen flat on my face because then I'd need you."

"That's not true," Tabitha protested. "All I want is for things to go back to the way they used to be."

"You mean when I'd whine about how scared I was to leave Kwaj, and you'd try to convince me I'd be fine?" There was a hint of scorn in Micah's voice.

Tabitha's patience finally snapped. "We had more going for us than that, and you know it. Next to Kira, you were my best friend in the entire world. I could talk to you about anything, and I thought you felt the same way about me. We knew everything that was going on each other's lives. I hardly know what you're thinking anymore. I mean, do you even go to church? Have you found a Christian group on campus?"

"Church isn't high on my list of priorities right now," Micah curtly informed her. "My main focus is on doing well in my classes."

"Yeah, right." Tabitha snorted. "You can find time to hit the clubs in Hono, but you can't find time for church? And you want me to believe it's because you're concentrating on school?"

"Get off my back," Micah snapped.

"You see? That's what I'm talking about." Tabitha was more sad than smug about having proved her point. "We used to have long discussions about faith. It was one of the things we had in common. Now you can't even be bothered to go to church."

"There's more to life than church."

Tabitha inhaled sharply. "Micah, what's the matter with you? Why are you acting like this?"

Instead of answering, Micah sneered, "You know what I think? You're jealous. You don't like it that I'm not wasting away up here without you. You want to be the most important thing in my life, and you can't stand it that you're not. So your solution is to get back at me by flirting with Sam and telling Kira the stuff you did this afternoon, knowing she'd tell me."

For several seconds, Tabitha was too stunned to speak. Micah mistook her silence for anger.

"Don't get me wrong," he went on in a gentler voice. "I'm not mad at you. I understand why you're doing what you're doing. You're scared I don't feel the same way about you that I used to, but you're wrong." He paused. "I still love you. I've met a lot of girls up here, but none of them compares to you."

Wow, that's a load off my mind, Tabitha thought sarcastically. She wished she were Cass and had the nerve to speak up for herself.

Aloud, she said lamely, "I'm glad."

"Are you really?" Micah asked softly.

Tell him the truth, urged a voice in Tabitha's head.

She couldn't. "Sure."

"So we're okay?" probed Micah.

The best Tabitha could manage was a lame, "I guess so."

"Good. Then this phone call was worth it. What?" Micah was distracted by muffled conversation in the background. A few seconds later, he was back. "Look, I've got to go. My roommate's waiting for a call. It was good talking to you ... Tabs."

Tabitha saw red. She wanted to shout at him to never—ever!—call her that again. As usual, she held her tongue. "Good talking to you too."

"I'll call you in a couple of weeks." Micah lowered his voice. "I love you."

For once, Tabitha found the courage not to respond. "Uh ... thanks. Bye." She hung up before Micah could say anything about her lack of a reply.

She lingered on the porch for a couple of minutes to regain her composure. Then, after replacing the phone, she went in search of Cass. She didn't have to look far. Cass was in the living room, watching a brainless sitcom. The moment Cass noticed Tabitha, she turned off the television.

"How'd it go?" she asked anxiously.

Tabitha passed a weary hand across her eyes. "I'd rather not talk about it right now. I just—" she sank down onto the coffee table, "really need you to pray about Micah and me. From the way the conversation ended, Micah seems to think we're doing fine." Her shoulders drooped. "But we're not. Sooner or later, I'm going to have to be honest with him."

"Do you want me to pray now?" Cass asked, sitting up.

Tabitha shook her head. "That's okay. Just add us to your list tonight. Oh, and throw in Kira's and my friendship too." Her face hardened. "If we have a friendship after I'm through talking to her, that is."

"She ratted on you?"

Tabitha's nod was grim.

"Are you going to call her now?"

Tabitha shook her head. "I'm too whipped to talk to anyone else." She slowly stood up. "I'm going to take a hot bath and go to bed."

"You want me to tuck you in and read you a bedtime story?" Cass grinned up at her.

"You'd do that for me?" Tabitha clasped her hands under her chin in mock gratitude.

"Are you nuts?" Cass shot back. "The only one I'd ever consider doing that for is our baby brother or sister. Maybe."

Laughing, Tabitha started across the room. "Thank you. I needed a laugh." She shot Cass an impish smile. "Looking at you wasn't enough to give me one this time."

"Ooh, good one." She waited until Tabitha was almost out of sight before calling, "I'm sorry you're having a rough time."

"That makes two of us, Sis," Tabitha replied sadly. "That definitely makes two of us."

CHAPTER 20

"Cass—" Dad appeared at her bedroom door. "Kira's on the phone for you."

It was two nights later. Cass turned from her desk where she was struggling to make sense out of her economics assignment. "Kira? For me?"

Nodding, Dad crossed the floor to hand her the receiver. "You're the one she asked for."

"Okay." Although she sounded doubtful, Cass accepted the phone. She waited until Dad left and closed the door behind him before speaking. "Kira?"

"The one and only," came the bubbly response. "What are you doing?"

"What else? Homework." Cass made a face. "I'm not even halfway through economics, and I still have Spanish to go."

"I hear you," Kira sympathized. "I won't talk long. I was just wondering if you and Sam would like to double-date with Jason and me tomorrow night."

Cass blinked her confusion. "Sam and I? Technically, there isn't any Sam and I. We're just friends."

"I know that," Kira said breezily. "But you'd really be doing me a favor if you'd go. Here's the deal. Jason asked me to dinner at the Yuk. I don't know him all that well yet, so I'd feel better if another couple came along. You know, to smooth over any awkward spots. I ran the idea by him, and he's fine with it. The first people I thought of were you and Sam."

Uncomfortable with the invitation, Cass tried to think of a way to politely weasel out of it. "What about Rianne and Greg? They're actually dating."

Kira hesitated then confided, "Don't get me wrong, I like Rianne a lot. But she's sort of a—how should I put this?—goody-goody. I'd rather be with people I can be myself with. First dates are bad enough without feeling like you have to be on your best behavior."

Cass couldn't decide if she was flattered or insulted by her remark. "I'd feel funny asking Sam to take me out to eat."

"I'll ask him for you," Kira offered.

The subtle approach obviously isn't working, Cass thought with a sigh.

"Look, I'll be honest. I'm not comfortable with the idea."

"But you and Sam get along great," Kira argued.

"It's not just the Sam thing." Cass took a deep breath. "I have a sneaking suspicion you're using me to get back at Tabitha. Ever since y'all had your big blowout the other day, you've been avoiding each other like the plague. Now, all of a sudden, you want me to double-date with you. It's too coincidental."

The silence grew so long on the other end of the line that Cass wondered if Kira had hung up. When she finally spoke, she was more subdued than Cass had ever heard her.

"I'm not using you. Honest. It's just ... I can't think of anyone else to ask. I don't have that many friends." At Cass' murmur of surprise, she insisted, "It's true. I know a lot of people, but you and Tabitha are the only ones I'm

really close to. Now that Tabitha's out of the picture ..."
Her words forlornly trailed off.

Oh, brother. Talk about being caught between a rock and a hard place.

"I'm not making any promises, but here's what I'll do," Cass replied. "I'll ask Tabitha how she feels about the dinner tomorrow night. If she has a problem with it, I'll have to turn you down. If it's okay, I'll call you back so you can call Sam. Deal?"

"Deal." Kira perked up considerably. "I'm going to hang up now. The sooner you talk to Tabitha, the sooner I can begin making plans."

Pressing the off button, Cass set the phone down on the desk. With Tabitha's anger toward Kira still running high, she didn't look forward to bringing up her name in conversation. But a promise was a promise. She reluctantly stood up.

After finding Tabitha's room empty, Cass went down the hall to the living room. Music played softly in the background while Mom and Dad sat on the couch talking.

"Taking a break?" Dad asked.

"Sort of." Cass glanced around the corner into the kitchen. "Mostly I'm looking for Tabitha. Is she on the porch?"

"She's out back," Mom answered. "She said she needed some fresh air to stimulate her brain cells. Apparently, her homework wasn't going well."

"I know the feeling," Cass muttered.

On her way outside, she stopped in the kitchen for a couple of apples. If all else failed, maybe she could bribe Tabitha into letting her double-date with Kira.

The moment she stepped out the door, a gust of wind set Cass' ponytail to dancing about her shoulders. Looking up, she smiled when she saw clouds scudding across the sky, obscuring the moon and stars.

"Looks like we might have rain tonight," she observed as she walked up behind Tabitha, who was sitting on a rock, looking out at the ocean.

Tabitha glanced over her shoulder. "What are you doing out here?"

Uh-oh, thought Cass. *Looks like she's in one of her moods.*

Settling herself on an adjacent rock, she held out one of the apples. After a brief hesitation, Tabitha took it. *So far, so good.*

"I need to talk to you about something."

To buy some time, Cass bit into her apple. Tabitha followed suit, and they chewed in silence for a few moments. Sneaking peeks at her, Cass couldn't help noticing how stern her sister's profile looked as she gazed out at the water. *She's really bugged about something. Maybe this isn't the right time to discuss Kira.*

"So, what do you want to talk about?" Tabitha asked around a mouthful of apple.

"It's not that important." Cass waved a breezy hand. "It can wait."

Tabitha shot her a skeptical look. "You go out of your way to track me down then you say it's not important? Right. What's going on?"

"Okay, here's the deal." Cass took a last bite of her apple then threw the core into the water for the fish. "Kira called a little while ago. She wants Sam and me to go out to eat with her and Jason tomorrow night."

"I see." Tabitha nodded slowly. "What's that got to do with me?"

"I told her I needed to check with you before I made a decision because I didn't want her using me to get back at you."

"What about Sam?" Tabitha asked. "Shouldn't you check with him too?"

"Kira's going to call him if you say it's all right," Cass

explained. She waited awhile. When Tabitha didn't say anything, she prompted, "What do you think?"

"I think, if you go out, I don't want to hear any more complaints about Logan and that girl, Shiloh," drawled Tabitha. "Dinner would definitely be considered a date, unlike Logan and Shiloh going to the movies with a group."

Bristling, Cass sat up straight and glowered as best she could in the dim light. "What does that have to do with anything? I want to know how you feel about me spending time with Kira."

Tabitha shrugged. "It's a free island. Do whatever you want."

"It doesn't bother you that Kira asked me instead of you?" Cass persisted.

"Not particularly. Think about it. Even if Kira and I were on speaking terms," reasoned Tabitha, "who'd be my date? It's not like I'm seeing anybody."

"I'm not exactly seeing Sam, you know," Cass defended herself.

"Maybe not officially, but you two spend an awful lot of time together." Tabitha pitched her apple core at the next wave. "What's he going to think when Kira asks him to escort you to dinner?"

"That we're doing a friend a favor?" Her response sounded lame, even to Cass' own ears.

"Yeah, right." Tabitha snorted. "Sure."

"Okay, I get your point," Cass huffed. Leaning back on her hands, she stared up at the sky where stars twinkled here and there between the clouds. "What do you suggest?"

"That depends on whether you want to consider it a date." Tabitha shook back the curls that the wind blew across her face. "Which means you have to figure out how you feel about Sam."

"He's a great guy," Cass replied immediately. "I like him

a lot." She paused to mull over the situation. "But only as a friend ... I think."

"So it might be something more?"

"Most of the time, I'm sure it's just a friendship. But every now and then—" Cass struggled to find the right words. "I look at him and think, wow, he's really terrific. Then again, if I try to imagine holding hands with him or even kissing him—" she pressed a hand to her stomach, "I feel really weird." She laughed. "How's that for a clear-cut answer?"

"It's honest." Tabitha folded her legs beneath her. "Where does that leave Logan?"

"The way I feel about Logan hasn't changed." Cass shifted to a more comfortable position on the rock. "But every time I get a letter from him, I'm afraid it's going to be the one where he tells me it's over. I can't believe our relationship is going to last. I mean, how many do?"

"Yours could be the exception."

"It could," conceded Cass. "But the odds are it won't."

"So Sam is what?" probed Tabitha. "Sort of an insurance policy in case Logan bails on you?"

Cass frowned. "It sounds so ugly when you put it like that."

"Hey—" Tabitha lifted her hands in a gesture of innocence, "I'm just trying to do what you do with me. I'm making you look at the facts. Which leads me to another question. Do you honestly consider Sam boyfriend material?"

"Hmm. Good question." Cass took her time answering it. "Like I said, he's a great guy, and I think the world of him. But ... there's no spark. Being with him is like being with Randy or Micah." Her forehead puckered in a worried frown. "Do you think he considers me a potential girlfriend?"

"I think it's possible. He sure likes spending time with you."

"He's never acted like we're anything more than

friends," Cass pointed out.

"Maybe he's biding his time until he thinks you're over Logan. Then he's planning to make his move." Tabitha didn't sound very thrilled about the idea.

"Oh, gee, I hope not," Cass fretted. "That would ruin everything."

"Then you might not want to go through with the date tomorrow night." Tabitha shrugged nonchalantly. "It could send Sam the wrong message."

About to agree, Cass suddenly straightened and peered intently at her. "Hey, wait a minute. Are you really concerned about Sam? Or is this your way of keeping me from going out with Kira and Jason?"

"I told you I don't care what you do, or don't do, with Kira." Tabitha crossed her arms and stared back at her. "Sam is another story. I don't want to see him hurt."

"Why do you care?" Cass asked quietly. "What's Sam to you?"

"The same as he is to you. A friend." Tabitha's tone dared her to argue.

Interesting, mused Cass. *She sounds pretty possessive for someone who's just a friend.*

Aloud, she advised, "Don't worry. I have no intention of hurting Sam. If we go out tomorrow night, I'll make sure he knows it's as a couple of pals. Okay?"

"I guess," Tabitha replied softly. "So you're going to call Kira and tell her yes?"

"As long as you're a hundred percent sure you don't mind."

"For the last time, I don't mind." Tabitha stood and brushed off the seat of her shorts. "I'd better go in and finish my homework. I've put it off long enough."

"Same here." Cass stepped off the rock onto the lawn.

"Don't forget to call Kira."

Cass shot her a cautious glance. Was that a snide tone

she heard in her voice? "I won't."

Before calling, she checked with Mom and Dad to make sure dinner out would be okay. Once she got the go-ahead, she headed straight to the phone.

"It's a go," she informed Kira when the other girl answered.

Kira's response was to squeal with delight. "Thank you! I owe you big-time. I'll call you back as soon as I talk to Sam."

Her indifferent attitude toward Tabitha bothered Cass. "Aren't you the least bit curious about what Tabitha said?"

"Not really." Kira's tone went from chipper to flat in the space of a second.

"Too bad because I'm going to tell you." Cass smiled to herself when Kira snorted with impatience. "She was very nice about it. In fact, she's fine with us going out."

"Oh. Well ... good." Kira was silent for a moment. "She didn't say anything negative at all?"

"Nope."

"I'm ... glad." Kira sounded anything but pleased.

"Good. I'll tell Tabitha." Cass stifled a laugh when Kira muttered something under her breath. "Anyway, I'll let you go so you can call Sam."

"All right. Bye."

After hanging up, Cass wandered into the living room. Mom was stretched out on the couch asleep, and Dad had moved to the recliner to read. Cass perched on the coffee table and gestured over her shoulder.

"How can she fall asleep so fast?"

Dad smiled. "Growing a baby is hard work." Eyes twinkling, he lowered his voice to add, "Especially at her age."

"If I have kids, I'm going to make sure I have them all before I'm 30," Cass declared.

"Make all the plans you want. Just remember—" Dad

playfully wagged a finger, "God's ultimately in charge." He set his book down in his lap. "Before you head back to your room, what's this about you and Kira double-dating?"

Cass briefly explained the situation.

"And Tabitha isn't upset that you're going out with Kira?" Dad looked skeptical.

"She said she isn't. That's all I have to go on."

"What does she think about you dating Sam?" Dad probed.

Cass squirmed a little. "She asked a couple of questions about it. But she eventually wound up saying it was okay."

"Are you using him?"

Cass' jaw dropped. "Dad! How can you think such a thing?"

"It's easy," he assured her. "You're missing Logan. You're afraid he's attracted to another girl. What's the best way to get back at him? Date another guy." He laughed at Cass' shocked expression. "I listen in on what's going on around here more than you girls give me credit for."

"Yeah, but your theory doesn't make sense," she argued. "Logan's 9,000 miles away. How's he supposed to know about Sam and me going out?"

Dad leveled a steady gaze at her. "I'm sure you'll figure out a way to let him know. Maybe casually mention it in a letter or phone call. Or make sure one of your friends does."

"That's ... I'm not planning ..." Cass sputtered to a stop because that was precisely what she planned to do.

"Hit a nerve, didn't I?" Dad observed mildly.

Cass shrugged.

"I know it's been hard for you since Logan left," Dad said softly. "But if you have a problem with him, talk to him about it. Don't use somebody else to make your point."

"How'd you get so smart?"

Dad grinned. "By making the mistakes I warn you and Tabitha about. Mom and I agree that's what 99 percent of parenting is. Telling you girls to do as we say, not as we did. Our hope is that you avoid the pitfalls we've encountered through the years."

"So you're saying you've used people in your life?" Cass found it difficult to imagine him doing something like that.

"I've been both a user and a usee," Dad replied. "And let me tell you, neither one is a good position to be in."

"Do you think I should back out of the dinner?"

"Not necessarily. It depends on why you're going. If it's as a favor to Kira and because you enjoy Sam's company then it's a good thing. But," Dad cautioned, "if it's to pay Logan back in some way, I'd advise you to call it off. Only you know what your real motivation is."

Sighing, Cass slowly stood up. "Life would be so much easier if you'd just tell me what to do."

"Making your own decisions is part of growing up," Dad reminded her.

"Sometimes there's a lot to be said for being a kid," grumbled Cass. She turned and headed for her room, adding over her shoulder, "Kira should be calling back any minute. Please pray I make the right choice."

"You got it, sweetie. That's what dads are for."

By the time Kira called with the news that Sam was happy to be her date, Cass had made up her mind to go through with it. Although a part of her enjoyed picturing Logan's reaction to hearing she'd gone out with another boy, the biggest part simply looked forward to spending time with people she liked. After finding out what time to meet, she hung up with an easy conscience.

CHAPTER 21

"Hey, Sam. I thought I heard the doorbell."

Cass walked into the living room only a minute after she heard the doorbell ring, but Tabitha, who had answered the door, and Sam already seemed deep in conversation. She glanced between him and Tabitha. A pleasant conversation, judging by the looks on both their faces. "Have you been here long?"

"Long enough to give Tabs her flowers." He presented Cass with another bunch of slightly wilted flowers. "Here you go. Fresh from the neighbor's garden."

Laughing, Cass examined the drooping plants. "Thanks. I think." She held them out to Tabitha. "Would you mind putting them in water?"

Tabitha took them with a dubious expression. "Sure, but I don't think it will help."

The threesome headed to the kitchen. While Tabitha stayed behind to take care of the flowers, Cass and Sam continued out the door to the lanai. They found Mom lazing in a chair and Dad grilling burgers.

"You two on your way out?" Dad waved at the smoke curling around his head.

"Yes, sir," Sam replied. He smiled at Mom. "How are

you, Mrs. Spencer?"

"I'm doing very well, thank you." She eyed his striped knit shirt and khakis. "You look nice this evening."

Sam glanced down at his outfit. "I clean up pretty good, if I do say so myself."

Dad moved around to the other side of the grill to get out of the smoke. "And, as usual, you're a vision, Cass."

She made a face. "Sure, throw me a bone."

"I mean it," Dad insisted. "In another few years, you might even be as beautiful as your mother."

Cass shot Mom a sidelong look. She used to think Mom was the most attractive woman she knew. But that was before the pregnancy had caused her to gain weight and look tired all the time.

"Yeah, I can't wait to look exactly like her," Cass responded with a distinct lack of enthusiasm.

Mom's sharp glance told her she'd picked up on the hint of sarcasm in her tone. Cass was suddenly ashamed of herself.

"No, really," she added with more sincerity. "I'm always flattered when people say I look like you."

"Thank you." Although Mom dipped her head in acknowledgment of the compliment, her mouth remained tight. "Well, we don't want to keep you. Have fun, and we'll see you at 10:00."

"I'll be here." Feeling guilty, Cass leaned down and kissed Mom's cheek. "Enjoy your hamburgers."

Mom's expression softened. "We will. If the group wants to do something after eating, call and we'll discuss it."

Cass walked her bike around front to where Sam had left his leaning against a tree. Passing the front door, they noticed Tabitha standing behind the glass and waved. She grinned and waved back.

"She sure is pretty," Sam murmured, almost to himself.

Cass automatically bristled, then, after another look at

her sister, nodded. "Yes, she is." They mounted their bikes and took off. "When we first met, it was the thing I resented the most. Everything about her was perfect—her looks, her clothes, her skin. I felt like a complete loser next to her. It took me a long time to get over feeling that way." She laughed self-consciously. "To be honest, I'm not entirely over it. Every now and then, I still find myself resenting her."

"You don't have any reason to," argued Sam. "You have a lot going for you too."

"I know. I know." Cass' sigh was composed of equal parts resignation and humor. "I have a great personality. There are days, though, when I'd trade it in for curly blonde hair, big blue eyes, and a figure good enough to stop traffic."

Sam abruptly applied the brakes and skidded to a halt. When Cass' head jerked around, he met her alarmed expression with an impish grin.

"There! Are you happy now? You stopped me in my tracks."

"You're a nut," Cass observed affectionately. She waited until they resumed riding to add, "By the way, the answer is yes. That did make me happy. I feel just like a femme fatale." She tossed her head so her hair streamed behind her in the wind. "The boys had better watch out. I'm on the prowl."

The evening was a success. Kira and Jason proved to be a fun couple to spend time with, and they talked about everything from classes to the upcoming fall formal. When the meal was served, the two couples launched into a conversation about possible college plans. Cass was amazed to learn that Sam was considering attending West Point.

"How weird. That's where Logan goes."

Sam rolled his eyes. "Duh. You only mention him about every other sentence. It's not like that piece of information has gotten past me."

Cass blushed and shifted uncomfortably in her chair. "Do I really talk about him that much?"

"Is Kwaj a teeny-weeny island in the middle of the Pacific Ocean?" Sam asked sarcastically. "Ask anyone. Logan Russell is your favorite topic of conversation."

"Is that true?" Cass demanded of Kira.

Her friend shrugged. "You do have a tendency to go on and on about him."

"Oh." Embarrassed, Cass suddenly concentrated on eating to avoid the others' gazes. She was surprised when Sam laid his hand over hers.

"No one's saying it's a bad thing," he assured her. "There's nothing wrong with talking about what interests you. Take me, for example. I generally talk about myself since that's what I find most interesting."

Everyone laughed, and Cass felt the awkward moment pass. She flashed Sam a grateful smile. "So, why do you want to go to West Point?"

"Actually, if I had my way, I'd go to Annapolis. That's the Naval Academy," Sam explained to Jason and Kira. "Call me crazy, but I'd really like to work on nuclear subs. Unfortunately, my father's a career army man. He'd die if I went into the Navy." He grinned wickedly. "Sometimes I think it would be worth applying just to see the look on his face."

"That's not very nice," Cass said.

"It's honest," Sam defended himself.

Once again, the group laughed.

I'm having a great time, Cass realized, studying Sam out of the corner of her eye as he chatted with Kira and Jason. *Maybe too good a time?* After thinking it over, she mentally shook her head. *No, what I feel for Sam isn't anything like what I feel for Logan.* Just then, he caught her eye and smiled warmly. Cass frowned. *Hmm. I wonder how he sees us, though. I don't want him thinking there's a possibility for something more between us. Maybe I should talk to him and make sure he understands we can't ever be anything more than friends.*

The more she thought about it, Cass decided that was exactly what she would do. In fact, she'd talk to him before the night was over. In case it was what Sam had in mind, she didn't want to risk ruining things by letting him think dating was an option.

The moment they parted company with the other couple, Cass turned to Sam and suggested, "Let's walk instead of riding. It's easier to talk."

"Sure." The always-amiable Sam shrugged and fell into step with her as they wheeled their bikes down the road. "You have something in particular you want to talk about?"

"Actually, I do." Cass took a deep breath. "You and me."

"Us?" His expression puzzled, Sam first pointed to himself then to her. "As in, like a couple?"

From the look on his face, Cass had the sinking feeling she had misjudged the situation. She desperately wished she hadn't started the discussion, but there was no way around it now. "Well ... yes. I ... uh ... I thought I should make sure you realize there is no ... us."

"Oh." Sam walked in silence for several seconds. "Uh ... I don't know how to say this without hurting your feelings, but I never thought about us as a couple. Well, maybe in the beginning I did," he corrected himself.

"Why'd you change your mind?" Cass couldn't decide if she was relieved or insulted.

"I don't know." Shrugging, Sam smiled. "You're ... Red. You're a pal. Pals don't date."

"True," Cass conceded. "And that's how I feel about you. You're a good friend."

"Maybe I shouldn't say this, but ..." Sam drew out the word until Cass reached over and playfully slugged his arm. "There's somebody I don't think of as a friend. In fact, I'm seriously considering asking her out."

Warning bells clanged in Cass' head. *Uh-oh, I think I know what's coming, and I'm not sure I want to hear it.*

Lowering his voice, Sam confided, "It's Tabitha. You think she'd go out with me?"

Despite expecting his announcement, Cass' stomach still lurched. She might not want to date Sam, but she didn't want Tabitha dating him, either.

God, what's the right thing to do? I know I shouldn't be selfish. But is it selfish to want Tabitha and Micah to stay together?

Realizing Sam was waiting for an answer, she swallowed hard and replied crossly, "How should I know? I'm not Tabitha."

Sam shot her a curious look. "I'm not asking for a definite yes or no. I'm just wondering what you think."

"Fine," snapped Cass. "She'd probably go out with you, but I'm not sure it would be right."

"What do you mean?"

"She is dating Kira's brother, Micah, you know." Cass didn't bother hiding her irritation.

"Huh." Sam glanced around as though looking for someone. "How can she be dating somebody who doesn't even live here? Besides," he went on before Cass could respond, "they're not engaged, are they? Tabitha's free to date. At least that's my understanding. Correct me if I'm wrong," he offered generously.

"You're not wrong," muttered Cass. She waved a dismissive hand. "Look, the two of you can go out every night for all I care."

Lost in thought, Sam gazed at the phosphorescence shimmering on the water before turning his attention back to Cass. "Are you mad that I want to ask your sister out?"

Now what do I say? she mused. *I can't lie, but I can't tell him it bothers me because he'll want to know why, and I don't know how to explain it.*

She settled for a tinkly laugh. "What do you think?"

"I think you are or I wouldn't have asked the question."

"The question is silly," Cass breezily assured him. "You and Tabitha are both free to do what you want."

"Yeah, but what I want to know is how you feel about it," Sam persisted.

"Like I said, it's your business." To forestall any more questions, Cass picked up the pace. "Get the lead out, Steele," she ordered over her shoulder. "My mom baked a German chocolate cake today, and it's calling my name. That sorry dish of sherbet at the Yuk wasn't nearly enough dessert to tide me over till the morning."

Lengthening his stride, Sam drew alongside Cass. "You think your mother might share a piece with me?"

"It's possible. For some strange reason, she likes you." She shook her head. "Sometimes there's no accounting for taste."

"If I weren't so good-natured, I believe I'd be insulted." Sam whistled a happy tune. "Luckily, my feelings don't get hurt easily."

They kept up a steady stream of quips throughout the rest of the walk. After parking their bikes on the lanai, they let themselves into the porch. Tabitha looked up from the swing where she was reading.

"Hey, you two. Back already?"

Cass made a face. "I hate those kinds of questions. I mean, it's obvious we're back. Why even ask it?"

Tabitha exchanged an amused look with Sam. "Poor you. Apparently she's in one of her moods. I know I speak for my parents when I say thank you from the bottom of our hearts for sparing us the misery of having her here."

As Sam tried to pretend his snicker was a cough, Cass tossed her head and sniffed. "While y'all yuck it up, I'm going inside to get some cake. And," she added, stalking to the door, "I'm not offering either of you a piece."

Before getting the cake, she stopped in the living room to say hello to her parents. Yawning, Mom looked up from the booties she was knitting. At the sight of them, Cass made a face.

She used to spend her free time working on stuff for Tabitha and me, she griped. *I can't remember the last time she made us something.*

Aloud, she said, "I'm home. Obviously. Sam's here too. Is it okay if we have some cake?"

"Of course. That's what it's there for." Mom produced her most entreating smile. "Would you mind cutting me a slice? And pouring a glass of milk while you're at it?"

"Sure," Cass replied without enthusiasm.

She turned away before the irritation could show on her face. Before the pregnancy, Mom was the one who waited on everyone. Now she asked people to do for her. It wasn't right. Parents were supposed to take care of their kids, and she definitely wasn't. Stiff with resentment, Cass stomped into the kitchen and yanked open the refrigerator door to get the cake and milk.

By the time she'd delivered Mom's snack and returned to the kitchen, Tabitha and Sam had wandered in from the porch. Cass scowled at them. They had no right to look so happy when she was in a bad mood.

"What are you smiling about?" she groused to Tabitha.

Her sister glanced shyly at Sam. He grinned back in a way that made Cass feel funny.

"What's going on?" she demanded.

When Tabitha didn't say anything, Sam spoke up. "I asked Tabs out for tomorrow night. And, lo and behold, she said yes. We're going to eat first then see a movie."

Cass' jaw dropped, and she rounded on her sister. "You're going on a date?"

Instead of shrinking under her withering glare, Tabitha nodded coolly. "Most people consider dinner and a movie a date."

"What about ... you know?" Cass slid an uneasy glance at Sam.

"You mean Micah?" He laughed, unfazed by the name. "Don't you remember we already discussed him on the way here? He's not exactly a state secret."

"We'll talk about this later," Tabitha hissed through clenched teeth.

"But—" Cass began.

"But nothing," Tabitha interrupted sternly. "We'll discuss it later. Get your cake, and let's talk about something else."

"I'm not hungry anymore." Cass' lower lip protruded in a pout as she returned her piece of cake to the refrigerator. "I'm going to my room." Unable to meet Sam's gaze, she looked over his shoulder and said woodenly, "Thanks for tonight. I had a good time."

"Same here." As Cass turned to leave, he caught her by the hand. "Would you come out on the porch for a minute? I need to talk to you." When she resisted, he coaxed, "Please? It's important."

"Oh, all right."

Cass reluctantly allowed herself to be led through the door. When they reached the porch, she jerked her hand out of Sam's, crossed her arms, and confronted him with an out-thrust chin.

"What do you want?"

"A straightforward answer would be nice." He stared her down until she averted her eyes. "You and I agreed we're friends. So why are you so worked up about Tabs and me going out? And don't tell me it's because you're worried about Micah's feelings. I may not be the brightest bulb in the chandelier, but even I know that would be a load of hogwash."

"I'm not upset," Cass hedged. "You just took me by surprise, that's all. I didn't expect you to ask her out so soon."

"That's not it, and you know it." Sam sighed. "Come on, Red. Level with me."

"I am," she insisted, telling her conscience to hush. Gathering her courage, she looked him right in the eyes.

After a moment's hesitation, he threw his hands up in defeat. "Whatever. You win. If you want to pretend everything's hunky-dory, there's nothing I can do about it. I just hope this doesn't ruin our friendship."

"It won't," Cass assured him without much conviction. Suddenly desperate to escape, she edged toward the door. "Nothing personal, but I really have to go. I feel a killer of a headache coming on."

Sam muffled a sigh. "Don't let me keep you then. Thanks again for tonight. Maybe we can do it again sometime."

"I'd like that." Cass left for her bedroom without a backward glance.

Fifteen minutes later, there was a knock at her door.

"Go away," she yelled. "I'm sleeping."

"You are not or you wouldn't have answered," Tabitha pointed out. She opened the door and poked her head around the side. "Can I come in?"

"No."

Tabitha walked in and sat down on the bed. Sighing gustily, Cass turned over to face the wall.

"So you think I'm being disloyal to Micah by going out with Sam." It was a statement, rather than a question.

Cass hunched a shoulder under the blanket.

"Do you also think I stole Sam from you?"

The blanket didn't move.

"The way I see it, I didn't. He told me the two of you had decided you'd never be anything more than friends. If I thought for one second that you were interested in him as a potential boyfriend I'd have turned him down flat when he asked me out." When Cass didn't say anything, Tabitha nudged her. "You do believe me, don't you?"

Actually, Cass did, but she didn't want to give her sister the satisfaction of a response. She smiled to herself as Tabitha grew increasingly agitated.

"I take it you're giving me the silent treatment. That's real mature," she jeered. "Can't we at least discuss this like a couple of semi-adults?"

Still, Cass held her tongue. The bed shifted as Tabitha stood up.

"Fine. You can play your stupid game for all I care, but you're not going to make me cancel my date with Sam." She marched to the door. "And you're not going to make me feel guilty about it, either. I'm looking forward to tomorrow night, and I won't let you ruin it for me."

After she slammed out of the room, Cass rolled onto her back and folded her arms beneath her head. *Is that what I want? To ruin their date?* She heaved a weary sigh. *I'm so confused. I honestly don't know what I want anymore. No, that's not true,* she corrected herself. *I want things to go back to the way they were a year ago, but that's not going to happen. I'm stuck in the present, and I hate it.* A tear made its way down the side of her face to pool in her ear. *I miss Logan so much. I miss the way life was when everyone was here, and we were one, big, happy group. Why do things have to change? Why can't they stay the same, especially when they're good? Lord, help!*

CHAPTER 22

The minute Cass rolled out of bed the next morning, she headed to the phone. Since she had no desire to watch Tabitha prepare for her date, her only option was to leave. She put in an emergency call to Rianne.

"Hello?" Her friend answered on the second ring.

"What are you doing today?" Cass didn't waste time with a greeting.

Rianne laughed. "Well, hello to you too, Cassandra. I'm fine. Thanks for asking. And how are you this glorious morning?"

"Cut the comedy," Cass grumbled. "I need to know if I can come over and spend the day with you."

Rianne refused to be serious. "What have you done now? Your family kicked you out, didn't they?"

Cass had to bite her tongue to keep from screaming. "Can I come over or not?"

"Of course," Rianne said, finally sounding normal. "*Mi casa es su casa.* You know that. Greg and I are going bowling, but that's not until tonight. We can pretty much spend the whole day together."

"Thanks. I'll hop in the shower then be on my way." About to hang up, Cass added, "Have you eaten breakfast yet?"

"No. I was just about to fix myself a bowl of cereal."

"Don't. As a token of my appreciation, I'll make you one of my super-duper omelettes."

"In that case, forget the shower," Rianne said. "My mouth is watering already."

When Cass emerged from the bathroom 20 minutes later, she met Dad in the hall. He gave her a curious look.

"What are you up to so early on a Saturday morning?"

"I'm heading out to spend the day with Rianne." Cass leaned around Dad to toss her nightshirt and robe on her bed. "See you."

"Wait a minute. Did you clear this with your mom?"

Cass frowned. "What's to clear?"

"She might want you to help out with something around here today," Dad suggested as a possibility.

Huffing her impatience, Cass jammed her hands into the pockets of her shorts. "Look, I'll be two minutes away. If Mom needs anything, all she has to do is call. Why are you making such a big deal about this? I go over to Rianne's all the time, and nobody ever says anything."

Dad's face tightened with displeasure. "Despite the fact that I don't care for your attitude at the moment, you have my permission to leave. However," he went on as Cass turned to go, "I don't want to hear a single complaint out of you if your mother asks you to come back. Understand?"

It took all her willpower not to reply snidely. With a curt nod, she assured him, "I understand."

"In that case, have a nice time. Call if you and Rianne decide to go somewhere so we know how to get a hold of you."

"Don't I always?" Cass muttered under her breath. At Dad's scowl, she assumed an innocent expression. "I mean, of course I will."

Cass and Rianne had to wait until they finished eating before they got a chance to talk privately. Rianne's younger brother, Robby, showed up in the Thayer kitchen just as Cass began assembling the ingredients for the omelette. She made him plead for two minutes before giving in and agreeing to cook him one too. While he ate, he entertained Cass and Rianne with stories of the girls he was pursuing in his class. After he left the table, they exchanged amused looks.

"He's a mess," Cass remarked.

"He takes after Randy." Rianne stood and collected the plates and utensils. "He's too good-looking for his own good."

Cass trailed her into the kitchen and leaned against the counter while she loaded the dishwasher. "Speaking of Randy, how's he doing? I haven't heard from him in a couple of weeks."

Rianne flashed her a brilliant smile. "Great. He's loving every minute of school. He and his roommate get along like long-lost brothers, and he's been out on a bunch of dates. Every time we talk he tells me how much he misses me, but I think he just throws that in to make me feel better. He's too busy to miss anybody, particularly his bratty little sister."

"I'm glad things are going so well." Cass used her nail to pick at a spot of dried egg on the counter. "Anyway, do you want to know why I'm here?"

"What do you think?" teased Rianne.

Taking a deep breath, Cass blurted, "Tabitha's going out with Sam tonight."

"Well, good for her." Rianne straightened up and nodded her approval. "Good for him too. He obviously has good taste."

Cass' eyes widened in surprise. "You're okay with them dating?"

"Sure. Why not?" Rianne once again bent down to arrange the plates in the dishwasher.

"What about Micah?" Cass demanded.

Rianne made a face. "According to Kira, Micah's whooping it up in Hono."

"So that makes it okay for Tabitha to whoop it up here?"

"Tabitha's not exactly the whooping type," Rianne drawled. "Besides, you've gone out with Sam lots of times."

"That's different," Cass coolly informed her.

"Oh, yeah? How?" Rianne challenged.

"They weren't dates." Crossing her arms, Cass fixed her with a smug stare.

"They weren't dates, huh?" Rianne raised an eyebrow. "If I remember correctly, you and Sam have gone swimming, picnicking, to the movies, and out to eat. Don't most normal people consider those kinds of activities dates?"

"Maybe people whose minds are in the gutter," snapped Cass.

"Ooh, sounds like I hit a nerve." Rianne reached for the sponge to wipe up the dried egg. "Are you mad because you want Sam for yourself?"

"I'm not mad," Cass hotly denied. "I'm ... concerned. I don't want Tabitha to get hurt. She's very vulnerable right now, what with missing Micah and all."

Rianne snorted. "Yeah, right. From what I've seen, she misses him like a bad cold. She's been a whole lot happier since he left."

Instead of arguing, Cass slumped against the counter. "You're right. There's no need to worry about her. Sam's another matter. What if she's using him?"

"You mean the way some people thought you were?" Rianne's eyes focused on Cass like two laser beams.

Cass squirmed under her intense gaze. "It's not the same."

"I know." Rianne dismissed her remark with a wave. "It's not the same thing. It never is with you. Everyone else is up to no good, but your motives are always pure."

"Why are you being so mean?" Cass frowned.

"Knock it off. Your 'poor, pitiful me' act doesn't work on me."

Cass dropped the pose. "Fine, but you should at least take my side. After all, you are my best friend."

"All the more reason for me to tell you the truth." Rianne's determined expression told Cass she planned to do exactly that. "You can't have it both ways. If you don't want Sam then let Tabitha have him with your blessing. If you are interested in him then be a woman and fight for him." She propped a hand on her hip. "So, which is it?"

Averting her gaze, Cass stared out the window at the flowers growing in the Thayers' backyard. They spilled out of planters and ran the entire length of the fence. They were a nice change from her own backyard view of the ocean.

"Hello?" Rianne snapped her fingers under Cass' nose. "Are you thinking or ignoring me?"

Blinking, she shifted her gaze back to her friend. "Thinking. It seems like that's all I do anymore. I spend most of my time trying to figure out how I feel about things. Do I like Sam as a friend or a guy? Am I happy about the baby or scared it's going to totally mess up my life? Should I trust that Logan and I will make it or break it off with him before he calls it quits?" She lifted her hands in a gesture of helplessness. "See what I mean? I'm completely mixed up. Do you have any advice?"

"Have you tried praying?" Rianne asked quietly.

"Sort of." Cass' smile was wry. "Nothing very serious. They've all been more of the quick, 'please help' kind of prayers."

"There's your problem," Rianne declared. "You need to get serious about it. Confess to God what a mess you're making of your own life—" Rianne paused to smile, "and ask Him for the direction and guidance you need. Then search His word and even talk to Pastor Thompson for that guidance."

Cass nodded. "I think you've hit on something. I've been running around like a chicken with its head cut off. I need to spend some uninterrupted time with God." Her mouth curled in an impish smile. "But first I want to spend time with you. It's been ages since we just hung out. You need to catch me up on what's happening with you and Greg."

"Well ... okay. If you insist." Laughing, Rianne pretended reluctance before turning back to the task of cleaning up. "Let me finish this, then we'll hole up in my room and have ourselves a nice, long chat." She winked. "Boy, do I have a lot to tell you."

Pushing off from the counter, Cass grabbed the sponge. "Then let's get this show on the road, girl. I'll rinse, and you stack. We'll be done in half the time."

Cass pushed aside the worries that had been weighing her down for the past several weeks. *Now's the time just to enjoy talking with Rianne,* she thought, *something we haven't done for awhile. I promise, God, I'll get to You when I get home.*

CHAPTER 23

"Cass, can I talk to you?" Kira made a show of glancing over her shoulder. Spotting Tabitha in line behind her, she grimaced and added pointedly, "Alone."

"Uh ... sure. After the meeting."

Along with nine other friends, Cass and Kira were making their way around the Spencers' dining room table, loading plates with fried chicken and potato salad. It was Sunday night, and, as usual, the youth group meeting was preceded by a meal one of the parents had prepared. A tingle of uneasiness had prickled Cass' nerves the moment Kira stationed herself directly behind her.

"It's important," Kira insisted. "Can't we go out on the porch and talk now?"

Cass firmly shook her head. Glancing behind Kira, she could see Tabitha watching them with undisguised suspicion. She realized her first priority was to remain loyal to her sister.

"You know my parents don't like us separating into little groups to gossip."

Kira's brows arched. "What makes you think I want to gossip?"

"Oh, please. I'm not stupid," Cass drawled. "Tabitha told

me she saw you and Jason at the movies last night. I assume that's what you want to talk about."

"It's not gossip if it's the truth." Kira's tone was as stubborn as her expression.

Cass emitted a brief, humorless laugh. "If it's meant to tear somebody down, it's gossip. No matter how truthful it is," she added pointedly.

"Whatever." Tutting, Kira held up a hand to signal the discussion was over. "Have it your way. I'll talk to you after the meeting."

Not if I can come up with a way to get out of it, Cass silently informed her. The last thing she wanted was to listen to Kira complain about Tabitha's date with Sam, especially when she still wasn't sure how she, herself, felt about it. It would be too easy to be pulled into a gripe session about her sister, which she knew would be wrong. *It's smarter to stay out of temptation's way altogether than to try to fight it while I'm smack-dab in the middle of it.*

The moment Cass sat down to eat, she realized she'd made a mistake. Instead of joining a group, she'd chosen an out-of-the-way spot where she could be by herself. It wasn't long before Kira plopped down beside her. Cass mentally kicked herself.

"The crowd's down tonight," Kira commented, glancing around the room.

Grateful for the safe topic, Cass immediately latched onto it. "Dad and I were talking about it the other day. The group's been hurting since so many people went off to college. He'd like to put a push on to recruit new members, but then again, it's easier this way on Mom. The fewer people we have, the less work it is for her."

"She's getting huge." Kira picked up a drumstick and tore off a chunk.

Cass' gaze darted to Mom's expanding waistline. "Tell me about it. The worst part is she still has four months to go. She's going to look like a beached whale by the time December arrives." She made a sour face. "Which means Tabitha and I will be doing even more around here. I can't imagine the doctor will let her ride her bike anymore so we'll have to run all the errands. I tell you, this baby's turning out to be more trouble than it's worth."

"Aw, you'll love it once it gets here," Kira breezily assured her.

"Yeah, right." Cass snorted. "That's when the hard part really starts. The smelly diapers and the crying all hours of the day and night. I've already asked Rianne if I can move in with her if it gets too bad."

"I don't guess Tabitha will be wanting to stay with me." Kira tossed her head. "Not that I care. I'm furious at her for running around on Micah."

"Kira," Cass warned, "I said we're not going to talk about this until after the meeting."

The other girl shot her an unrepentant smile. "Just seeing if you were paying attention." Kira glanced back towards Tabitha, who was sitting with Rianne and two other girls. "Look at that, she's avoiding me. She's acting like I'm not even here."

Cass looked, and her stomach gave a disturbing lurch. *What's wrong with this picture? Here I am, sitting with Kira, who used to be Tabitha's best friend. And there's Tabitha, sitting with Rianne, who's supposed to be my best friend. Are things mixed up or what?*

"You two haven't exactly been on the best of terms lately," she reminded Kira. "Don't blame it all on her date with Sam. You were mad at her before that."

"Sam." Kira hissed the name as if it left a bad taste in her mouth. Her eyes narrowed as the front door opened, and he walked in. "Well, speak of the devil. Let me guess who invited him."

"Will you please stop!" Cass ordered irritably. "It's not

like this is the first time he's been here. You're blowing everything out of proportion."

"Excuse me for looking out for my brother's interests," Kira said hotly.

"It might help things if Micah cared enough to look out for his own interests," Cass retorted.

Kira bristled. "What's that supposed to mean?"

"He acts like he doesn't give a rip about what Tabitha's doing." The argument robbed Cass of her appetite, and she set aside her plate. "His letters and calls are all about him."

"She should be grateful he still keeps in touch with her, seeing as how she wants a break from him." Kira heaped potato salad on her fork. "It was like a knife in his heart when I told him how she felt."

Cass' head jerked up, and she glared at Kira. "Thanks for reminding me. I've been meaning to talk to you about that. You had no right—"

"Howdy, Red." Sam's voice lost some of its enthusiasm as he added, "Kira."

Cass smiled up at him. "Hey, Sam. I'm glad you're here."

Kira sniffed and looked away.

Her reaction brought a mischievous gleam to Sam's eyes. "That's what I like about Christian groups. Everybody is so—" he raised his voice for emphasis, "friendly and accepting."

Kira's face twitched, but she didn't say anything.

"Yup," Sam continued, "they sure take seriously Jesus' command to love their neighbors as themselves."

"Okay, okay." Kira relented with an exasperated sigh. "Hello. There, are you happy now?"

"I'm tickled pink. You've made my day." Sam executed a bow and a flourish. "Well, my work here is done. Ladies, it's been a pleasure. I'll be going now."

"Gee, I wonder where he's going," Kira drawled loud enough for him to hear.

Cass rounded on her with a furious scowl. "For pity's sake, you're acting like a total snot."

Sam apparently decided it was a good time to leave. With a one-fingered wave at Cass, he slipped away to join Tabitha and her group.

"Thanks a lot for embarrassing me in front of him," Kira blazed.

"I wasn't about to let you get away with being rude," Cass coldly informed her. "After all, Sam's a guest in my house."

"What am I?" snapped Kira. "Chopped liver?"

"Girls," Mom broke in before Cass could reply, "if you insist on fighting, take it outside. Your behavior is affecting the rest of the group."

Looking up, Cass discovered Mom frowning down at them. She squirmed under the intensity of her gaze. Kira, however, didn't seem at all fazed by the scolding.

"She started it." She pointed at Cass.

"Me?" Cass squeaked, pressing a hand to her chest. "I didn't—"

"That's enough. I mean it." Mom looked ready to explode. "If you can't behave, you're going to have to leave."

Cass blushed a bright crimson. *How humiliating. To be called down in front of everybody by my own mother.*

Mustering what shreds of dignity she had left, she looked Mom right in the eyes. "I'm sorry. I know better than to make a scene in front of the group." Without sparing a glance for Kira, she stood up. "I'm going to my room for a few minutes. I'll be back out in time for the prayer and lesson."

Mom patted her back and murmured, "I appreciate you listening. I'm sorry if I embarrassed you."

Cass was subdued when she rejoined the group as they settled down to pray. Noticing her anxious look around the circle, Mom came over and squatted beside her.

"Kira decided to go home," she whispered.

Cass' face crumpled. "Great. It's all my fault. Should I call her and ask her to come back?"

Mom shook her head. "No, leave her be. She needs time to cool off. You'll see her in school tomorrow."

Cass nodded in agreement, although she would've preferred to settle the matter immediately. However, she couldn't concentrate on either the prayer or the lesson. She barely listened as Mom and Dad taught about the Sermon on the Mount and didn't participate when they opened the floor for group discussion. Even though it didn't do any good, she continued to fret about the situation with Kira. The dirty looks Tabitha kept shooting her way didn't help things any.

Everywhere I turn, someone's mad at me, she lamented. *How did things get so messed up?*

Chapter 24

As soon as the last guest left, Mom groaned and collapsed on the couch. Dad hurried to her side, followed slowly by Cass and Tabitha.

"Honey, are you all right?" Dad alternated between hovering and patting her hand.

"Can I get you something?" Tabitha asked anxiously.

Cass gazed down at her with only a smidgen of sympathy. "The group's getting to be too much for you, isn't it?"

Mom managed to open an eye. "I'm afraid so. I wanted to talk to you and Tabitha, but it's going to have to wait until tomorrow. I'm exhausted." She struggled to a sitting position. "I'm going to bed. G'night, all."

With Dad's help, she shuffled down the hall to the bathroom. When he returned, Cass and Tabitha were already cleaning up.

"How's she doing?" Tabitha turned from the sink to ask.

"Fine. She just overdid it tonight." Dad crossed to the dining room table to help Cass clear it. "Your Mom knows two speeds—fast and faster. She needs to pace herself better."

"Did she tell you what she wants to talk to us about?" Cass stacked plates and utensils to carry to the kitchen.

"No, but I've been meaning to have a chat with you." Dad followed her to the counter.

Cass exchanged a nervous glance with Tabitha. Her sister shrugged as if to say, *I don't have a clue.*

"Are we in trouble?" Cass ventured.

Dad smiled wryly. "Trouble is such a harsh word. I prefer to say you need a stern talking-to."

Cass' heart sank. "Just me? Or both of us?"

"I originally planned to talk to you," Dad replied. "But what I have to say applies to you both."

"Oh, goody," Tabitha drawled. "A lecture. Just what I'm in the mood for."

Dad deposited his load on the counter. "That's exactly what I want to talk about. You girls are carrying some good-sized chips on your shoulders, and it's time you got rid of them. It's making life around here pretty unpleasant."

"For example?" challenged Tabitha.

Cass busied herself with scraping leftovers into the garbage, content to let Tabitha stand up to Dad.

Leaning against the counter, he folded his arms and crossed one ankle over the other. "For example, you've been a bear since Micah left. One minute you're up, the next you're down. I never know which Tabitha I'm going to be dealing with when I walk in the door. Being upset at Micah doesn't give you the right to take it out on the family. One way or the other, it's time to settle things with him."

Tabitha arched an eyebrow. "What do you mean, one way or the other?"

"Either reach an understanding you can live with or break it off," advised Dad. "You can't keep living in this in-between state forever. It's not doing you—or the rest of us, for that matter—any good."

Seemingly about to protest, Tabitha abruptly closed her mouth and swung back around to the sink. Turning the water on with a jerk, she resumed rinsing dishes with a vengeance.

"What about me?" Cass made herself ask. She smiled tentatively. "How long is your list of complaints?"

"There's only one." As Cass started to relax, Dad added, "But it's a major one."

She inhaled deeply to prepare herself. "Okay, shoot."

"It's time for you to stop resenting the fact that your mom's having a baby."

Cass flinched and darted a furtive glance at Tabitha. Fortunately, her sister was too wrapped up in her own misery to pay any attention to her.

"Wh-what makes you think I'm resentful?"

Dad regarded her with a steady gaze. "Don't play games, Sweetie. One of the things I've always admired about you is your willingness to face the truth about yourself. You know what I'm talking about. You haven't been yourself since we announced Mom's pregnancy."

"It has taken some getting used to," conceded Cass.

"Not for me," Tabitha piped up.

Cass rounded on her. "Butt out! I didn't put in my two cents while Dad was talking to you."

When Tabitha opened her mouth to quarrel, Dad held up his hand. "Cass is right."

"Cass is right," Tabitha echoed bitterly. "Why am I not surprised? She's always right." Muttering, she picked up the sponge and furiously wiped off a dish.

"Anyway, let's get back to what we were talking about before we were so rudely interrupted." Dad stifled a smile when Tabitha snorted loudly. "At times, you've been downright surly to your Mom. You've made it clear you're put out by the extra demands on your time."

"Sorry," Cass grumbled, sounding anything but. "What am I supposed to do? Act like everything's hunky-dory?"

Tabitha snickered. "Hunky-dory? Who says that anymore?"

"Me. Duh," Cass shot back. "In case you haven't noticed, so does your friend, Sam."

Dad ignored their bickering. "After everything your mom has done for you, I expect you to be pleasant and cooperative now that she needs you. Stop thinking so much of yourself and start thinking a little more about her. Got it?"

Chastened, Cass lowered her eyes. "I guess."

"Good." Dad pulled Tabitha over and draped his arm across both girls' shoulders. "I'm glad we had this little talk. How about you ladies?"

Cass made a sound that could have meant anything. Tabitha shrugged out of his embrace and moved to the sink.

"It was thrilling. I can't wait till we do it again."

"Do I detect a note of sarcasm?" teased Dad.

"Gee, you tell me," Tabitha retorted sweetly.

Dad ruffled her hair then followed up the gesture with a loud kiss on her cheek. Tabitha smiled, and Cass watched them, her insides twisting with jealousy.

"You girls finish up here. I'm going to check on Mom. She looked beat." Dad sighed. "I bet she'd appreciate a back rub."

Cass and Tabitha didn't say anything for several minutes after he left. Cass' plan was to complete her chores as quickly as possible and flee to her room. Along with Dad's scolding, she needed to think about what had happened with Kira. A gusty sigh escaped her.

"What was that for?" Tabitha placed the last glass in the dishwasher then closed and latched the door.

"Nothing." Cass made a face. "Everything."

"There's a clear-as-mud answer." Tabitha handed her the sponge to wipe down the counter.

"It's the best I can do at the moment." Cass snatched the sponge and began furiously scrubbing the counter. "I spent an hour last night trying to make sense out of my life. I thought I did pretty well, but after the incident with Kira and the talk with Dad, I'm back to square one."

"Speaking of Kira—" Tabitha hesitated for a moment, "what was your fight about?"

"Believe it or not, I was sticking up for you." Cass tossed the sponge into the sink. "She started in about you and Sam so I brought up the way Micah's been acting. After that, it was all downhill. I know I shouldn't have said anything, but I let my temper get the best of me."

"Wow, I feel like a royal jerk. I assumed the two of you were having a grand old time raking me over the coals," Tabitha confessed. "That's why I couldn't figure out why you were arguing."

"I'm really mad at myself for letting her get to me." Walking to the dining room, Cass pulled out a chair and sank down into it. "During my prayer time last night, I promised God I'd do a better job of acting like a Christian. You know, being nicer to people. Stuff like that." She raised her hands in a helpless gesture. "You see how well I did. I couldn't even last 24 hours."

"Don't be so hard on yourself." Tabitha sat in the chair beside hers. "I appreciate you taking my side against Kira."

"It was the right thing to do," agreed Cass. "I just shouldn't have been so snotty about it."

"But, Sis—" Tabitha took her hand and gave it an encouraging squeeze, "that's the way you are. For you to stop being a snot would be the same as not breathing."

"Don't make me laugh." The twitching at the corners of Cass' mouth belied the irritation in her voice.

"Me?" Tabitha rounded her eyes into innocent saucers. "How could I possibly make you laugh? Everyone knows *you're* the comedian in the family."

"You've been spending too much time with Sam," Cass

good-naturedly groused. "You're starting to sound just like him."

"He's a great guy," Tabitha acknowledged.

"He sure made a beeline for you tonight." Cass smirked. "You should have seen the look on Kira's face when he hightailed it over to sit with you. She looked like she'd just bitten into the world's sourest pickle."

"She doesn't understand what I see in him." Angling her body away from Cass, Tabitha propped her feet up on an adjoining chair.

"What is it you like about him? Other than the fact that he follows you around like a lovesick puppy, that is?"

"He does not!" Tabitha vehemently defended Sam. "He has more class than to do something like that."

"Then what's the attraction?" Cass persisted.

Tabitha flashed her an uncertain look. "Don't take this the wrong way, okay? It's because," she took a deep breath then finished in a rush, "he reminds me of Logan."

Cass' eyes immediately narrowed to suspicious slits. "Don't tell me you've had a secret crush on Logan all this time."

"Don't be silly. I mean, Logan's a terrific person," Tabitha hastily explained when Cass swelled with indignation, "but I've never thought of him as boyfriend material. The way Sam's like him is that they're both decent, solid guys. They're not flashy, but they have this—I don't know—kindness and caring about them. Sam really listens when I talk to him. It's not like he's waiting for me to finish so he can get his turn. He wants to know what's going on with me, and he doesn't get annoyed if I hog the conversation."

"Unlike Micah," observed Cass.

Tabitha's shoulders slumped. "Yeah, unlike Micah." She raised troubled eyes. "I know it's not fair to compare them, but I can't help it. Whenever I'm with Sam, I keep thinking how different he is from Micah."

"Micah used to listen to you, didn't he?" Cass had a sick feeling that Tabitha was on the verge of telling her it was over with Micah, and she wasn't sure she was ready to hear it.

Tabitha nodded slowly. "Before we started dating, I could talk to him about anything. Once we began going out, I realized he did most of the talking. It was frustrating because I couldn't figure out why things had changed. The couple of times I got up the nerve to ask him about it, he acted like he didn't know what I was talking about. As far as he was concerned, everything was great."

"Does Sam do anything else that reminds you of Logan?" Cass wondered what else Tabitha admired about Logan.

A shy smile spread across Tabitha's face. "I used to envy the way Logan thought you were the most beautiful girl he'd ever seen. That's how I feel around Sam. With Micah, I always felt like I didn't measure up."

"Micah is pretty spectacular-looking," conceded Cass. "But then again you're no slouch in the looks department."

Tabitha slanted her a sidelong look. "Thanks for throwing me a bone."

"No, I mean it." Cass playfully swatted her arm. "I've always said you're gorgeous."

"I hardly ever felt that way with Micah." Propping her elbow on the table, Tabitha leaned her head on her hand. "I think, deep down, he considers himself God's gift to women. He knows how handsome he is, and he sort of struts about it. Sam, on the other hand"—her face lit up— "never looks around to see who's checking him out. I like his looks, but they're no big deal to him. He has more important things to think about." She grinned. "Like me."

Cass drew up a leg and rested her chin on her knee. "You're making me miss Logan more than ever. I'm going to ask Mom if I can try calling him tomorrow. The problem is it's so hard to get through since cadets don't have phones in their rooms." Her expression turned wistful. "It sure would be nice to talk to him."

Tabitha hesitated, then asked, "Have you decided what you're going to do about Kira?"

Cass rolled her eyes. "I have no idea. I'm almost scared to talk to her. She blows up at the littlest thing."

"She's very protective when it comes to Micah." Sliding her feet off the chair, Tabitha swung around to face Cass. "Do you think I'm cheating on him?"

Here's my chance to drive a wedge between her and Sam, Cass realized. She thought about the time she'd spent praying the night before. *But do I really want to do that? I'm 90 percent sure I don't want him for myself, so what right do I have to try to bust them up?*

She shook her head. "No, you're not cheating. Just like I wouldn't be cheating on Logan if I dated somebody else." Her stomach clenched. "Of course, if he goes out with Shiloh, I would consider that cheating."

"That's not going to happen," Tabitha assured her. "He's crazy about you. You two are going to get married someday, have a half-dozen kids, and live happily ever after."

"Except for the part about the six kids, I hope you're right." About to say something else, Cass was distracted when Dad reappeared. "Hey, there. Did you give Mom a back rub?"

"Yup. She said she's eternally in my debt." He went into the kitchen. "Now she's sleeping like the proverbial baby." Opening the refrigerator, he took out the milk and gave it a shake. "Would either of you like a drink?"

Placing her hands on the table, Cass pushed back her chair and stood. "Not me, thanks. I have an English paper to write."

Dad frowned. "Is it due tomorrow?"

Cass teasingly stuck out her tongue. "No, sir. It's not due

until Tuesday."

"I don't want any, either." Tabitha also got up. "I think I'll turn in early."

"Fine. Abandon me." Pretending to be insulted, Dad dismissed them with a curt wave. "It doesn't hurt my feelings that nobody wants to spend time with me."

"That's good," Cass good-naturedly shot back. "I'd hate to think we upset you."

Dad laughed. "You are one heartless young woman."

Grinning, Cass curtsied. "I know. It's one of my more endearing qualities, don't you think?"

With that, she and Tabitha headed down the hall, going their separate ways into their rooms.

CHAPTER 25

A host of butterflies careened off the walls of Cass' stomach as she biked to school the next morning. Sam had come by to ride with Tabitha so she was on her own, which gave her too much time to contemplate what she'd say to Kira. She couldn't make up her mind whether she should approach Kira or wait until the other girl made the first move. Either possibility caused her to break out in a cold sweat. The closer she got to school, the slower she pedaled.

"Hi, Cass."

At the sound of Rianne's voice, she sagged with relief. Now she didn't have to make a decision. She'd ride the rest of the way with Rianne and not worry about tracking down Kira.

"Hey, Rianne. Greg." *Great—two people is even better,* she thought. "Sorry I didn't get a chance to talk much with y'all last night."

Rianne made a comical face. "We understand. You were kind of busy."

"Kind of busy?" echoed Greg. "For awhile there, I thought you and Kira might actually start slugging it out."

Cass winced at the memory. "Let's not talk about it, okay? I'm not proud of what happened."

"Okay." Greg shrugged agreeably. "Did you do your

economics assignment?"

"First thing Friday so I wouldn't have it hanging over my head the rest of the weekend. What about you?"

"I'm a wait-until-the-last-minute kind of guy," Greg replied. "I was up until 11:30 last night doing it."

Rianne heaved a sigh of exaggerated patience. "I'm trying to break him of the habit but so far, I'm not having any luck."

Greg shot her a grin. "Has it occurred to you there's a method to my madness? I figure, as long as you consider me a project, you'll stick around. If I shape up, you might move on to greener pastures."

"Aw, how sweet," Cass drawled. "I'm going out on a limb here, Rianne, but I think he likes you."

Crimson spots blossomed on her cheeks. "Nah, he just appreciates somebody taking an interest in him."

"I don't know how to tell you this," Greg said, moving up closer to Rianne, "but Cass hit the nail on the head."

"Oh." Blushing furiously, Rianne stared straight ahead. "Uh ... good."

Cass giggled. "Would you two like to be alone?"

Greg laughed while Rianne pretended not to hear. Seconds later, they arrived at school.

After parking their bikes, the trio entered the building and headed to their lockers, all located in the same hall. Cass faltered when she spotted Kira at her locker a few feet away from hers. She thought about ducking into a class-room to wait until she left, but squared her shoulders and marched to her locker. She'd never been one to avoid confrontation, and she didn't plan to start now.

"Good morning, Kira," she said as brightly as she could.

Scowling, Kira grunted something that might have been a greeting.

Cass wracked her brain for something to say. "How's it going?"

Talk about lame, she chided herself.

"What do you care?" sniffed Kira.

"Aw, come on," Cass wheedled. "Don't be like this. Everyone has disagreements every now and then."

Kira slammed her locker shut. "It would be one thing if it were every now and then. But they're happening all the time now, and I'm sick of it. I'm also sick of always being in the wrong. I can't wait to get away from here. Five days in Hawaii won't be nearly long enough."

Cass raised an eyebrow. "You're going to Hawaii? When?"

"When I got home yesterday, my parents and I talked about it, and they decided to send me up to Hono over Labor Day weekend. Not," Kira added with a disdainful toss of her head, "that it's any of your business."

Cass struggled to hold onto her temper. "Cool. You'll get to see Micah. I'll bet he's excited."

"Not half as excited as I am at the thought of being away from all this for awhile." Kira swept her arm in a semicircle. "I can't decide if it's the island or the people that's starting to close in on me."

"Maybe a little bit of both." Cass bit her tongue to keep from adding a nasty remark. "When do you leave?"

"Next Thursday, and I'll be back Monday night." Shifting her books to her other arm, Kira turned to go. "Be sure to tell Tabitha, on the off-chance she might want to send something for Micah."

"Why don't you tell her yourself?" Cass suggested.

"Yeah, right," Kira flung over her shoulder. "And while I'm at it, I'll see if she wants to do something after school." Snickering unpleasantly, she walked away.

Rianne came over to stand next to Cass. "She's really hurting. We need to do something."

"What's this 'we'?" Dropping her backpack on the floor, Cass bent over the combination lock. "I'm not the least bit interested in being nice to her."

"I know things are tense between you two," Rianne said.

"So I guess it's up to me then."

Cass' expression softened. "You truly are a good person. You'd go out of your way for anybody."

"I wouldn't say that." Rianne hunched her shoulder in embarrassment. "It's just ... we've all been friends for a long time. It would be a shame for it to end before we graduate, especially like this."

"You're right." Cass frowned. "We've lost too many relationships as it is. We can't afford to lose anymore."

"Exactly." Rianne gazed down the hall in the direction Kira had taken. "I'll go see if she feels like talking. If not, maybe she'll agree to get together after school."

"Thanks." Cass briefly rested a hand on her arm. "Every group needs someone like you."

"Whatever." Rianne brushed aside the compliment. "I'm just doing my Christian duty."

Her words stayed with Cass after she left. *If she's doing her Christian duty then what am I doing?* she mused as she extracted the books she needed for her morning classes. *Obviously my Cassandra duty. I'm doing what feels good and makes me happy, whether it's the right thing or not. I'm ashamed to admit it, but Rianne cares way more about other people than I do.* She sighed. *Once again, Lord, I have to ask Your forgiveness. I know I sin every day, but some days—or, in my case, months—are worse than others. Please give me a heart for doing Your will.*

Cass was subdued as she made her way to homeroom a few minutes later. When Rianne didn't appear, she assumed her friend had succeeded in getting Kira to talk.

Unfortunately, their discussion didn't seem to have helped matters. When Cass, Tabitha, and Rianne gathered at their usual table for lunch, it was immediately apparent that Kira was missing.

"Did she have to stay after class?" Tabitha asked Rianne, who had Spanish with Kira right before lunch.

"Not that I know of." Rianne glanced around the cafeteria. "Uh ... there's your answer." Without being obvious, she pointed to a table halfway across the room.

Kira sat in the middle of a group, talking and wildly gesturing. The girls surrounding her periodically erupted in laughter. Tabitha's mouth tightened.

"She's showing me she has other friends," she said darkly. "Fine. Two can play at this game."

"Don't," Rianne ordered quietly. "There are already enough problems. Don't add fuel to the fire."

Tabitha sagged back in her seat. "I know you're right." Her gaze wandered back in Kira's direction, and her eyes filled with tears. "I hate that it's come to this. Kira and I used to swear we'd always talk things out. We'd never play games with each other. Now look at us." She covered her face with her hands, murmuring through her fingers, "I never should have started dating Micah. But who knew it would lead to this?"

Cass and Rianne sat on either side of her, shielding her from curious stares. While Rianne crooned soothing words, Cass struggled to come up with a solution to the situation. No matter how hard she tried, she kept drawing a blank.

At one point, Cass noticed Kira glancing their way. In response, she glowered so ferociously that the other girl hastily averted her gaze.

There I go again, she berated herself. *I could have smiled. But no. I had to be nasty. I'm hopeless. I don't know why God even bothers with me.*

Tabitha gave a final sniffle, shook herself, and lowered her hands. "Okay, I'm better. It just got to me for a moment there." She pasted on a phony smile. "See? Good as new."

"Liar." Cass' tone was affectionate as she bumped shoulders with her. "Is there anything we can do? Go over and get Kira so y'all can patch things up?"

"I don't think the cafeteria's the best place for that."

Tabitha managed a weak laugh. "One of us might start throwing food, which could get ugly."

"That, I'd pay to see." With the worst of the storm over, Cass settled down to eat. She was glad when Tabitha emptied the contents of her lunch bag onto the table. "Kira told me earlier that she's flying up to see Micah next week."

Tabitha set down the sandwich she'd been about to bite into. "Really? Any special reason why?"

"I guess she just wants to spend time with him." Cass crunched into a potato chip. "She might also be planning to tour the campus, but I don't know that for sure. She did say to tell you, if you have anything you want to send up for Micah, she'll be happy to deliver it to him."

"How about a 'Dear John' letter?" Suddenly agitated, Tabitha raked her fingers through her hair. "Forget I said that. I didn't mean it." She began breaking her sandwich into little pieces. "I can't decide if I'm jealous she's going to be seeing Micah or relieved it's not me. Plus, I don't know if I should send something or not. If I do, what should I send?"

Rianne took her wrist and gently shook her. "Hey, calm down. You have a week to think it over. You don't have to decide this very second."

Tabitha expelled her pent-up breath with a whoosh. "You're right." She smiled wanly. "As usual. I appreciate you not slapping me to snap me out of it the way they do in the movies."

"That was my second choice if shaking didn't work." Rianne released her wrist. "I'm trusting you not to go crazy on us."

"I'll try to behave." Tabitha popped a piece of sandwich into her mouth.

"At least warn us if you feel another spell coming on," Cass requested.

This time Tabitha's smile was genuine. "You have my word."

CHAPTER 26

The week passed quickly. Cass and Tabitha's relationship with Kira remained frosty, and Kira didn't seem open to anything that would make it better. She skipped both church and the youth meeting. After a great deal of thought, Tabitha opted not to send anything with her so the two girls didn't talk before Kira left.

The Saturday following her departure Cass and Tabitha laid out at the pool, soaking up the sun.

"Are you up to talking?" Tabitha asked.

"Not for long." Cass opened up a lazy eye to glance at her sister and stifled a yawn. "You'd better hurry."

"I've been lying here, wondering what Kira's doing. It's strange to think that right this very moment she's probably talking to Micah. Sometimes I can hardly remember what he looks like." Tabitha shot her a curious glance. "Does that ever happen with Logan?"

"No. My problem is I think about him all the time." Cass watched a bead of sweat make its way down her arm. "I think about what he looks like, what he sounds like, what it feels like to hold his hand." She smiled wryly. "I guess you could say I'm obsessed with him. I can't believe it's been over two months since I last saw him."

"You got a bunch of letters from him the other day," Tabitha reminded her. "Plus, he sent that tape so you got to hear his voice."

"That was nice," conceded Cass. "He said he'd try to call me this weekend, but it's already Sunday there." She frowned. "I guess he couldn't get to a phone."

"There's still tomorrow." Tabitha abruptly flipped over and stood up. "I'm about to burn up. I've got to cool off. Are you going to join me?"

"You go ahead. I'll be there as soon as I muster the energy to get up."

Cass had just found the energy to get up when the gate opened, and she saw Dad beckoning to her. She jogged over to him.

"Hurry," he urged. "Logan's on the phone."

Cass' heart cartwheeled. "I'll be right there. I need to get my sandals. Don't let him hang up."

Dad disappeared while Cass hurried back to her towel, where she'd left her flipflops. Tabitha had swum to the side of the pool and hung there, waiting to find out what Dad had wanted. Cass wasted no time in telling her.

"Way to go, Logan!" Tabitha cheered as Cass jogged out of the pool area.

Mom was on the phone with him when Cass burst into the house. Her wet skin erupted in goosebumps from the air-conditioning, but she barely noticed. Nothing mattered except the phone. Mom handed it to her with a smile. Cass immediately walked out to the lanai.

"Logan? Hey!"

"Man, do I ever miss hearing you say 'hey' like that. Sorry to interrupt your swimming," he teased.

"Just don't let it happen again." Cass sank down into a wicker chair. "How are you?"

"They haven't killed me yet. But school starts the day

after tomorrow, and that might be what does me in." Logan didn't sound like he was joking.

"Take it one day at a time, and you'll do fine," advised Cass.

"How are you doing in school?"

"I'm getting 90s and 100s on my tests so I guess I won't flunk."

"Grades like that are good enough to get you into this place," Logan said. "Have you ever thought about coming here?"

Cass laughed. "Yeah, me with a gun. Now there's a good idea."

"Hmm. I didn't think of that. Maybe you're right." There was a pause, then, in an oh-so-casual tone, Logan asked, "Anything new with that guy, Sam, you told me about?"

He sounds jealous. Cass smiled to herself. *I like that.*

Aloud, she replied, "He and Tabitha have really hit it off. They've been out a couple of times. When he comes to youth group, he always finds a way to sit next to her." In her own ultra-casual tone she inquired, "What's up with Shiloh?"

Logan's hesitation raised the hairs on the back of her neck. *Uh-oh.*

"There was a dance last night, and we went," came his reluctant response.

"Together?" Cass squeaked. "As in a date?"

"No," Logan said hastily. "We both happened to be there, and we started to talk, and the next thing I knew, we'd spent the entire time together."

"Did you dance with her?" Cass made herself ask.

"A couple of times."

"Any slow ones?" Cass squeezed her eyes shut to block out the images of Logan with another girl.

"Just one."

"Oh."

"Cass, you don't have anything to worry—" Logan began at the same time she croaked, "I can't talk anymore right now."

"What?" Logan asked.

Cass repeated her statement.

"Don't hang up," he pleaded. "Let me explain."

"I have to go." It was hard for Cass to breathe. "I'm not playing games. I honestly can't talk."

"I'll call you back in five minutes." Logan sounded panicky. "I'll stand by the phone to make sure no one else uses it."

"No." Cass rubbed her throat as if to massage away the fear clogging it. "I'll call you."

"When?"

"I don't know."

"Soon?" Logan asked desperately.

"I don't know," Cass repeated. "Bye, Logan."

Pressing the off button, she collapsed in tears. For the first time, they'd ended a conversation without Logan praying. Cass clutched her stomach, bent double by the pain.

It's over. He's found somebody else. Not that I blame him. What good is having a girlfriend who's 9,000 miles away? She raised her tear-streaked face to the cloudless sky. *Jesus, You're going to have to get me through this. I can't do it on my own. It hurts too bad.*

Cass cried for 10 minutes before finally dragging herself into the house. She gave her parents a summary of what had happened, but unable to tolerate their sympathy, she escaped to her room. Except for meals and church, she holed up there for the rest of the weekend.

When she emerged Tuesday morning for school, she was hollow-eyed, but calm. She figured she'd survived the worst of it. She hadn't called Logan back yet, but that would have to wait until she was stronger.

Tabitha had passed up riding to school with Sam and had stuck close to her side. Halfway there, they were joined by Rianne who took up her post on Cass' other side. They maintained the same position as they entered the building and headed to their lockers. They paid little attention to Kira standing in the middle of a crowd of girls until it quickly became obvious that she wanted them to hear what she was saying.

"I tell you," she declared in a voice loud enough to rouse the dead, "college life is *fu-un*. The parties everyone talks about?" She fanned herself. "*Who-ee!* They're everything people have said they are and more." She whistled. "A lot more."

"Was there drinking?" someone asked.

"Girl, the beer flowed like water," Kira said with a grin. "But it sure didn't have the same effect as water."

"Did you drink?" another girl asked.

"That's about all I did from the time I stepped off the plane," bragged Kira. "I partied hard, believe me."

Cass, Tabitha, and Rianne exchanged uneasy glances. Was she telling the truth or showing off?

"What about guys?" a third girl questioned.

Kira laughed. "Mmm-mmm. I had my pick. I could tell you stories that would make you blush."

Tabitha had heard enough. Tugging on Cass' and Rianne's shirts, she gestured toward a nearby classroom, and they slipped inside.

"I can't take any more of this," she hissed. "Micah and I are messed up. Kira and I are messed up. So are Cass and Logan. Now Kira seems to be into drinking and partying.

Something's got to be done. But what?"

She looked at Cass, who shrugged and lowered her gaze. She couldn't solve her own problems, let alone anyone else's.

Rianne shrugged. "We need to pray," she said.

Tabitha shook her head. "I've tried that."

"Me too," Cass added.

"I mean now. Here." Rianne gave each of them a stern look. "Wherever two or three are gathered in His name ..."

"Okay," Cass reluctantly agreed after a quick look around to make sure they were alone. "But make it snappy. I don't want an audience."

"It'll be short and sweet," Rianne promised.

"But hopefully effective," Tabitha added.

Although Cass still felt a little embarrassed, they bowed their heads. While Rianne whispered an urgent prayer, Cass and Tabitha silently added their requests. *Maybe it will help*, Cass thought. At the very least, she felt better when they were done.

CHAPTER 27

"Do you think Kira's ever going to talk to us?" Cass asked Tabitha as they rode home from school two days later.

"It looks pretty doubtful." Tabitha gave a concerned glance at the sky. If they hurried, they might just beat the rain home. "She seems to have settled in with her new group."

Cass made a face. "I don't like those girls. They're trouble."

"They do have a reputation for being wild," conceded Tabitha. She put on a burst of speed as the first raindrops began to fall.

"Kira's even giving Rianne the cold shoulder." Cass ducked her head against the stinging drizzle. "She's the last person who deserves to be treated badly. All she wants is for everyone to get along."

"I keep thinking I should try one more time to talk to Kira," Tabitha said, "but I can't bring myself to do it. I don't want to give her the chance to rip into me." Braking, she hopped off her bike. "I guess I'm being a coward."

"If you are, then I'm one too." Cass hurried into the house. A gust of wind slammed the porch door shut behind her. "That should let Mom know we're home."

Instead of being greeted by a cheery hello from the living room, they walked into a silent house. Not finding a note from Mom on the counter saying she'd gone out, they headed down the hall to the master bedroom where they discovered her curled up on the bed. Cass stifled an impatient sigh while Tabitha walked to the bed and gently shook Mom's shoulder.

"Hey, sleepyhead," she murmured. "We're home."

Mom rolled onto her back, and Cass felt a stirring of alarm. Her face was flushed, and her eyes glittered unhealthily. Perching on the edge of the bed, Tabitha brushed damp tendrils of hair off Mom's forehead.

"You don't look so good. Do you feel all right?"

Mom smiled. "I think I may have come down with a touch of something. Nothing serious," she assured them. "Even pregnant women get the flu."

"Are you sick to your stomach?" Cass hovered over Tabitha's shoulder. She didn't like what she saw. Maybe she should call Dad.

"I am a little queasy," Mom admitted. "Why?"

"Because you're holding your stomach like it's bothering you." Cass reached past Tabitha to lay the back of her hand on Mom's forehead. "You feel feverish. Have you taken your temperature?"

Mom's face lit up with genuine amusement. "Since when did you become a medical expert?"

"I took notes back when you used to doctor me." Her mother's good humor relieved some of Cass' concern. "The first thing you always did was check to see if I had a fever."

Mom laughed. "I did, didn't I? And here I thought you weren't paying attention." She tried to sit up, but closed her eyes and hastily lay back down. After a moment she looked at them again and smiled. "Listen, you two worrywarts, I'm fine. Stop looking like you expect me to up and pass out any second. I'm temporarily under the weather. It happens. All I need is a few hours of bed rest, and I'll be good as new."

"I'm going to call Dad." Getting up, Tabitha started for the door.

"Sweetie, don't. Don't you think I'd call him if I thought for one second something were seriously wrong? Believe me, I'm not about to take any chances when it comes to the baby."

"She has a point," Cass said. "She wouldn't risk the baby's health."

"I guess you're right," Tabitha grudgingly conceded. "In that case, can I get you something? Juice maybe? Or a snack?"

Mom's reply was cut off by the ringing of the telephone. Tabitha took off down the hall at a jog. After she left, Mom glanced out the window where a full-fledged storm lashed the palm trees, whipping them into a frenzy.

"Looks like you beat the rain home," she commented.

"We got sprinkled on, but it could have been a lot worse." Cass moved to the window and sat down on the ledge. Choosing a raindrop, she traced its path down the glass. "I'm sort of looking forward to the rainy season. It reminds me of fall."

"Are you missing Tennessee again?" Mom asked softly.

Cass shrugged. "Sort of. Mostly I keep thinking about Logan being in New York and how the season's probably starting to change up there."

"You haven't written to him since his phone call last week, have you?"

"He hasn't written to me, either." Cass' indignation ebbed as quickly as it had flared. "Besides, I don't know what to say to him. He has every right to date anyone he wants. But—" her face crumpled, and she twisted her hands together in her lap. "I hate it. Every time I think of him dancing with that girl, Shiloh, I get sick to my stomach."

"I know the feeling." Mom ruefully rubbed her own middle then patted the bed. "Come here, Sweetie. We need to talk. I should have done it sooner, but—"

She was interrupted by Tabitha's reappearance. "Sam's on the phone," she informed Cass. "He's wondering if we'd like to meet him and some others at the library to study for the economics test tomorrow."

Cass shot Mom a quizzical glance. "Will you be okay here alone?"

"Of course." Mom reached for the afghan at the end of the bed. "All I plan to do is sleep. I can do that whether you're here or not."

Uncertain, Tabitha shifted from one foot to the other and consulted Cass. "What do you think?"

"I suppose we should take her word for it," Cass said with a shrug.

"Don't talk about me like I'm not here," Mom complained good-naturedly from her cocoon.

Cass got up from the window ledge to walk over and pat Mom's head. "If you're well enough to gripe at us, you should be all right by yourself." She nodded at Tabitha. "Tell Sam we'll be at the library in about 15 minutes." As Tabitha turned to deliver the message, Cass added, "Ask him if he's called Rianne. If not, I'll do it." Cass turned back to Mom. "Are you sure you don't want anything?"

"No, thanks, Sweetie. Just bring me the phone so I'll have it nearby in case I need to call Dad."

Cass frowned. "Do you think you're going to need him? Because if you do, I'll stay."

Mom pulled back the afghan to make a comical face. "You know me. I don't like to leave anything to chance."

"Okay." Cass moved toward the door. "I'll bring it in as soon as Tabitha gets off."

Heading to her room, she sighed with relief. She was

looking forward to spending time with her friends, even if it was to study. She definitely wouldn't have liked having to stay behind. Tabitha met her in the hall.

"Sam talked to Rianne and Greg on the way home from school. They'll be there, along with three or four other people."

"Great." Cass nodded her approval. "After we're through studying, maybe we can head downstairs to the bowling alley for pizza. Let's take money."

"Good idea." Tabitha walked past her into her room. "I'll be ready to go in a few minutes."

Before leaving, Cass got the phone and placed it on the bed beside Mom, who briefly opened her eyes and murmured her thanks.

"Try not to get too wet," she advised sleepily.

Laughing, Cass leaned down to kiss her. "Yeah, right. With the way the wind's blowing, our ponchos aren't going to do much good. We might as well wear our bathing suits."

"If you do, don't let your father catch you. He'll haul you out of the library so fast you won't know what hit you."

"I'm glad you're up to joking. I don't feel so guilty leaving you here by yourself." Cass affectionately ruffled Mom's hair. "I'll call you if the group decides to stay and eat. Otherwise, we'll see you around 5:00."

Once they gathered in the library, their biggest problem was keeping the noise down. Since there were no other patrons for them to bother, the easygoing librarian left them alone. Her only warning was an occasional, tolerant smile.

Two hours passed quickly. Amid the chatter and laughter, they managed to get a fair amount of work done. They had just decided to end the session and head downstairs for pizza when the phone rang. The librarian answered, listened a moment, then set down the receiver and approached their table.

"Is one of you Cass Devane?" she inquired.

Cass' heart sank. *Great. Ten to one it's Mom, and she needs me to come home.* She raised a hand. "I'm Cass," she reluctantly identified herself.

"Your father's on the phone."

Cass locked eyes with Tabitha before jumping to her feet. She hurried to the phone with Tabitha close on her heels. Her hand shook as she lifted the receiver.

"Dad?"

"Hi," he replied tersely. "Is Tabitha there?"

"She's standing right next to me. Do you want to talk to her?"

"No." Dad took a deep breath. "I need you girls to come to the hospital. They just admitted your mom. The doctor's afraid she might be—" his voice broke, and he struggled to compose himself, "losing the baby."

"Oh, Dad, no." Cass gripped the phone so tightly that her knuckles turned white.

Tabitha urgently shook her arm. "What's the matter?"

Cass waved at her to shush. "We'll be right there. Tell Mom—" tears welled in her eyes and she had to swallow hard before continuing, "we love her, and we're praying like crazy." The moment she hung up, she turned to Tabitha, whose face had gone ashen. "Mom's in the hospital. There might be a problem with the baby."

Tabitha's hand flew to her mouth. "We should have never left her alone."

Grim-faced, Cass nodded. "I know. I'll never forgive myself if the baby—" She couldn't complete the thought.

The girls dashed to the table where their friends had already surmised something was amiss. After listening to their hasty explanation of the situation, Rianne assured them she'd take care of their books and urged them to hurry. They shot out the door and clattered down the steps without looking back. Reaching the bike racks, they slipped on their ponchos before racing off into the rain.

Jesus, I take back every nasty thing I've thought and said about not looking forward to the baby, Cass prayed silently. She swerved to avoid a puddle and nearly lost control of the bike. Once she regained control, she added, *Please don't punish the baby for my sins. I promise to love him or her with all my heart. I'll never again resent helping Mom. Just please, please keep her and the baby safe.* Instead of the usual peace she felt when she prayed, her nerves continued to jangle as her heart thumped painfully against her chest.

CHAPTER 28

By the time they arrived at the hospital, Cass couldn't tell where her tears left off and the rain began. Parking their bikes, she and Tabitha ran to the entrance, slamming through the double doors at the same time. A quick look around the waiting room told them Dad was nowhere to be seen. Tabitha led the way to the front desk.

"Can you tell us where Mrs. Donna Spencer is?" she gasped.

The nurse frowned at the rain dripping off Tabitha's poncho and puddling on the counter. "Would you mind stepping away from the desk while I look up the information?"

Cass gaped in astonishment as her normally meek-and-mild sister snapped, "You bet I mind. This is my mother I'm talking about. She might be having a miscarriage, and I want to know where she is. Now."

Before the nurse could respond, Dad appeared. He called to them as he came down the hall.

"Tabitha! Cass! Over here."

With a final glower at the nurse, Tabitha wheeled around and, taking Cass by the hand, jogged to him. His expression sent Cass' spirits plummeting.

Swallowing hard, Cass forced herself to ask, "How's Mom?"

Dad gestured for them to follow him to a seat in the corner. He waited until they were seated before replying, "She's having contractions. The doctor's monitoring them to see how strong they are and if they're getting closer together. He's also running some tests to see what might be causing them."

"She wasn't feeling well when we left for the library," Tabitha confessed. "She said something about the flu. We asked about staying with her, but she said she'd be okay."

Cass covered her face with her hands. "Even though I offered, I didn't want to stay. I'm sure Mom knew it, which was why she told me to go on." She choked back a sob. "I've been awful about the baby, and now she might lose it."

Tabitha turned haunted eyes to her father. "If the baby does wind up coming now, there'd be no way it could live, right?"

Dad nodded slowly. "It's too early. It wouldn't survive."

Cass inhaled sharply. Even though it was the answer she expected, it still pained her to hear it. Beside her, Tabitha moaned and wrapped her arms around her middle, hugging herself for comfort. "Is Mom scared?" Cass whispered.

For the first time, a ghost of a smile creased Dad's face. "She's got rock-solid faith. She keeps telling me, and anyone else who will listen, everything's going to be fine. The doctor just shakes his head, but even that doesn't discourage her. If she's told me once since we got here, she's told me a thousand times that the baby's going to be born healthy and at the right time."

"How does she know?" Cass wanted something—anything—to hold onto.

Dad lifted his hands in bewilderment. "She says it's a

combination of trust in God and mother's intuition."

"Can we see her?" Tabitha asked.

"I'm afraid not yet. In fact—" Dad stood and glanced towards the hall with worried eyes. "I should get back. I'll let her know you're here. It'll mean a lot to her. She said to tell you to storm heaven on the baby's behalf."

"We will," Tabitha vowed, speaking for them both.

Cass nodded her agreement. Getting up, she threw her arms around Dad's neck. "That's for you and Mom and the baby. Tell Mom I love her and that I'm praying like I've never prayed before."

Dad squeezed hard before releasing her. "She'll appreciate that." He turned to Tabitha and gathered her close.

"Tell Mom I love her and the baby, and that I'm praying for both of them." Sniffling, she buried her head in his neck. "I love you."

"Me too," Cass piped up.

Dad pulled her to him for a group hug. "I love you girls. I'll be back out as soon as we know something."

"We'll be here."

Cass stepped back and reached for Tabitha's hand. Their fingers entwined, Cass watched Dad disappear down the hall. When she could no longer see him, Cass pulled away from Tabitha and sank down into a green vinyl chair.

"It doesn't sound good," Cass said glumly as Tabitha sat down next to her.

"Mom seems to think it'll be okay," Tabitha replied.

Cass snorted. "You know Mom. She could be in the middle of a raging blizzard, and she'd still find a silver lining."

"You don't think she'd lie to Dad, do you?"

"I wouldn't call it lying." Shifting in the chair, Cass tucked her legs up beside her. "She doesn't want to add to his worrying."

"She wouldn't want to give him false hope, either,"

Tabitha insisted. "If she thought she was losing the baby, she'd tell him so he could prepare himself and us."

Cass shrugged. "Maybe."

Tabitha glanced over her shoulder at a wall phone. "Maybe we should call some people and get a prayer chain going. I doubt Dad's had time to think about it."

Grateful for something to do, Cass nodded enthusiastically. "Good idea. Let's start with Pastor Thompson. He'll know who to call."

Cass had just stood up when the entrance doors blew open. Sam, Rianne, and Greg hurried inside, anxiously scanning the waiting area. Rianne spotted them first.

"There they are." She pointed in their direction.

Sam went immediately to Tabitha's side, while Rianne and Greg flanked Cass.

"How's your Mom?" they chorused at the same time.

"They're doing tests to find out what's going on," Tabitha said, leaning against Sam.

"Is the baby okay?" Concern shadowed Rianne's eyes as she turned to Cass.

"They don't know yet." The honest reply made Cass shiver. "Mom's having contractions. If they're not stopped—" She couldn't bring herself to say out loud what might happen.

Rianne slipped a steadying arm around her waist. "They'll stop," she predicted.

"But what if they don't?" Cass pressed a hand to her chest in an attempt to slow her galloping heart. "What if the baby comes today and—and doesn't make it?"

Tabitha emitted a soft cry. Sam took her hand and sandwiched it between his.

"We'll cross that bridge *if* we come to it," Rianne said. "Whatever happens, we have to keep trusting God is in control, and He's working everything out according to His perfect will."

"And if His will is for the baby not to make it?" Cass couldn't let it go.

"It would be tough to accept," Rianne acknowledged. "All I can tell you is that I believe with all my heart that God is in charge of everything that happens."

"Even the bad things?"

Rianne's nod was firm. "Absolutely."

A strange peace settled on Cass. For the first time since Dad's call, she relaxed. Glancing at Tabitha, she saw that her sister also appeared calmer. Turning back to Rianne, she smiled wanly. "How does it feel to be an answer to prayer?"

"It feels weird." Rianne made a face. "I'm just here to do whatever you need me to do. Where should I start?"

Tabitha remembered the phone. "We were about to call Pastor Thompson. Maybe you could do it. I wasn't sure I'd be able to tell him what's happening without breaking down."

"I'll get right on it."

Rianne moved to the telephone and picked up the phone book.

"How about I get you something to snack on?" offered Greg. "You left before you could eat. You must be hungry."

As if on cue, Cass' stomach growled, and everyone laughed.

"Well, now that you mention it ..." she quipped.

"I'll be right back." Fishing in his pockets, Greg headed for the vending machines on the opposite side of the room.

That left Cass, Tabitha, and Sam. Eyeing the couple's clasped hands, Cass realized she wasn't upset by the affection it indicated. She was glad Tabitha had someone to lean on. In that moment, her longing for Logan was so fierce it took her breath away.

I don't care if he and Shiloh have been out dancing every night. First chance I get, I'm calling him and telling him how much I appreciate the way he's always been there for me, she vowed.

Sam motioned toward the chairs. "There's no sense standing when we can sit."

Tabitha and Sam settled in side by side chairs, scooting them closer so the armrests touched. Smothering a smile, Cass looked away. *Micah*, she addressed her distant friend, *I do believe your days as Tabitha's boyfriend are numbered. She's found herself one truly nice guy.*

Rianne and Greg returned at the same time. While Greg distributed bags of peanuts and cans of cola, Rianne sat down next to Cass.

"Pastor Thompson is going to make several calls before coming here. He said to tell you both that he's praying for your family and to remind you that everything's in God's hands."

Cass eyed her suspiciously. "Did he really say that? Or did you throw it in to make it sound like he believes the same thing as you do about God controlling everything?"

Rianne laughed. "He said it. I can't help it if I'm as smart as the minister."

"Maybe you are, and maybe you're not," Cass retorted. "I know one thing for sure, though. You need to work on your humility."

"Hey!" Greg protested in Rianne's defense. "She's the humblest person I know. She has no idea how wonderful she is."

The others emitted exaggerated groans, and Cass went so far as to make gagging noises. Tabitha suddenly bent forward and buried her face in her hands.

"Listen to us. How can we joke when Mom's lying in a room, maybe losing our little brother or sister?"

Cass instantly sobered. "You're right. We should be praying, instead of clowning around."

Sam awkwardly patted Tabitha's back and looked around the group. "Does anyone want to ... uh ... you know ... pray?" His expression was apologetic. "I would, but I've never prayed out loud in front of people."

Greg took the lead. "I'll start. Feel free to jump in, anybody, if you get the urge. Then how about we close with the Lord's Prayer?"

One by one, they joined hands until the circle was complete. As Greg began his prayer, Cass closed her eyes and focused her thoughts on God.

"Jesus," Greg started, "You know why we're here, and what we want to ask. The Spencer baby is in trouble, and we're calling on You to help. Please keep the baby from being born too soon. Heal Mrs. S. of whatever it is that's making her sick and putting the baby in danger." He paused for a moment. "I guess that's it. Thank You for hearing this prayer. Amen."

Silence reigned for several seconds. The only sounds were the rain lashing at the windows and muffled sniffles from Cass and Tabitha.

"Lord God," Rianne murmured, "please give the Spencers—" she opened an eye to smile at Cass, "and Cass the strength they need to get through this difficult time. Let them know they're not alone, that You're with them every step of the way. In Jesus' name, amen."

Nobody else jumped in, so after a long pause, Greg began, "Our Father, who art in heaven ..."

As Cass joined in on the familiar words and let their meaning sink in, she felt herself relax. The God who provided everything from daily bread to salvation was in control. She slowly sat up and stretched, smiling as everyone else did the same. Nodding with satisfaction, Sam looked at each person in turn. His gaze lingered on Rianne and Greg.

"You guys pray good," he observed. "How'd you learn to

do that?"

Rianne smiled shyly. "Going to the youth group has taught me a lot. I never used to pray, either out loud or to myself." She giggled. "Well, not exactly to myself. I meant, to God, in my head."

Looking amused, Greg tapped her shoulder. "It's okay. We understand." He turned his attention back to Sam. "I grew up praying. My parents are strong Christians. In my family, praying's about as natural as breathing."

"Cool." Sam leaned back. "I kind of envy you. My folks decided it was more enlightened to let us kids choose what we want to believe in."

"How does that work?" wondered Cass. "Do they give you books on different religions? Or do they have you try one out one year and another one the next year?"

Sam laughed. "I don't know how it works in other families, but my parents have never pushed anything on us. When we visit my grandparents, we go to church with them. Which, by the way," he added, "I've always liked. But that's been about it when it comes to religious training."

"My Dad and I didn't become Christians until a few years ago," Tabitha said softly. "I'm very glad we did. I don't know how I would've gotten through the past year otherwise." She blinked back tears. "More importantly, I don't know how I'd get through this without God."

"Amen to that," Cass agreed fervently.

"Hanging around with you guys makes me want to learn more about the Bible and stuff." Sam teasingly mussed Tabitha's hair. "And I'm not saying that just to score points with Tabs here."

She stuck her tongue out at him. "That's good because it's not working anyway."

"Man—" Greg whistled his appreciation, "she got you, buddy."

Sam flicked at his shoulders as if brushing off the insult. "That's okay. I'm big enough to take it."

"I hate to break this to you," Tabitha leaned close to confide, "but you're not all that big. I mean, how tall are you? Five-eight, five-nine?"

While Greg hooted his approval, Cass and Rianne erupted in laughter. Suddenly a harsh voice broke into the merriment.

"Is this incredible or what? The minute Pastor Thompson called, I jumped on my bike and raced over here because I thought you might appreciate having a shoulder to cry on, Tabitha!" Kira raged. "But what do I find instead? You yucking it up with your pals." She threw her hands up in disgust. "I got drenched for nothing."

Sam snorted. "Is that all you care about? That you got wet? You haven't even asked how Mrs. S. is doing."

Glaring, Kira advanced on him, wagging her finger. "Don't you dare lecture me! I've known Mrs. S. way longer than you have, and I care about her more than you ever could. It's not getting wet that bothers me," she sneered. "It's seeing Tabitha and Cass carrying on like nothing's wrong."

"Now wait just a minute," Tabitha said, standing up to glare at Kira. "I resent the implication that Cass and I don't care about what's happening to Mom."

Kira tinkled a brittle laugh. "What implication? I'm not implying anything. I'm saying it right out. Your behavior is disgraceful." She shot Sam a venomous sidelong glance. "Honestly! Flirting with that ... that snake while your mother and the baby are in danger. I'm ashamed to call you my friend."

"Then don't." Tabitha coldly returned her glower. "With friends like you, who needs enemies?"

Cass had enough. "Knock it off, y'all," she ordered irritably. "If you're not careful, you're going to say something you'll regret. Everyone's emotions are running pretty high. This isn't the time or the place to discuss your relationship."

Tabitha and Kira continued to glare at each other until Tabitha's shoulders finally sagged. "Cass is right," she mumbled. She motioned toward a nearby chair. "You're welcome to stay if you'd like. I appreciate you coming."

Kira sat down. "I love your mom. I had to come." She looked down at her hands folded in her lap. "How is she?"

Cass repeated the information about the tests and the monitoring, adding, "I hope Dad has another report soon. I'm on pins and needles, waiting to hear something."

"We all are," Rianne chimed in.

"I don't know what I'll do if the baby—" Cass paused to take a deep breath, "doesn't make it. And I can't imagine how Mom and Dad will cope."

"Their faith is strong," Rianne quietly assured her. "God will get them through if the worst happens."

"My faith isn't as strong as theirs." Cass' insides twisted with fear as she made this confession. "What if I ... I wind up hating God?"

There, she thought. *I've finally made myself say out loud what I'm most scared of, other than losing Mom or the baby.*

Tabitha gaped at her in astonishment. "I thought I was the only one who was worried about that. I've been sitting here thinking that, compared to you, I haven't been a Christian very long. I'm afraid I won't pass this test, that I'll lose my faith."

To Tabitha's surprise, Kira spoke up first. "First of all, I don't think that will happen," she predicted confidently. "But even if you waver, Christ is real and solid and He'll go on loving you no matter what."

"You really think so?" Tabitha whispered.

A genuine smile curved Kira's lips. "We go back a long way. Have you ever known me to say something just to make somebody feel good?"

Tabitha laughed. "Now that you mention it, no." Gratitude softened her features. "Thanks. I needed to hear that."

Kira offered an airy wave. "Hey, what are friends for?"

"For this, right here." Cass gestured around the circle. "For supporting one another." A gust of wind hurled raindrops at the window, making them sound like pebbles hitting the glass. Cass smiled. "For coming out in the middle of a tropical storm because they want to help." Ducking her head to hide her tears, she finished gruffly, "Y'all are great. I'll never forget this as long as I live."

Embarrassed murmurs greeted this remark, and Sam quickly changed the conversation to something lighter.

CHAPTER 29

Half an hour later, the doors swung open to admit Pastor Thompson. He walked immediately to the group, bending down to hug first Tabitha then Cass.

"How are you holding up?" he asked.

"Pretty well, all things considered," replied Tabitha.

Cass responded by holding out her hand and waving it from side to side, indicating her shaky state of mind.

Pastor Thompson frowned in concern. "I know you're worried, Cass. Is there anything I can do for you?"

Cass started to shake her head, then remembered the horrid nagging thought she couldn't displace. "Well—"

She stood up and stepped away from the group. Pastor Thompson followed, laying a comforting hand on her shoulder. "I just have this feeling—" she stopped, swallowing hard. "It's not my fault, is it?" she asked in a rush. "I mean, that something's wrong. You don't know how much I've resented this baby—how much I've resented Mom—"

"You're feeling guilty about resenting the baby," Pastor Thompson reflected. "You think God is punishing the baby because of what you have thought, right?"

Cass felt the air rush out of her. "Yes," she said softly, "I think it's my fault and I'm really sorry ..."

"No, Cass," Pastor Thompson said gently, "God is not punishing the baby for your sins. Jesus took on Himself the punishment for all our sins—including those that happen today, including your resentment. So whatever is happening with your mom and the baby—It's not your fault. But He knows you're sorry for feeling the way you have, and He forgives you. Do you believe that?"

Cass glanced up at his comforting face. She smiled. "Yes, I do," she said truthfully, feeling relief and peace flood through her. "Thank You."

He smiled in return, "No problem. Now, where's your dad?" Pastor Thompson glanced around the room.

"He's with Mom," Cass said.

"I wonder if I'm allowed to see them. There's only one way to find out." Pastor Thompson headed to the desk.

"I'm sure they'll let him in," observed Rianne. "See?" She nodded with satisfaction when the nurse pointed down the hall to Mom's room. "What'd I tell you?"

Pastor Thompson came back to speak to the girls. "I'm going to see your parents. Can I deliver a message from you?"

"Uh—" Cass glanced at Tabitha who shrugged, "tell them we're still praying, and we want to see Mom as soon as we can."

"You've got it." Pastor Thompson gave them a two-fingered salute. "See you in a bit."

Although the others started a quiet conversation after he left, Cass was unable to sit still. She got up and wandered to the window, amazed to see that night had fallen. The rain had let up, and the palm trees swayed in a gentle breeze. Cass imagined she could hear the fronds clacking, a sound that had become as familiar to her as her own breathing in the past year. A hand descended on her shoulder, and she glanced back to see who it was.

"How's it going?" Rianne murmured.

"Not so great." Folding her arms, Cass leaned her forehead against the cool glass. "I know I need to stay here until we hear something. But there's a part of me that would like to go off by myself so I can think some things through. The situation is making me look at stuff I should have looked at sooner."

"Like what?" Rianne kept her back to the others so nobody could overhear their discussion.

"That's the thing. I can't talk about it yet. I need to think first." Cass blew on the glass and wrote Logan's name in the condensation. Realizing what she'd done, she quickly erased it. "I will tell you one thing. I wish Logan were here. Except for you and Tabitha, he's my best friend in the whole world. A person really needs her friends at a time like this."

"Are you going to call and tell him what's going on?"

"I thought about it, but it's the middle of the night in New York." Cass made a face. "There's no way he'd be allowed to come to the phone. It's times like this that I wish he were going to a regular school."

Rianne lowered her voice. "Tabitha didn't call Micah, did she?"

A ghost of a smile crossed Cass' face. "What do you think?"

"I'm thinking no." Rianne laughed quietly. "Which is another black mark against her in Kira's book."

Cass snickered. "Like anyone could tell at this point. She has so many—"

Rianne cut her off with a nudge. "Here comes your dad."

Her stomach lurching, Cass spun around from the window. Tabitha spotted him at the same moment and jumped up. Cass hurried over to him and he opened his arms wide to draw both her and Tabitha close for a hug.

"Everything's fine," he said. "Thank God. It turns out your mom has a minor infection. The doctor says it frequently causes contractions in pregnant women. He's put her on antibiotics, and he wants to keep her overnight, just to make sure there aren't any complications. She should be permitted to go home in the morning."

Cass' relief was so great she burst into tears, which triggered an identical reaction in Tabitha.

"What's happened?" Greg's voice brought Cass back to the present. The others, having noticed the tears, had gathered around, faces all showing deep concern.

"It's-it's—" Tabitha could barely get the words out between her hiccups. "It's good news."

"Yes, we're happy," Cass wailed.

"Man, I'd sure hate to see you two upset," Sam said.

"Maybe I'd better explain." Dad dug in his pockets for tissues for the girls. They gratefully accepted them and began mopping their faces. "It turns out it's nothing serious. My wife has an infection, and the doctor has started her on medication. She'll be spending the night here, but he fully expects to release her tomorrow."

"Praise the Lord!" Rianne said, clapping. "Thank You, God."

"Amen to that," Greg added.

Tabitha recovered enough from her crying to ask Dad, "Are you staying here tonight?"

He nodded firmly. "Absolutely."

"You can spend the night at my house," Kira invited Tabitha. Remembering Cass, she added, "You too."

Cass didn't know how Tabitha felt, but she preferred to sleep in her own bed in her own house. Not wanting to sound ungrateful, she replied carefully, "Thanks for the offer. But, if it's okay with Dad, I'd rather go home."

"Same here," Tabitha agreed. "All I want to do is take a long, hot shower and curl up on the couch. No," she corrected herself, "first I want to see Mom then I want to do those other things."

"You're in luck," Dad said. "The doctor has granted you two a five-minute visit."

"Then can we go home? Or don't you want us staying alone?" Cass asked.

"Mom and I discussed it, and we decided to let you stay by yourselves, if that's what you wanted."

"I believe I speak for us both when I say we definitely want to stay by ourselves," Tabitha declared.

"For once, I can't argue with you." Moving to Tabitha's side, Cass linked arms with her. "So, Sis, are you ready to go see our Mom?"

"Girl, I've been ready for a couple of hours now."

When they reached Mom's room, Cass had to take a deep breath before letting Tabitha open the door. Once they stepped inside, Pastor Thompson, who'd been sitting beside the bed, stood up, murmured something to Mom, and left. The girls tiptoed across the floor.

"You don't have to walk on eggshells around me," Mom teased. "I'd prefer it if you'd just be your normal, noisy selves."

"Hey," protested Cass, working hard at being natural, "I resemble that remark."

"I don't." Tabitha tossed her head and assumed a pious expression. "I'm always quiet as a mouse."

Mom snorted. "Unless you're yelling at your sister or arguing with some decision Dad and I have made."

Cass relaxed at her joking tone. Moving to either side of the bed, she sat down and picked up Mom's hand.

"How are you feeling?" Cass laced her fingers through Mom's.

"Not bad, now that they've started the medication." She indicated the IV tube attached to her other hand. "In fact, I'm actually getting hungry, which is a good sign."

"Have the contractions stopped?" Tabitha asked.

Mom shook her head. "Not yet. But Dr. Howell said they should before morning." Despite her fatigue, her eyes danced with merriment. "Did Dad tell you they did another sonogram to see how the baby was doing?"

"No, I guess he forgot." Tabitha glanced at Cass. "Unless he mentioned it to you."

"Nope." Cass turned her attention back to Mom. "I take it everything was okay?"

"Better than okay." Mom smiled at them. "We found out what the baby is."

Cass' face lit up. "Cool! What?"

"We haven't decided whether to tell you or not." Mom folded her arms above her stomach and grinned.

"No fair!" Tabitha objected.

"Oh, well." Laughing, Mom shrugged. "Dad and I are going to talk about it tonight then let you know our decision tomorrow. Speaking of which," she continued before the girls could comment, "you will be able to get yourselves up and out to school without any problem, won't you?"

"We'll set all the alarm clocks in the house," promised Cass.

"It's strange to think about you two spending the night by yourselves." Mom assumed her most threatening expression. "No wild parties."

"Like we're the wild party types," Tabitha scoffed.

Mom patted both of their arms. "It's nice to know we can trust you." She lay back against the pillows. "Perhaps we should call it a night. I'm pretty tired. It's been an exciting day."

"I can do without this kind of excitement," muttered Cass. Standing, she took Mom's hand and squeezed before reluctantly releasing it. "I love you, and I'm really, really glad you and the baby are all right."

"Thank you, Sweetie. It meant a lot to know you girls

were praying for us." Mom laid a protective hand over her midsection. "Someday I'll tell the baby about how his—or her—big sisters prayed us through this crisis."

"When you get home, I want to talk to you about what I learned from the experience." Cass leaned down to kiss her cheek.

"First chance we get," Mom vowed. She turned to Tabitha. "I love you, Sweetie. I'll be thinking of you tonight."

"Not as much as I'll be thinking about you." Tabitha kissed her forehead. "Take care of yourself and—" she briefly touched Mom's stomach, "our little one."

"Will do." Mom yawned then smiled apologetically. "Sorry. Would you send Dad back in when you leave?"

Cass laughed. "There's a hint if I've ever heard one. Fine. We're leaving."

"Don't go away mad," Mom replied. "Just—"

"Go away," Tabitha finished for her. "That one's as old as the hills."

Blowing kisses, they exited the room and ran into Dad where he loitered just outside the door.

"Everyone left," he said. "They all said they'd call later. I'll be by in a couple of hours to see how you're doing."

"You mean to check up on us," Cass retorted good-naturedly.

"That and to tuck you in," Dad said with a laugh. "Be sure to eat something when you get home."

"Would you like us to bring you a sandwich?" Tabitha asked.

Dad shook his head. "I'll fix myself something when I stop in. I'm not too interested in trying the cafeteria food here."

"We'll go on then." Backing toward the entrance, Cass waved. "See you."

Tabitha kissed her father then joined Cass. They walked

out into the warm night air, filled with fragrances released by the recent shower. Cass raised her face to the sky.

"What a day."

"You can say that again."

Flexing her shoulders, Cass sighed. "I feel like the weight of the world's been lifted off me."

"Because you know Mom and the baby are okay?" Tabitha led the way to their bikes.

"Yes, but also because God has opened my eyes about a bunch of things." Cass backed her bike out of its slot. "If I make supper, will you let me tell you what I've discovered?"

"Even before you tell Mom?" The face Tabitha turned to her was amazed. When Cass nodded, she added, "Sis, you've got yourself a deal. I can't wait to hear this."

Without another word, they climbed on their bikes and headed home.

CHAPTER 30

Cass and Tabitha didn't linger after school the next day. Eager to see if Mom was home, they bid their friends a hasty farewell and pedaled home as fast as they could. Whipping around the side of the house, Cass noted Dad's bike parked on the lanai and took that to be a good sign.

"I think she's here," Cass said, leaning her bike against the fence that enclosed a portion of the patio.

Tabitha pushed down the kickstand on her bike. "I do too." She grinned. "Isn't this silly? It's not like she was away for days and days. It was just overnight, but I really missed her."

"Same here." Cass opened the porch door and held it for Tabitha to pass through. They rounded the corner from the kitchen to the living room and, to Cass' delight, found Mom lying on the couch. Dad looked up from where he sat in the recliner. Both parents appeared to have recently awakened from a nap.

"Hey," Cass softly greeted them. Walking to the coffee table, she perched on the edge. "I'm glad to see they released you. Was it for good behavior or because they couldn't take you anymore?"

"You're not home five seconds, and you're already picking on me," Mom pretended to gripe. "I think I'll go back to the hospital. They were nice to me there."

"Don't you dare!" Tabitha ordered with a laugh. "Cass and I were just saying how much we missed you last night."

"Well, you could have fooled me," Mom said darkly, although the corners of her mouth twitched. "I see you managed to get yourselves up and out in time this morning."

"Actually, no," Cass teased. "We rolled out of bed at 11:00, had cookies and cake for breakfast, and spent the day lounging at the pool."

"Hah! Caught you," crowed Dad. "We got back here a little after 10:00, and you were long gone."

"You even washed the breakfast dishes." Mom pressed a hand to her chest. "When I saw that, I thought I'd have heart failure."

"Now who's picking on who?" Cass leveled her an accusing look.

Mom stuck out her tongue. "Turnabout's fair play."

"It's good to see everything's back to normal around here." Laughing, Tabitha sat down in the rocker. "Did the doctor give you a clean bill of health, or are there things you shouldn't be doing?"

"He said I should rest for the next few days, then I can gradually resume my regular activities." Mom's smile was impish. "I hope you girls are prepared for me to take advantage of the situation. I believe I'm going to like being waited on hand and foot."

"You won't hear any complaints from me," Cass assured her. "I definitely learned my lesson with the scare you gave us yesterday."

"She did." Tabitha's nod was vigorous. "We talked for a long time last night about the wake-up call it was for both of us."

Curiosity sparkled in Mom's eyes. "Do you feel up to

sharing your discussion with me? Or, knowing you like I do, do you need to get something to eat first?" She smiled at Dad. "You should see these two when they get in from school. You'd think it had been weeks, instead of hours, since they last ate."

Ignoring her teasing, Cass slid off the table. "A snack sounds good to me. Do you want something, Tabitha?"

"Sure. What are you having?" Tabitha stayed seated and rocked gently.

"Cinnamon toast," Cass said. "If you want something else, you'll have to get it yourself."

"In that case, cinnamon toast sounds great." Tabitha glanced at her parents. "How about you? Can Cass get you something?"

"Way to offer my services," Cass complained good-naturedly.

Tabitha shrugged. "Didn't you say you weren't going to complain about helping Mom?"

"Yes, I did," Cass acknowledged. "But I didn't say anything about turning into a servant for you and Dad. No offense, Dad," she added.

He laughed. "None taken."

She headed to the kitchen, asking over her shoulder, "Now that we have that settled, would you and Mom like something?"

"A glass of lemonade would be nice," Mom said. "And cinnamon toast is starting to sound pretty good."

"I'll have what she's having," Dad chimed in.

"Then it's cinnamon toast and lemonade all around." Cass reached into the breadbox just as the phone rang. "I'll get it."

She picked up the receiver. "Hello?" The pause on the other end told her it was a long-distance call.

"Hi. Who's this?"

Cass hated it when a caller began a conversation with

that question. "Who do you wish to talk to?" she asked frostily.

A familiar chuckle rumbled across the line. "Hi, Cass. Feisty as always, I see. It's Micah."

"Hey, Micah." Leaning over the counter, she gestured to Tabitha.

"Kira called me last night and told me about your mom. How's she doing?"

"She's home. The doctor told her to take it easy for the next couple of days." Cass motioned again to Tabitha, who seemed to be taking her sweet time getting up. "Other than that, she's in good shape."

Micah exhaled a relieved breath. "Whew. I'm glad to hear it. Kira's call scared me. I think the world of your mother."

"I know. She'll appreciate that you called." Cass gave up being subtle and madly waved to her sister. "Do you want to talk to Tabitha now?"

"Not particularly."

Cass' arm dropped to her side like a lead weight. Uncertain she'd heard right, she asked, "Excuse me?"

"I said, not particularly," Micah repeated. "Kira told me about Sam being at the hospital with her last night. It sounded like he did a bang-up job of comforting her. I figure she doesn't need any sympathy from me."

"What a ... totally ... absolutely ... rotten thing to say!" Cass sputtered. "That's why you called, isn't it?" She went on without giving him a chance to respond. "You're not interested in how my mother's doing. You just want to get your digs in at Tabitha. Honestly, how low can a person sink?"

"That's not true," Micah defended himself. "I did call to check on your mom."

"I don't believe you." Cass wasn't in the mood to mince words. "You know, all this time, I hoped you and Tabitha could work things out. Now I'm not so sure I want that to happen. She deserves better than your crummy treatment. If Sam's going to treat her the way she should be treated then I'm all for them going out."

"Now wait just a minute," blazed Micah. "You have no right—"

"No, you wait," Cass interrupted, not caring if she upset him. "Who do you think you are, getting on your high horse about Sam being there when Tabitha needed him? From what I've heard, you're partying hard up there in Hono. Is your mind so twisted that you think it's okay for you to act like a wild man, but Tabitha making a new friend is wrong?"

"You don't know the first thing about what my life is like so quit acting like you do." Micah's voice shook with anger.

"Are you calling your own sister a liar?" Cass taunted.

Something tugged at her arm, and she shook it off. There was another tug, and she whirled around. Tabitha stood behind her with her hand held out.

"Maybe I'd better take it from here," she suggested, her tone amused.

About to give her the phone, Cass suddenly winced and quirked a smile. "Too late. He hung up." Rubbing her ear, she pressed the off button. "And hard too. Sorry."

Tabitha patted her head as she would a 2-year-old's. "That's okay. It sounded like you were doing a terrific job of sticking up for me."

"He made me mad." Cass replaced the receiver in its holder. "To be fair, I made him mad too."

Feigning unconcern, Tabitha asked casually, "What did he say that got you so riled up?"

"He made a snide remark about Sam being at the hospital yesterday." Cass impatiently shook her head. "Honestly! What does Kira do? Call in a daily report to him about where you go and with who?"

Tabitha's mouth tightened. "I'm beginning to wonder." She shrugged. "We can talk about it later. Right now, we have a couple of hungry parents waiting to be fed."

"For pity's sake, they're as bad as kids." Cass rolled her eyes at her sister.

"We heard that," Dad called from the living room.

"Good. You were supposed to," Cass shot back.

In no time, the girls had prepared four slices of toast and poured four glasses of lemonade. Tabitha fixed a tray for Mom, complete with a plate and a cloth napkin. Cass delivered Dad's toast to him on a paper towel.

"Hey!" he protested. "No fair. How come she gets the royal treatment?"

"Because—" snickering, Cass dropped a kiss on the top of his head before returning to the kitchen for her and Tabitha's snacks, "she's the one who was in the hospital. Plus, she's carrying our baby brother."

As Dad opened his mouth to speak, Mom held up a warning hand. "Don't say anything. She's hoping to trick you into telling her what the baby is."

Dad shot Cass an admiring look. "Wow, you're sneaky."

Returning to the room, she curtsied. "Thanks. I try."

"It's not a good thing to be told you're sneaky," drawled Mom.

"It's not?" Cass rearranged her features into a mock scowl. "In that case, I'm insulted."

In between bites of toast, Cass went into more detail about her conversation with Micah. Then, after fielding several more calls from friends who wanted to know how Mom was doing, Cass collected everyone's crumpled paper towels and piled them on Mom's tray. Setting the tray on the counter, she retrieved the pitcher of lemonade and refilled the glasses. Finally, she set the answering machine to pick up after one ring and returned to the couch where she sat down in the corner opposite Mom.

"There," she announced, pleased with herself. "Now we can talk without being interrupted."

"Sounds like you're planning on a serious discussion," Dad said, a slightly amused look on his face.

"I guess I am." Cass tucked her legs underneath her. "Like Tabitha said, we talked quite awhile last night." She smiled. "I don't think I should tell you how late we got to bed. Anyway, the first thing I want to do is apologize for my attitude the past few months. Since there's no other way to put it, I'll just admit outright that I've been a crab. No matter what was happening, I wasn't happy. First, I was thrilled about the baby. Then I started getting bugged about it, especially the way being pregnant was affecting you, Mom. I didn't want Sam as a boyfriend, then I did, now I don't again." She lifted her hands in a helpless gesture. "Do you see what I mean?"

After glancing at Dad, Mom nodded. "We discussed what we saw going on and the possible reasons for it."

"What did you come up with?" Cass asked stiffly. Although she was getting used to it, it still bothered her that Mom talked about her with Dad.

"Logan's leaving was difficult for you. You worked hard at being a good sport, but ..." Mom let the rest of the sentence trail off. "Then, along with coping with his departure, you've had to deal with the reality of the baby coming. Since this hasn't been an easy pregnancy, you've been forced to take on responsibilities you're not used to. And, let's face it, you've resented it."

Cass would have liked to argue, but she couldn't. Instead, she hung her head. "You're right."

Mom nudged her foot. "I didn't say that to make you feel guilty, but to let you know Dad and I understand what you've been going through. It's been a confusing time."

Cass' nod was vigorous. "That's exactly the word I'd use. Confusing. Half the time, I didn't know from one day to the next if I was mad, sad, happy, or scared."

"Mom and I talked about it during lunch, and we decided there's been an outbreak of discontentment around here," observed Dad.

Tabitha and Cass switched their attention from Mom to him. Tabitha's eyes narrowed, and she asked, "What do you mean by discontentment?"

"Basically, nothing's pleased you two for several months," Dad explained, then corrected himself, "No, that's not true. Some things have, but you've each been bothered about different aspects of life."

Cass exchanged an uneasy look with Tabitha. They'd been down this road before, and she wasn't sure she wanted to travel it again. "I have a feeling we're about to be blasted," she muttered, making a face. "Or at least I am. You usually come out smelling like a rose in these kinds of discussions."

"Not this time." The corners of Tabitha's mouth drooped. "I've been just as bad as you."

"I wouldn't say that," Dad teased. At Cass' glower, he laughed and raised his hands in self-defense. "Whoa there. I was just kidding." When she subsided, he went on, "There's enough blame to go around for all of us."

"You and Mom included?" Cass sounded skeptical.

"Believe it or not, yes," replied Mom.

Cass' frown revealed her puzzlement. "What do you mean?"

"As happy as we are about the baby, Dad and I have had our own adjusting to do." At Tabitha's murmur of surprise, Mom smiled. "Just because we're in our thirties doesn't mean things automatically come easy to us. We've fretted about starting over with a baby at our age, the financial burden of having another child with you two in college, whether we should have a second baby—and how soon—so this one doesn't grow up an only child like you girls did."

Tabitha's eyes rounded into saucers. "You haven't even had this baby, and you're already thinking about having another one?" She peered at Cass. "Did you know about this?"

"Nope. And it's a good thing too," she replied with heartfelt sincerity. "I have enough on my mind without worrying about another rug rat being added to the family."

Amused, Dad shook his head. "You have such a way with words. Anyway, to pick up where Mom left off, we haven't been having a peaceful, contented time of it ourselves."

Tabitha raised her hand as if she were in class. "I'd like to 'fess up too." Dad nodded for her to continue. "It's like I told Cass last night. The thought of the baby hasn't bothered me. Neither has having to help out more around the house. Not much, anyway," she added truthfully. "What's gotten on my nerves is the situation with Micah. I go back and forth in my head over what to do about him. When you throw Sam into the mix, it really gets crazy. Life used to be so simple. But, lately, all it's been is one, big hassle." She chuckled humorlessly. "I don't even want to get into the deal with Kira. We'd be here the rest of the night."

Cass' expression grew thoughtful. "It sounds like we've all been going through the same thing, but in different ways." She peered around at the others. "Does that make sense?"

"Perfect sense," Mom assured her. "What Dad and I concluded is that we've allowed ourselves to be controlled by circumstances, instead of relying on God. When that happens, peace and contentment go right out the window."

"Boy, you can say that again." Cass wearily leaned her head back against the cushions. "I thought last year was hard after we first moved here, but this has been a thousand times worse. I hated not being able to figure out how I feel about things. It was like ... like—" she waved toward the window facing the ocean, "being caught in a big wave. I kept getting tossed this way and that, and I couldn't find any footing."

"That's an excellent description of what we've all experienced." Dad smiled his approval.

"Yeah, but now that we know what's been happening and why," put in Tabitha, "what are we supposed to do about it?"

"Funny you should ask." Dad stood suddenly and headed down the hall to his and Mom's room. "I'll be right back."

"Uh-oh," Cass said in mock despair. "He didn't draw up charts and diagrams, did he?"

Tabitha groaned. "I wouldn't put it past him. The man does like to organize things, especially other people's lives." Changing the subject, she turned to Mom. "So, are you really thinking about having another baby?"

"We have you worried, don't we?" Mom uncurled her legs and stretched.

Tabitha frowned. "I think I have a right to know exactly how big this family is going to get."

Mom smiled. "Dad and I have decided to take it one baby at a time. We'll have this one and see how it goes. Of course," she added, "we might find we like it so much that we'll go on and have two or three more."

"Oh, brother." Cass covered her face with her hands. "Please tell me you're not serious."

"I'm not—" a mischievous twinkle appeared in Mom's eyes, "sure. Anything can happen."

"You're a real comedian, Mom," Cass said darkly. "I can hardly contain my laughter."

Fortunately, Dad chose that moment to reappear. He held his Bible, one finger keeping his place between the pages.

"I found the Scripture we were talking about earlier, Donna." He sat down and opened the Bible on his lap. "It's

Philippians 4, verses 11 and 12. '... For I have learned to be content whatever the circumstances. I know what it is to be in need, and I know what it is to have plenty. I have learned the secret of being content in any and every situation, whether well fed or hungry, whether living in plenty or in want.' "

After waiting for him to continue, Tabitha urged, "So, tell us. What's the secret?"

Once again, Dad read from the Bible, " 'I can do everything through Him who gives me strength.' "

Cass' head shot up, and she stared at Mom. "Hey! That's the verse you gave me last year to help me deal with the changes in my life."

"That's right. Now it seems we all need the two verses that come before it." Mom smiled ruefully. "We've become a discontented bunch. We forgot that true peace is found only in Jesus, who really has given us everything we need—most importantly, salvation through His death and resurrection. When we rely on our circumstances to make us content, we go up and down like yo-yos. But if we trust that God is in control, no matter how difficult or confusing things appear, we'll stay on an even keel."

A wry smile quirked Cass' lips. "And we won't be so crabby?"

"Our crabbiness quotient will drop dramatically," Mom solemnly assured her.

"We'll also quit worrying about what other people are thinking and just do what it seems God's leading us to do, huh?" Tabitha stopped rocking to lean forward and ask her question with quiet intensity.

"Yup." Dad winked at Mom. "Donna, I do believe they're catching on."

Drawing up her legs, Cass wrapped her arms around them. "But the problem is we still have the same old problems. How does being content solve what I'm supposed to do about Logan?"

"It all goes back to the trust factor." Dad regarded her with a steady gaze. "Do you believe God is in charge of your relationship with Logan? Be honest," he added when Cass began to reply. "Or do you believe you're actually controlling it?"

Lowering her forehead to her knees, she mulled over the question. "Sometimes I like to think I'm calling the shots," she finally responded. "But, deep down, I know God is."

"Then all your fretting is a waste of time," Dad pointed out. "It just leaves you worked up and—"

"Crabby," Cass finished for him and grinned. "Or, to use your word, discontented. I see what you're getting at. If I believe God's working everything out, I can relax. I can be content—" she smirked at Dad, "because, even if things don't turn out the way I want them to, I trust God knows best."

"As Romans 8: 28 says," Mom reminded her, " 'And we know that in all things God works for the good of those who love Him.' Not in a few things or even in most things. *In all things.* If that doesn't give you peace, I don't know what will."

"So I should quit worrying about what life is going to be like after the baby gets here? And what's going on with Logan and Shiloh? And whether or not I should date?" When Mom nodded, Cass made a show of mopping her brow. "Whew! That's a load off my mind."

"Now that you've solved Cass' problems, what about me?" Tabitha waved to get her parents' attention. "How can I find peace when things are so messed up with Kira and Micah?"

"Keep your eyes on Jesus. No, I mean it," Dad insisted when Tabitha scowled.

"That's easier said than done," she argued.

"Of course it is. It's often difficult to trust in Jesus. But remember, He *is* with us. He's promised us. He gives us so many promises in His word. And just last Sunday He was with us in holy communion. But why is this so important? Because the only way we really find contentment is in Jesus." Dad settled himself more comfortably into the recliner before continuing. "But contentment doesn't come all at once—it doesn't come naturally."

"Sometimes I get tired of waiting," Tabitha confessed in a soft voice.

"We all do, Sweetie," observed Mom. "That's why God gives us all the help we need, through His Spirit, through His Son, through His Word—even through fellow Christians supporting and encouraging one another. And I can tell you the rewards are worth it."

"I know." Tabitha smoothed imaginary wrinkles in her shorts. "Living by my own rules the past few months sure hasn't made me happy. Or content." Like Cass, she flashed Dad a smile.

"Then I suggest we take on learning to be content as a family project." Dad tapped the Bible that remained open in his lap. "I'll copy down these verses and post them on the refrigerator so we all can be reminded of where true contentment comes from. Plus, every few days, we'll talk about how well we're doing in the contentment department. How does that sound?"

"To tell you the truth," Cass spoke up when no one else did, "kind of corny." Dad's jaw dropped, and she laughed. "But I like it. It's so ... organized."

"I like it too," Tabitha chimed in, stifling a snicker. "I'm sure it'll help a lot. In fact, do you know what would make it even better? Charts and diagrams."

"You girls are making fun of me, aren't you?" Dad demanded. He glared at Mom. "Do you think my idea's corny?"

"Of course not, dear." She appeared shocked at the very suggestion she might. "It's sweet and so typically ... you."

Dad threw his hands up in disgust. "Women! I could live to be 100, and I'll never understand you people."

"If you get me a dish of ice cream, I'll tell you what the girls were laughing about," Mom bribed.

Dad tilted back his head and looked down his nose at her. "For your information, I can't be bought. But—" he erupted with a grin, "I can be rented. How much ice cream would you like?"

When he left to get it, the girls also stood up.

"I have a ton of homework I need to get to," Tabitha announced.

"Same here. Every teacher handed out assignments today." Cass turned to go then looked back. "Is supper taken care of or should I make something?"

Tears instantly pooled in Mom's eyes. "Thank you, Sweetie. Your offer means more than you'll ever know." She blinked away the tears and smiled. "Lucky for you, though, Mrs. Simpson called earlier to say she'd be bringing over a casserole and dessert."

"Is there anything else you need me to do before I lock myself in my room to start on my homework?" Cass offered.

Beside her, Tabitha snorted. "What's going on? Are you competing for the mother's pet award?"

Cass fought back a surge of annoyance. "I deserve that," she admitted to Mom and Tabitha's obvious surprise. "I haven't exactly been willing to help out around here. But I meant what I said last night. I'm turning over a new leaf, starting immediately."

"If you don't mind," Mom said, "would you ride over to the post office and see if we have mail? Ed Nishihara announced on the radio that a couple of tons came in on this morning's flight."

"My pleasure." Cass glanced at Tabitha. "Do you want to ride along?"

"Sure. Why not?" She disdainfully kicked the backpack lying at her feet. "The longer I can put off doing homework, the happier I'll be."

On their way out to the lanai, they passed Dad returning with Mom's ice cream.

"We're off to get the mail," Tabitha informed him.

"I heard." Dad raised the ice cream out of her reach when she attempted to scoop out a taste with her finger. "I appreciate you doing it. I'm pretty pooped from last night. It's hard to get any sleep sitting in a chair."

"You know what they say." Placing her hand over her heart, Cass recited, "Neither rain nor snow nor gloom of night shall keep the mailman from his—or, in this case, her—appointed rounds."

"Whatever." Tabitha rolled her eyes. "Like we have to worry about snow around here." Taking Cass by the arm, she pulled. "Let's go before you get really patriotic and start singing the Star-Spangled Banner."

That was all the incentive Cass needed. As Tabitha hustled her toward the door, she burst into the opening lines of the national anthem.

Chapter 31

Arriving at Macy's, Cass and Tabitha parked their bikes in a rack and bounded up the steps to the porch that led to the rows of post office boxes. Cass greeted several friends as they made their way to the family box. Leaning over, Tabitha peered inside.

"Yippee! It's stuffed full with letters," she reported.

Cass leaned against the porch railing while Tabitha spun out the combination to open the box. Gazing to her left, she watched the endless procession of waves and experienced a sense of peace she hadn't felt in a long time.

"Isn't it amazing to think how far the waves have to travel before they finally hit us?" she remarked.

"I guess." Tabitha opened the door and began pulling out mail. "I never really thought about it. How far do they travel?"

Cass shrugged. "Actually, I don't know. But it has to be thousands of miles."

"Gee, they must be tired then," Tabitha said sarcastically.

"I can see you're not the slightest bit interested in the subject," Cass said darkly.

She pushed off from the railing to look over Tabitha's shoulder as she started through the envelopes. Her heart lurched when she saw there was a letter from Logan. Tabitha handed it to her.

"Here. I believe you might like this." She riffled through two more letters. "Ooh. Here's another one." Coming to the end of the stack, she drawled, "Gee, nothing from Micah. Why am I not surprised? But there's a notice we have a package. Do you want to stay here and read your letters while I go inside and pick it up?"

"Sure."

Cass didn't really know if she wanted to open Logan's letters, but she obediently walked to one of the benches lining the porch. Sinking down, she studied the postmarks on the envelopes to see which one had been written first. Both letters had been sent before their disastrous conversation. When Tabitha returned a few minutes later, Cass was sitting with the letters still unopened in her lap. She sat down next to her.

"Hey—" she bumped her shoulder against Cass', "what gives? How come you haven't ripped into those letters like you usually do?"

"I decided not to read them here." Cass smoothed her hand over the envelopes, her expression wistful. "It's too public. Besides, I need to make sure I have this contentment thing down pat before I open them. I'm serious about working on that, and I don't want to blow it so soon after the talk with Mom and Dad."

"Are you afraid he might have written something to upset you?" Tabitha set the box she'd retrieved beside her on the bench and piled the mail on top of it.

Cass nodded. "Lately, I've managed to find something in every letter to be mad about," she confessed. "No matter what he wrote, I wasn't satisfied. Either he didn't tell me enough times that he missed me. Or he said it too much, and I felt guilty because I was having a good time with Sam." She hung her head. "I could go on and on. But you get the picture.

Basically I'm slime, and I don't deserve to live."

"Like that's a news flash," Tabitha joked.

Cass' head jerked up and around so she could glare at her. "I'm being serious."

Tabitha assumed her most innocent expression. "So am I."

The corners of Cass' mouth started to twitch. "You're just trying to make me laugh," she accused.

"Is it working?" Tabitha bounced on the bench like a hyperactive 5-year-old. "Is it? Huh? Huh?"

"Knock it off," growled Cass. "You're embarrassing me."

"Nope." Tabitha continued to bounce. "Not until you tell me if it's working."

"Okay, okay. It's working." Cass bared her teeth in an ear-to-ear grin. "See?"

Tabitha settled down. "Good. My work here is done." Standing, she picked up the box and letters. "Let's go."

Shaking her head, Cass followed her off the porch. "I've said it before, but I really mean it this time. You're spending way— I mean, way!—too much time with Sam. His weird sense of humor is rubbing off on you."

"Thank you. That's the nicest thing you've ever said to me." Tabitha wheeled her bike out of the rack and dumped her load into the basket. "Do you want to go straight home or would you like to stop off someplace to read your letters?"

"Let's go home," Cass decided. "Then I think I'll go out back and sit on the rocks to read them."

"Sounds like a plan." Tabitha climbed on her bike and turned it toward home.

After delivering the mail, and finding out the box contained a quilt Mamaw had sewn for the baby, Cass took her letters outside. The tide was out so she walked along the shore until she discovered a comfortable-looking rock to lean against. With the sun warming her head and shoulders, she picked up the first letter.

"Jesus," she murmured, "please help me stay peaceful, whatever this says. I want to rely on You for my contentment, not the circumstances surrounding me."

Having prayed, she slid her thumb under the envelope's flap and opened it. A single sheet of paper was all it contained. Unfolding it, she began to read.

Dear Red (just kidding—I know that's what Sam calls you),

It's almost lights-out so I don't have much time. Just wanted you to know I'm thinking about you. When I have time to think, that is. The pace here is unbelievable. I hit the floor running every morning and don't stop until I crawl into bed at night. Then, 45 minutes later, I get up and it starts all over again. Ha-ha, just kidding again. I actually get an hour-and-a-half of sleep every night. Anyway, whenever I get a free moment, I think about you. Everyone's sick of me talking about you. Shiloh told me this morning if I said your name one more time, she was going to scream. I did. She didn't. Talk about empty threats. I sure miss you. I hope to talk to you soon. It helps a lot to hear your voice. Well, they're blowing taps so I'd better go. Don't ever forget how much I care. Write soon.

Logan

Coming to the end, Cass refolded the letter and slid it back into the envelope. *Nice note,* she thought. *Unfortunately, he had to ruin it by tossing in Shiloh's name.*

She was immediately stabbed by guilt. *Oops, there I go again, finding fault instead of being grateful that he wrote.* Shaking her head, she picked up the second envelope. *Learning to be content is going to be even harder than I thought.*

Although the second letter was longer, it didn't contain much more news. What it did contain, to Cass' irritation, was four—she recounted to make sure she had it right—references to Shiloh. After she was finished reading, she had to restrain herself from ripping the letter to shreds and scattering the pieces to the breeze. Drawing up her legs, she draped her wrists over her knees and stared moodily at the water.

"Everything okay?"

Tabitha's voice made Cass jump. She glanced at her watch. Almost 15 minutes had passed since she finished reading Logan's letters.

Cass shrugged as Tabitha lowered herself next to her in the sand. "Everything's peachy keen." Cass nonchalantly flicked her fingers at the letters in her lap. "You can read them if you'd like."

Tabitha frowned. "I don't want to read your mail. It's private."

"Not really." Cass dismissed the comment with a derisive snort. "Half of what Logan wrote was about Shiloh. How private is that?"

"Half?" Tabitha's eyebrows formed two skeptical arches. "Are you sure you're not exaggerating just a tad?"

Cass scooped up a handful of sand and let the grains trickle out between her fingers. "Okay, maybe it's not half." Her expression became stubborn. "But it's close."

"You know, it's too bad Logan's letters came today," Tabitha remarked.

"Why?" Cass shot her a sidelong glance.

"You were just starting to work on being content then they had to go and ruin it." Tabitha sorrowfully shook her head.

Cass' eyes narrowed with suspicion. "I know you're getting at something. Why don't you quit beating around the bush and spit it out?"

Instead of taking offense, Tabitha grinned. "Who'd have believed a year ago that we'd get to where we know each other so well? I thought I was being sly, but you saw right through me." At Cass' impatient sigh, she went on, "Anyway, my point is our peace is supposed to come from God. You're letting what Logan wrote upset you, which means you're depending on your relationship with him to make you happy. Or, in this case, unhappy."

"Gee, Mom, do you have any more words of wisdom for me?" Cass drawled, her face tight with annoyance.

"Nope, that should do it." Standing, Tabitha brushed the sand off the seat of her shorts. "I'm going back inside now to start my homework."

"Wait," Cass ordered before she could take two steps. Pivoting on her bottom, she peeered up at Tabitha. "Are you telling me you have being content down pat? After one discussion on the subject?" She sounded as doubtful as she looked.

"Of course not. I won't find out how much of what the folks said stuck until I'm put to the test." Tabitha moved back a few steps into the meager shade of a palm tree. "I don't know how I would have reacted if I'd heard from Micah today. I learned something from watching you, though. No matter how good your intentions were, it was really easy to take your eyes off God and focus on your circumstances. When you did that, you might as well have kissed peace and contentment goodbye."

"Well, excuse me for not reacting perfectly," Cass huffed.

"I'm not criticizing you," Tabitha hastened to assure her. "I'm sure I wouldn't have done any better. I hope, when it's my turn to deal with Micah, you'll remind me, the way I tried to with you, that staying focused on the Lord is the only way to go."

Lowering her gaze, Cass studied the envelopes in her lap for several seconds. When she raised her head, she felt the tension drain from her face. "You're right. I let my old habits get the best of me. I'm tired of going up and down all the time like I'm riding an emotional roller coaster. I'm ready to make some changes."

"Me too." Tabitha slid her hands into her pockets and shrugged. "The question is, how do we make them?"

Cass quirked a wry smile. "Obviously it's going to take time. And we definitely can't do it on our own. The Holy Spirit will help us to rely each day on God's promises to forgive us and renew us. You know—put into practice what Pastor Thompson is always talking about—daily repentence and renewal. And of course we're going to need to keep checking with one another to see how we're doing."

Tilting her head to the side, Tabitha grew thoughtful. "And we'll have to be honest. You know, tell one another what's really going on. No fudging."

"Yup." Cass squinted up at her. "Does that scare you?"

Tabitha mulled over the question before replying, "Nope. You're my sister. If I can't be honest with you, who can I be honest with?"

Cass scrambled to her feet and joined Tabitha in the palm's shade. "That means a lot, especially since I feel like I can tell you anything too."

Tabitha emitted a low whistle. "Wow. A year ago, who'd have thought we'd ever get to the point where we'd trust each other with our deepest, darkest secrets?"

"God knew all along we'd wind up like this." Cass linked arms with Tabitha, and they started toward the house. "That's why He brought us together." She patted her back pocket where she'd placed Logan's letters. "So you could find me and give me a much-needed pep talk."

"God sure is smart."

"Amen to that," Cass fervently agreed. "And the best part is He's just getting started with us."

Tabitha chuckled. "Cool. I can't wait to see what else He has up His sleeve. I mean, He's done an excellent job so far."

CHAPTER 32

"So how's my baby sister doing this morning?" Cass chirped, coming through the kitchen on her way to school.

Busy at the stove fixing scrambled eggs for Dad, Mom glanced over her shoulder and grinned. "Exactly how stupid do you think I am?"

"Apparently not stupid enough to fall for my ploy." Since Tabitha was nowhere to be seen, Cass stopped and propped a hip against the counter. "You're not going to tell us what the baby is, are you?"

Mom shook her head. "Dad and I decided it would be more fun for you girls to wait for the birth."

"But that's a whole three months away," whined Cass. Her voice dropped to a conspiratorial whisper. "How about you tell me? I promise I won't breathe a word to Tabitha."

With a furtive look around to make sure they were alone, Mom leaned over and pressed her lips to Cass' ear. "Nope." Returning to her cooking, she added, "Coincidentally, Tabitha asked me the same thing."

Cass bristled with indignation. "She wanted you to tell her what the baby is, and not tell me? The nerve of her."

"Hello?" Mom waved to get her attention. "Isn't that what you wanted?"

"Yes, but—" Cass sputtered. "It's different. You're my mother. I have a right to know what you're expecting."

"I'm as much Tabitha's mother as I am yours," Mom reminded her. "If I tell one of you, I'm obligated to tell the other."

"I know." Instead of taking offense, Cass shrugged. "Oh, well. It was worth a try." Her eyes narrowed suspiciously. "You don't think she'll talk Dad into telling her what we're having, do you?"

Mom flashed her a broad smile. "I've warned your Dad not to be taken in by either of you. He's much more susceptible to your charms than I am. I'm afraid you girls have him wrapped around your little fingers." She abruptly grew serious and placed a hand on Cass' arm. "I like what you said just now about what we're having. It tells me your attitude toward the baby is changing."

Cass accepted her remark with a shyly bowed head. "Last night I started working again on the baby's afghan. Of course—" a sly expression stole across her face, "I could start over, using pink or blue yarn, if I knew which color would be appropriate."

"That's one of the things I admire about you." Turning off the burner under the frying pan, Mom moved to the cupboard for a plate. "Your never-say-die attitude. You don't give up without a fight."

"I'm going to weasel the baby's gender out of you before December if it's the last thing I do," Cass vowed. She smirked at Dad as he entered the room. "If not you, then the weak link here."

After dropping a kiss on top of Mom's head, he turned to Cass with a mock scowl. "I believe I've just been insulted, but I have no idea why."

Handing him his plate, Mom gave him a push toward the table. "I'll tell you after the girls leave. Sit down before your eggs get cold."

Tabitha appeared a few seconds later, and she and Cass left out the back door to retrieve their bikes. They pedaled to school under a gloomy sky.

"It looks like the rainy season may arrive early this year," observed Cass.

"That's fine with me." Tabitha's mouth was set in a thin, discontented line. "It suits my mood perfectly."

"What's going on now?" Cass shot her a curious look.

"Same old, same old. No," Tabitha corrected herself, "actually, this is different. Very different," she added for emphasis. "I stayed up until 1:00 this morning writing Micah a letter and I didn't hold anything back. I let him have it with both barrels. How disappointed I am with his partying and his attitude toward me. Everything. I figure we're talking make or break time with this letter. Whether or not we have a future will depend on how—or even, if— he responds. I gave it to Dad to mail on his way to work because I didn't want to run the risk of changing my mind and not sending it."

"Good for you," approved Cass. "It's about time you laid it on the line with Micah. Is there any particular way you'd like me to pray about his answer?"

Tabitha thought a moment before shaking her head. "Not really. I just want him to write back. It would be awful not to hear anything, like my letter disappeared into a black hole or something."

"Then that's what I'll pray for." Cass swerved to avoid a sandpiper in the road. "Dumb birds. They just dare you to run over them. I doubt they'd move even if a tractor-trailer was headed straight for them."

"They do have an attitude," Tabitha agreed. "Anyway, now that I finally got up the courage to come clean with Micah, why don't you do the same with Logan?"

"What do you mean?" Cass' tone was wary. She had the sneaking suspicion she was about to hear something she wouldn't like. "I was straight with him the last time we talked. I told him exactly how I felt about him and Shiloh."

"Be honest now. That's not what's really at the heart of the matter, is it?" Tabitha's gaze homed in on Cass like a laser.

She squirmed under its intensity. "Since you obviously have something specific in mind, why don't you stop beating around the bush and tell me what you think is going on? So I can tell you how wrong you are," she added under her breath.

"I heard that," Tabitha blithely informed her. Before Cass could reply, she continued, "You know as well as I do that the problem you're having with Logan is, deep down, you're convinced your relationship won't last. It didn't with Jan and your other friends back in Tennessee, so you assume the same thing's going to happen with Logan. In your mind, long-distance relationships don't work."

"Not just in my mind," Cass pointed out coolly, hating that Tabitha had hit the nail on the head. "In my experience. Yours too. Look at what's happened to you and Micah."

"We're not talking about Micah and me. For the record, though," Tabitha couldn't resist adding, "our situation is way different from yours and Logan's. We were having problems long before he left. But we put up a good front and pretended everything was fine."

"You're right," Cass grudgingly conceded. "But that doesn't mean I've been harboring a secret fear Logan's like Janette, and he's going to dump me the first chance he gets."

"Oh, no?" Tabitha's expression was as skeptical as her tone. "You've dropped some pretty broad hints that's precisely how you feel."

Cass' brows drew together in a thunderous glower. "You're reading too much into a few innocent remarks."

"I don't think so," Tabitha lilted in a singsong voice. "But now is not the time to go into it." She smiled in the direction of Sam, who just came into view ahead of them. "Just think about what I said."

"Who died and left you mother?" grumbled Cass.

Tabitha fixed her with a stern stare. "I'm your sister. In some ways, that gives me even more say in your life. I know stuff Mom doesn't."

Cass' defiance melted under her gaze. "Whatever. Go on and catch up with Sam. I know that's what you want."

"Gee," drawled Tabitha, "I can't keep anything from you. You read me like an open book."

"Go." Cass snapped her fingers then pointed. "I don't feel like putting up with your sarcasm one second longer."

Laughing, Tabitha went. Cass realized she didn't experience an inkling of jealousy as she watched her sister pull alongside Sam.

Maybe this contentment thing really works, she mused. *Now if only I can figure out how to apply it to Logan and me.*

After school, Tabitha announced that she and Sam would be stopping by Surfway on their way home so he could pick up a few things for his mother. Since Cass didn't feel like accompanying them, she headed straight home, promising Rianne she'd call her about getting together later. Arriving home, she was pleased to find Mom rolling out a piecrust on the counter.

"Hey." Cass sniffed appreciatively. "You've been busy. Is that spaghetti sauce I smell?"

"Yup." Mom gave the crust a final swipe before setting aside the rolling pin. "And we're having cherry pie for dessert."

"Are we celebrating something?" Cass moved to the cookie jar and helped herself to a couple of oatmeal cookies.

"Two things. I have to wait to share one of them until Tabitha and Dad are here." Mom reached for the pie pan and began positioning the crust into it. "The other one is for you. Logan called a short while ago. He said he'd call back at 3:00." She eyed the clock. "That's 10 minutes from now."

"I can tell time," Cass snapped, then instantly regretted it. "Sorry. I'm a little on edge. What did he say? How did he sound?"

"He sounded good. Same as ever." Having fitted the crust into the pan, Mom started trimming the edges. "After Rianne talked to Randy about my stay in the hospital, Randy called Logan to tell him. First off, Logan wanted me to know he's been praying for me, then he wanted to talk to you."

"And he didn't sound mad or upset?" Cass checked again.

"Not in the slightest. If anything, he seemed quite eager to talk to you." Brushing a hand on her apron, Mom reached out and patted Cass' cheek. "Don't work yourself up into a dither. He'll be calling any time now, and you'll hear for yourself how he sounds."

"Okay." Cass took a deep breath that was meant to calm her jangling nerves, but which did nothing of the sort. "I'll wait here by the phone."

She took up position next to the wall and stared at the receiver, willing it to ring. Mom turned back to her baking, but not before Cass saw the smile curving her lips.

The moment the phone rang, Cass pounced. Snatching it up in mid-ring, she croaked, "Hello?"

"Hello, yourself," came Logan's greeting. "Are you okay? You sound kind of hoarse."

"I'm fine," Cass assured him. "How are you?"

Way to make conversation. She mentally kicked herself. *That'll keep him coming back for more.*

"Not bad," Logan replied. "But I sure could be a whole lot better."

"How?" Cass asked before she could stop herself. It belatedly occurred to her that she might not want to hear his answer.

"By knowing things are okay between us."

"Oh." Cass' spirits soared. "Well, what do you want to know?"

"For starters, why don't you trust me?" Logan's tone was testy. "Other than one crummy dance with Shiloh, what have I done that's so bad?"

Recalling Tabitha's comments that morning, Cass decided to be truthful. "It's not you as much as it is me," she confessed, moving out onto the porch. "Ever since you left, I've been waiting for the letter or the phone call telling me to take a hike."

"But why?" Logan persisted.

"I figured it would be like it was with Janette," Cass explained in a rush, needing to get everything said before she lost her nerve. "We'd go along for awhile, acting like nothing had changed. Then, little by little, we'd stop calling and writing as much. When we did talk, it'd be about nothing important until one day we'd wake up and realize a couple of weeks had passed without any communication. It was hard enough when it happened with Jan. I couldn't face it happening with you."

"So you decided to take matters into your own hands and break up with me before I could break up with you," Logan concluded.

"No— I ..." Cass stammered before admitting, "Yes." Even though he couldn't see her, she hung her head.

"You should know me well enough by now to know I'd never do anything so underhanded," Logan gently chided. "Give me some credit for being a decent human being, will you? Do you really think I wouldn't be honest with you about Shiloh if I considered her a potential girlfriend?"

"Since you put it that way, no." Cass ran her fingers through her hair, mussing her ponytail. "All I can say in my defense is that I wasn't thinking clearly. Life's been weird since you left. Dad talked to us yesterday about how discontented we've all been lately. Then he gave us a Scripture verse about being content, no matter what the circumstances. It's going to take awhile to sink in, but I'll keep plugging away until I get it right."

Logan's laugh was affectionate. "I don't doubt that for one second. You're nothing if not persistent. Once you set your mind to something, you're like a dog with a bone."

"Excuse me?" Cass pretended to huff. "No girl likes to be compared to a dog. What are they teaching you at that place?"

"Not to put my foot in my mouth, that's for sure. That's something I learned all on my own." Logan paused then said softly, "Look, you and I have something special, and I'm not about to throw it away."

"I'm not either." Cass blinked away the tears that pooled in her eyes. "The problem is I got so mixed-up about stuff that I wasn't thinking straight. Mom going into the hospital and Dad talking to us really helped put everything back into perspective, including our relationship."

"I'm glad. I don't know what I'd do if I couldn't pick up the phone and talk to you." Logan's laugh held very little humor. "I'd probably go nuts."

"You're sure talking to Shiloh wouldn't help?" Cass felt secure enough to tease.

"Now that you mention it, it would," Logan shot back. "Thanks. I'll keep her in mind."

"No way, buddy." Cass refused to let him have the last word. "I'm the only one you're allowed to think about."

"Man, are you demanding," Logan pretended to gripe. Serious again, he asked, "So we're okay now?"

"We're better than okay. We're terrific," Cass assured

him. "Thanks for talking and for listening."

"We'll be fine as long as we keep communicating. It's when we stop talking that we run into problems." Logan carried on a muffled conversation with someone on his end of the line then came back on the phone. "I hate to cut this short, but a guy from my company wants to make a call. Let me pray first, though." Lowering his voice, he murmured, "Father, thank You for allowing Cass and me to talk. Take care of us while we're apart, and let everything about our relationship be pleasing to You. In Jesus' name, amen."

"Amen," echoed Cass. "I'll sit down tonight and write you a nice, long letter."

"I'll look forward to getting it. Bye, Sweetie."

"Bye."

Pressing the off button, Cass set the receiver down on the porch swing where she'd been sitting and stood up. She moved to the window and gazed at the horizon where a line of dark, forbidding clouds inched ever closer.

It'll be raining by tonight, she predicted, then, breaking out into a huge grin, hugged herself. *But who cares? It may be gloomy outside, but inside I'm all sunshiny. Logan and I are okay.*

Her thoughts were interrupted by the opening of the porch door. Swinging around, she saw Tabitha and Sam entering. To her sister's surprise, Cass dashed over to her and grabbed her hands.

"Dance with me," she invited.

Shooting Sam an embarrassed glance, Tabitha tried to free her hands, but Cass held fast.

"What's gotten into you?" Tabitha hissed.

"Contentment. Peace. Joy." Cass executed a jig, despite Tabitha's refusal to participate. "I just got off the phone with Logan."

"Ah." Understanding dawned, and Tabitha nodded sagely. Over her shoulder, she informed Sam, "She just talked to Logan."

"So I heard." Grinning, he cocked his head to the side. "Is this how you react when I call?"

"Sort of." Tabitha's eyes sparkled with mischief. "If you leave out the dancing and giggling, it's exactly the same."

Sam clutched his heart and staggered back a step. "Man, you really know how to hurt a guy."

Feigning irritation, Cass waved to get their attention. "Hey! We were talking about Logan and me. We can discuss y'all later."

"She has a point," Tabitha conceded to Sam. Squeezing Cass' hands, she demanded, "All right, give. What did you and Logan talk about that has you so fired-up?"

"He told me he doesn't—" Cass paused for dramatic effect, "like Shiloh. Even better, he doesn't plan to. He says he doesn't want to give up what we have."

Squealing, Tabitha seized Cass and began jumping up and down with her. Sam just stared at them and laughed.

With a last squeeze, Tabitha released Cass' hands. "Didn't I tell you everything would work out?"

"Yes, but you're hardly ever right," Cass teased. "It was hard to put any faith in what you had to say." Laughing, she skipped out of reach when Tabitha playfully swatted at her.

Tabitha turned to Sam. "Can you stay for awhile?"

"You bet. Since we already dropped off the stuff for my mother, I don't have to hurry home."

As it turned out, he stayed until Dad arrived home from work. Although the trio gathered around the dining room table on the pretext of studying for an economics test, they did more chatting and laughing than actual work. The hours passed quickly, so Cass was surprised when Dad walked into the kitchen. Sam immediately stood up.

"Hi, Mr. Spencer. Is it quitting time already?"

Dad gave him a friendly wave. "It better be or I'm in big

trouble."

"With who?" Cass challenged. "You're the boss. You can do whatever you want."

Mom and Dad exchanged amused smiles before Dad shook his head. "Boy, do you have a lot to learn. There's always someone to answer to."

Cass nudged Tabitha and made a face. "Tell us about it. We're the experts on having to answer to people."

"Yeah, like you have it rough around here," Mom jeered good-naturedly. "You don't know the first thing about having demanding parents."

Holding up his hands, Sam backed away from the table. "As much as I'm enjoying listening to your family fight, I should get going." He checked an imaginary wristwatch. "It's about time for my family to start our nightly battle, and I really hate to miss it."

After he left, Dad flashed Tabitha an approving smile. "I like that boy. He has a great sense of humor."

"He'd have to, to be interested in Tabs," Cass quipped.

"Stop. You're killing me." Tabitha slapped her knee in feigned merriment before turning her attention back to Dad. "Do you like Sam more than Micah?"

He frowned. "I don't like comparing people. Sam and Micah are very different, and I like both of them for different reasons."

"Spoken like a true diplomat," Mom murmured as she passed him to slide a loaf of garlic bread into the oven. "Girls, clear your things off the table and set it. Honey, wash up. We're eating in five minutes."

After they sat down, they joined hands for prayer. "Father," Dad prayed, "we thank You for the food You have provided for our physical nourishment and for the love we share that nourishes our spirits. In Jesus' name, amen."

When everyone's plates were filled, Mom tapped her

glass with her spoon. "As I told Cass earlier, this is a celebration supper," she announced when three pairs of eyes swung toward her. "My mother called this afternoon to let us know Linda had the baby today."

"And?" Cass prompted when she stopped.

Her eyes shining, Mom replied, "It's a girl. Rebecca Louise. She's named for Linda's mother and Mamaw. She's eight pounds, three ounces, and 20 inches."

Tabitha turned to Cass and high-fived her. "All right! A girl cousin! Remember when you used to play with baby dolls? It'll be like having one again. We can dress her up and take her out to show her off."

Cass firmly snuffed out the resentment that flared at Tabitha claiming Rebecca as a cousin. "I can't wait to see her. I wish we were going to Tennessee for Christmas." As soon as the words were out of her mouth, she regretted them. She turned a stricken face to Mom. "I didn't mean that the way it sounded. Honest. What I meant—"

"It's okay," Mom assured her. "I know what you meant because I feel the same way. I'd like nothing better than to spend time with my niece. Babies have a habit of growing much too fast."

Cass' smile was grateful. "That's what I was trying to say."

"Mom and I have been discussing the possibility of flying home during your winter break." Dad laughed as Cass and Tabitha's heads immediately swiveled in his direction. "We can show off our baby and visit colleges in the area since that decision is looming on the horizon."

"You mean it?" Tabitha bounced with excitement. "That'd be great. If money's a problem, you don't have to buy us Christmas presents. Anything, as long as we get to go home."

"Hey, wait a minute," Cass protested. "Speak for yourself. I'm not giving up Christmas just to see Tennessee. And since when do you consider Tennessee home? I thought Kwaj was heaven on earth as far as you were concerned."

"It is." Shrugging, Tabitha grinned. "But I've discovered I can like two places at one time, and I've come to really like Tennessee." She tilted her head to the side. "You honestly wouldn't give up Christmas in order to fly back?"

Put on the spot, Cass nibbled at her thumbnail. "I guess I would," she allowed. "You surprised me, that's all."

"I'm full of surprises." Tabitha twirled her fork in the spaghetti. "Sometimes I don't even know what I'm going to do next."

"I bet I know what you're going to do." Cass gave her a saucy wink.

"Oh, yeah? What?" Tabitha popped the spaghetti in her mouth and waited.

"Start an all-out campaign to get Sam to take you to the fall formal."

Tabitha choked and reached for her glass of milk. Cass beamed a triumphant smile at their parents.

"Am I wrong?" she purred when Tabitha finally caught her breath.

"Absolutely, 100 percent wrong." Tabitha returned Cass' smug look with one equally as smug. "There won't be any campaign because Sam's already hinted around about taking me."

Cass was outraged. "Sam asked you to the dance, and you didn't tell me? I'm your sister, for pity's sake! We're supposed to share these kinds of things. It's in the sister handbook."

"He hasn't come out and asked me in so many words," Tabitha defended herself. "I said he's been hinting around."

"That's as good as an invite in my book." Cass jostled Tabitha's arm. "Come on, girl. Get with the program. We need to look at patterns and find out who's going to Hono

246

so they can shop for dress material."

The eyes Tabitha raised to Cass held a hint of uncertainty. "It won't bother you if I go to the formal and you don't?"

Cass thought about dismissing her question with a breezy wave, then decided she deserved an honest answer. "As it gets closer, it'll probably start to bug me. But right now it doesn't. Besides"—she made a comical face—"you never know who might crawl out from under a rock to ask me, so there's still hope."

"It wouldn't be as much fun without you," Tabitha said.

"Of course it wouldn't." Cass pretended to preen then made a scale out of her hands. "Think about it, though. You have two choices. Stay home with me." One hand went up several inches. "Go to the dance with Sam." She lowered the other hand. "Stay home. Go to dance." She seesawed her hands a few times then dropped one to the table. "Looks like going to the dance wins."

Laughing, Tabitha clasped her hand and squeezed. "You're a good sister."

Cass put a finger to her lips. "I know, but don't let it get out. I do have a reputation to maintain."

"What reputation is that?" Dad asked suspiciously.

"Duh," Cass teased. "As Kwaj's biggest grouch, of course."

"I'm so proud." Mom pretended to wipe her eyes with her napkin. "I've always wanted you to excel at something. This is a happy day for me."

After sharing a laugh, the family settled down to eating. Cass told Dad about Logan's call, and they discussed the possibility of making a quick side trip to New York if the Tennessee trip materialized.

Climbing into bed that night, Cass' heart fluttered at the thought of seeing Logan in four months. *Now that*, she decided, *would be worth giving up Christmas*.

CHAPTER 33

Over the weekend, Sam mustered the courage to ask Tabitha to the dance. She came home from their bowling date walking on air. Waltzing into Cass' room without knocking, she flung herself on the bed. Cass turned from the desk where she was writing a letter to Logan.

"I take it you have something to tell me?"

Rolling onto her stomach, Tabitha propped her chin on her palms and grinned. "Uh-huh."

Cass heaved a sigh of mock irritation. "You want me to guess what it is." When Tabitha nodded, she made a face. "Gee, let me think. What could it possibly be? By any chance, did Sam invite you to the formal?"

"Ding-ding-ding! Right answer!" Tabitha imitated an excited game show host. Flipping over, she sat up and hugged her knees. "You should have been there. He was so sweet when he asked me."

Cass regarded her with a wry gaze. "I doubt he'd have said anything if I were there." Dropping the pose, she leaned forward in her seat. "So what did he do that was so sweet?"

Tabitha's expression grew dreamy. "I always think of Sam as being so confident. But when he began to ask me, he got all tongue-tied and he kept wiping his hands on his shorts like they were sweaty. He even shuffled his feet a couple of times."

"How cute." The image of the joking, self-assured Sam Steele reduced to a little boy made Cass smile. "How long did it take him to finally pop the question?"

"At least five minutes." Tabitha laughed at the memory. "He looked so pathetic that I just about decided to put him out of his misery and tell him I knew what he wanted to ask me. Then he just blurted it out."

"What were his exact words?" Getting up from the chair, Cass moved to the bed to sit next to Tabitha.

"He said—" Tabitha took a deep breath and started again, "He said, 'Tabitha, would you do me the great honor of allowing me to escort you to the fall formal?' " Laying her forehead on her knees, she whispered, "He never calls me Tabitha. It really made the invitation special."

"I'll say." Cass swallowed the lump that had formed in her throat. "Wow. He actually used words like *great honor* and *escort?*"

"Yup." Tabitha lifted her face to reply.

"Cool." Cass nodded her approval. "What was his reaction when you told him yes?"

"This is where it gets even better." Tabitha shivered at the memory. "We were standing out back on the rocks. He took my hand and kissed it, like they do in the old movies. And he said, 'I don't know what a beautiful girl like you sees in a lunkhead like me. But when I go home, I'm going to get down on my knees and thank God for making my dream come true.' "

Pressing her hands to her heart, Cass breathed, "That's so romantic. What a classy guy. Do you think he'd be willing to write to Logan and give him some lessons?"

"From what you've told me, Logan does just fine on his own." Tabitha scooted back several inches until she leaned against the wall. "Sam made me feel like a princess tonight, like I was doing him a favor instead of the other way around. It was nice."

"That's the way it should be," Cass declared stoutly. "If anyone deserves to be treated like a princess, it's you. I mean, look at you." Shifting to her knees, she leaned over and fluffed Tabitha's hair. "You have golden curls, big, blue eyes, and perfect skin like princesses are supposed to have."

Tabitha shook her head. "I'm not talking about the outside. That's not important. It's the inside that counts. Sam makes me feel special and important on the inside."

"In that case, my dear princess—" Cass grinned, "I'd say he's your knight in shining armor."

"He is, isn't he?" There was a note of soft wonder in Tabitha's voice. "I'm going to have to tell him." She raised worried eyes to Cass. "If you don't think it'd be too corny."

"I've discovered boys don't mind a little corn every now and then, especially if it feeds their egos." Cass sat back on her heels. "Are you going to tell Kira about going with Sam or wait for her to find out through the grapevine?"

The corners of Tabitha's mouth drooped. "I prefer to take the chicken's way out and let her hear about it, but I owe her more than that." She glanced at the clock. "Unfortunately, it's not too late to call her so I guess I should do it now and get it over with."

"I'll be praying for you." Cass delivered an encouraging pat to Tabitha's back as she slid past her off the bed. "I hope she doesn't take it too hard."

"You and me both, pal," Tabitha muttered.

Dialing Kira's number, she implored silently, *Please don't let her be home. I'm not sure I'm ready to face her. Please let her be out with those other girls.*

Kira answered on the first ring. "Hello?"

So much for wishful thinking, Tabitha mused. Aloud, she chirped nervously, "What were you doing? Sitting on the phone?"

"Just about," Kira replied. "I can't believe I'm home on

a Saturday night. I've been waiting for somebody—any-body—to call."

"Well, here I am. The answer to your prayers." Tabitha tinkled the brittle laugh she used when she was tense.

"Are you stuck home too?" A hint of warmth crept into Kira's tone.

"I went out earlier. With ... uh ... with ... Sam," Tabitha forced herself to respond.

"I see." The frost returned to Kira's voice. "Is that why you called? To tell me you and Sam had a date?"

"Sort of. I ... uh ... " Tabitha paced the length of the porch and back again. "I decided it would be best if I told you myself that he ... he ... asked me to the fall formal ... and I accepted," she finished in a rush. The silence that greeted her announcement went on so long she concluded Kira had hung up. "Hello? Kira?"

"I'm here."

Her terse reply told Tabitha she was furious.

"I guess you're upset, huh?" she ventured.

Instead of the tirade Tabitha expected, Kira answered with a heavy sigh. "I don't know what I'm feeling anymore. Everything's been such a mess for so long that I'm utterly and completely confused."

"I know what you mean," Tabitha sympathized.

"You weren't too confused to say yes to Sam," Kira shot back.

"True," Tabitha conceded without anger. "Believe it or not, it was one of the easiest decisions I've had to make lately."

"I don't get it." Kira sounded thoroughly bewildered. "What do you see in him? He's so ... ordinary."

"That's what I like best about him. Plus," Tabitha went on, her voice softening, "it's not just what I see in him. It's what he sees in me. Like I told Cass when we talked before, he makes me feel like a princess."

Kira groaned. "It's over between you and Micah, isn't it?"

"I think so," admitted Tabitha. "I wrote him a letter, and a lot depends on how he responds. But I'm not holding my breath that it'll make a difference. I think we've drifted too far apart."

"You sound so calm," Kira complained. "Doesn't breaking up bother you at all?"

"I've done my share of crying, believe me." Tabitha stopped at the window and gazed at the phosphorescence glittering on the water. For some strange reason, the sight brought tears to her eyes. "Even if I lose Micah as a boyfriend, I don't want to lose him as a friend." She paused then added quietly, "I don't want to lose you, either."

"I almost wish you and Micah had never started dating because it makes things so difficult now." Kira hesitated. "I don't know whose side to be on. If this were any other guy, I'd back you, no questions asked. But Micah's my brother, and I love him." Her voice thickened with emotion. "As hard as it is to admit, he's changed a lot in the past couple of months. It's like he's forgotten everything he used to believe. Or said he believed. When I was in Hono, I went along with whatever he wanted to do, and it was kind of fun at the time. But now, when I think about the parties and stuff, it makes me nervous, for him and for me. I wonder if I'm going to go crazy like he has when I go off to college."

"You won't if you don't want to. It's not something that automatically happens." Tabitha frowned. "I don't think it does, anyway."

"It doesn't matter. What may or may not happen 10 months from now isn't the issue," Kira pointed out. "What's going on with you and Micah, and how it affects us, is. How do we stay friends?"

"I don't know," Tabitha replied truthfully. "But I'm willing to try if you are."

"Of course I'm willing," Kira said hotly. "I'm the one

who brought it up, aren't I?"

Tabitha laughed. "Ah, there's the Kira I've known and loved all these years. Next to Cass, you're the touchiest person I know."

"I guess, if we've managed to stand each other for 10 years, we should be able to make it through this." Kira hesitated then grudgingly asked, "So what are you going to wear to the formal?"

Appreciating what it cost Kira to ask, Tabitha launched into a description of the patterns she'd already looked at. When Tabitha hung up 10 minutes later, it was with the feeling that they'd made great strides in restoring their shaky friendship. Tabitha headed back to Cass' room, eager to tell her how the conversation had gone.

Over the next several days, Tabitha found herself jumping every time the phone rang and anxiously flipping through the mail Dad brought home. There was a part of her that couldn't wait to see Micah's reaction to her letter and a part that dreaded it. As the days passed, she decided the worst scenario would be no response. She could live with anything but not knowing. When his letter finally arrived, she'd just about given up hope of hearing from him.

"Hi, Sweetie," Mom greeted Tabitha when she returned from school the following Friday. "You and Cass both hit the jackpot when I picked up the mail today. You each have three letters."

Tabitha's stomach flip-flopped, leaving her with a faintly sick feeling. "Anything from Micah?" she asked as casually as she could.

Mom nodded. "Yes. Plus one from your grandmother in Oregon and one from Randy. He also wrote to Cass so I guess he figured it was time to catch up on his correspondence."

"Randy's good about staying in touch. Unlike someone else I know." Tabitha's gaze strayed to the counter where the mail was piled, and her face tightened in a sour expression. "I suppose I should read Micah's letter and get it over with." She riffled through the envelopes until she located the one from him. "I think I'll take it out back."

"If it's bad news, you won't do anything drastic like throw yourself off the rocks into the water, will you?" Mom teased gently.

"I might have a few months ago." Tabitha smiled to let her know she was joking. "But I've learned that Micah isn't the be-all, end-all of my existence. If it's over, it's over. I'll survive."

"That's the spirit." Mom patted her cheek. "I'm here if you need to talk."

Tabitha turned to leave then swung back around to hug her. "I know. Thanks." Giggling, she rested her hand on Mom's stomach. "You feel like you have a beach ball in there." She made a show of making sure they were alone. "Come on. Won't you tell me if it's a boy or a girl?"

"I would," Mom solemnly assured her. "But then I'd have to kill you."

"Oh, well, since you put it that way—" Tabitha held up her hands and laughed, "forget it."

With a lighthearted wave that hid the tension jangling her nerves, she headed out the door. She met Cass who'd just parked her bike on the lanai.

"Where are you going?"

Tabitha held up the letter. "Out back to read this."

"Oh." Cass' smile disappeared. "Is it from Micah?"

"I'll give you three guesses, and the first two don't count."

"You want company?" Cass offered.

"No, thanks. This is something I need to do on my own. But," Tabitha added with an impish smile, "if I'm not back in an hour, why don't you check on me just to make sure I'm okay?"

"You got it." Cass set the timer on an imaginary watch. "See you in an hour."

Instead of settling on the rocks directly behind the house, Tabitha turned left and walked down the beach several yards. Sinking down onto the sand, hidden by rocks and beach grass, she said a quick prayer took a deep breath, and opened Micah's letter. She unfolded the three pages in her lap and carefully read what he had written.

Thirty minutes passed before Tabitha became aware of a shadow falling across her. Shading her eyes, she turned to see who it was.

"Hi. What are you doing here?"

Dad stepped off the rock onto the sand beside her and sat down. "Mom called and said you got a letter from Micah. Since Ed showed up early, I asked him to take over and came on home." Drawing up a leg, he draped his wrist over his knee. "You want to talk about it?"

About to say no, Tabitha abruptly changed her mind and nodded. "The short version is Micah told me to butt out of his life. He made it clear he doesn't answer to me and that he's free to do what he likes when he likes. He said he still loves me, but that his definition of love doesn't include one person controlling the other. If I ever come to my senses, I'm welcome to get in touch with him, and we'll take it from there. In the meantime, he doesn't care to hear from me anymore."

"Whew." Dad whistled under his breath. "That's quite a load to have dumped on you. How are you holding up?"

"Pretty well, actually." Tabitha brushed back the curls the wind had blown across her face. "It's not like I wasn't expecting it. The handwriting's been on the wall for quite awhile. I'm sorry we can't stay friends, but maybe that'll come in time. The good news is now I can date Sam with a clear conscience."

"Sam's a fine young man." Dad nodded his satisfaction

then his forehead puckered in a frown. "Did I hear right that you and Micah have talked about love?"

Tabitha squirmed uncomfortably. "Yes, but don't worry. When I told Cass, she gave me a long lecture about what a mistake it is for people our age to talk in terms of love. I only said it to Micah once. After that, I promised myself I wouldn't say it again until it was to the man God's chosen to be my husband."

"I'm glad to hear it." Dad pretended to mop his brow in relief. Leaning back, he regarded Tabitha with a steady gaze. "You've really grown up in the last few months. You're becoming quite a young woman."

"It's been rough, but you, Mom, and Cass have seen me through." Tabitha grinned. "Oh, and God, of course. I can't forget Him."

"Nope, because He never forgets us." Standing, Dad reached down a hand to her. "What do you say we go inside and invite the others to join us in a celebration dinner at the Yokwe Yuk?"

Accepting his hand, Tabitha allowed him to pull her up. "What are we celebrating?"

"Life. Love. Peace. Contentment. Growing up." Dad playfully tapped her nose. "All the good things God has given us. Uh-oh." He pointed to the pages of Micah's letter that had slipped from Tabitha's lap when she got up and were blowing toward the water. "You'd better catch them."

Slipping her arm through Dad's, Tabitha turned her back on the pieces of paper. "Let them go. I'm ready to move on. I'll never forget Micah, but he's part of my past. I'm looking forward to what tomorrow holds."